from *your* heart

By Shannyn Schroeder

For Your Love

Under Your Skin

In Your Arms

Through Your Eyes

From Your Heart

The O'Learys

More Than This

A Good Time

Something to Prove

Catch Your Breath

Just a Taste

Hold Me Close

Hot & Nerdy

Her Best Shot

Her Perfect Game

Her Winning Formula

His Work of Art

His New Jam

His Dream Role

from *your* heart

SHANNYN SCHROEDER

ZEBRA BOOKS
KENSINGTON PUBLISHING CORP.

http://www.kensingtonbooks.com

ZEBRA BOOKS are published by

Kensington Publishing Corp.
119 West 40th Street
New York, NY 10018

All Kensington titles, imprints, and distributed lines are available at special quantity discounts for bulk purchases for sales promotion, premiums, fund-raising, educational, or institutional use.

Special book excerpts or customized printings can also be created to fit specific needs. For details, write or phone the office of the Kensington Sales Manager: Attn.: Sales Department. Kensington Publishing Corp., 119 West 40th Street, New York, NY 10018. Phone: 1-800-221-2647.

Zebra and the Z logo Reg. U.S. Pat. & TM Off.

First Printing: April 2018
ISBN-13: 978-1-4201-4649-3
ISBN-10: 1-4201-4649-1

eISBN-13: 978-1-4201-4650-9
eISBN-10: 1-4201-4650-5

10 9 8 7 6 5 4 3 2 1

Printed in the United States of America

Chapter One

Sixteen months ago

Kevin O'Malley stood against the bar at O'Leary's Pub and watched the party unfold in front of him. Although he'd known the O'Learys his entire life, they were becoming family. He still couldn't believe that his older brother Jimmy had fallen in love with Mouthy Moira.

He tilted his bottle of beer to his lips with a smile. Watching Jimmy and Moira over the last six months or so had been jarring. Jimmy, who had always been the rock of their family, the man who took care of everyone, who told everyone what to do, was knocked off his game by a red-headed bombshell.

And they were so fucking happy that Kevin was a little jealous.

The jukebox blared music in the back room and people were dancing. Jimmy and Moira greeted every guest and thanked them for coming out in the cold to celebrate their engagement.

O'Learys and O'Malleys filled the entire bar and most were more than halfway to drunk. Their families knew how to throw one hell of a party. Unfortunately for him, he had a breakfast meeting in the morning and showing up hungover wouldn't bode well for his career. He'd worked too hard over the last few years to throw it away for an engagement party.

Not that any of that would stop him from messing with Moira. As she turned the corner toward the dance floor without Jimmy, Kevin saw his chance. He set his beer down and ran up behind his soon-to-be sister-in-law.

"Moira, baby. You owe me a dance." Before she could respond, he had his arm on her waist and led her to the dance floor.

"Why do you feel the need to fuck with me?" Moira said with a clenched jaw.

"What? I have precious few chances remaining to prove you chose the wrong O'Malley brother."

His quip did what he'd hoped, and she burst into snorting laughter. She relaxed in his arms and allowed him to lead in a dance.

"In all seriousness, I'm glad he has you."

Moira pulled back in his arms and studied his face. "How drunk are you?"

"Not at all."

"Sincerity from Kevin O'Malley? Hell must be freezing over."

"Tell anyone and I'll deny it till my dying breath." He paused and said what he wanted her to know. "You make him extraordinarily happy, and there's nothing more any of us could ask for him." He pulled her close again for the remainder of their dance.

In his ear, she whispered, "Does this mean you're finally calling a truce, and you're going to be nice to me?"

Now it was his turn to laugh. "No way, babe. Messing

with you is one of life's greatest pleasures. It's bound to only get worse once you're family."

She shook her head slowly. "That's what I was afraid of."

Their dance ended, and he released her so she could return to Jimmy. Kevin went back to the bar and scanned the crowd to see if he could find some female company that he wasn't related to.

As he looked over his choices, his gaze landed on a tall brunette. Her long brown curls bounced wildly down her back, drawing attention to her luscious ass. It definitely looked like a firm handful.

He shifted to order a couple bottles of beer to use as a means of introducing himself. Before he got the bartender's attention, the woman turned and he caught a glimpse of her face.

Kathy Hendricks.

Kevin's mouth went dry at the realization. He hadn't seen her in almost four years. Not since she'd blown him off.

But before that, they were hot together.

Suddenly Moira was once again at his side.

"Don't even think about it," she said.

"I wasn't anywhere near you."

"Not me. Kathy. You leave her alone."

Her stern comment had him turning away from the bar to fully face her. She wasn't kidding. This was no playful warning. "Kathy and I have history."

"Yeah. You did a number on her."

"What?"

Moira stared at him for a full minute. It was the quietest minute he'd ever had with her. "You really are clueless," she said.

"When it comes to whatever you're rambling about right now, yeah."

"I don't know how it happened, but when you were dating Kathy, she was totally falling for you." He started to grin until she continued, "And you broke her heart."

"I did not."

Moira's hand flashed up in his face. "I'm not going to argue with you about something that happened years ago. I'm just saying that you need to leave her be."

Then she flounced off, leaving Kevin to order and drink a beer alone. He waved the bartender over and got his drink. When he turned to the crowd again, a tall man had an arm slipped around Kathy's shoulders. So even without Moira's crazy warning, Kathy would be off-limits. His days of sleeping with a woman regardless of her relationship status were long over.

The more he thought about Moira's words, the more they gnawed at him. He and Kathy had been scorching for a while.

Memories came flooding back. They'd been good together and then she disappeared. Totally ghosted him.

He hadn't broken up with her. Or done anything to break her heart.

All of his residual anger surfaced and he swallowed it down as he guzzled his beer. He had no idea what Kathy had told Moira, but if there was a victim here, it was him.

It wasn't like he'd never been dumped, but it usually came with some form of *fuck off*. They'd been having a great time. They were good together in bed and out. Kathy hadn't said good-bye or anything. He'd called and gone to her apartment, but she never answered. She'd sent a clear message without saying a word. That bothered him more than he'd like to admit. But he had no problem moving on to the next warm woman who'd been willing to join him.

At least that's what he told himself as he finished his drink.

Kathy laughed with Maggie, Moira's little sister. She hadn't seen Maggie in a long time because Maggie had taken off and lived in Ireland for over a year. Ray was bored out of his mind at this party because he knew next to no one, except Moira and Jimmy, but he was being a good sport about it.

Moira came up beside Maggie and took hold of one of Maggie's hands and one of Kathy's "We need to talk. Come with me." She began tugging at both of them.

Kathy pulled to a stop and looked up at Ray. "Will you be okay?"

"I'm fine as long as Moira doesn't keep you too long. You still owe me a dance." He kissed her cheek.

Moira resumed her pulling.

"What the heck is the rush?" Maggie asked.

"You'll see."

When they got to the back hallway of the bar near the bathrooms, Maggie said, "If you're gonna puke, I don't think you need both of us. Kathy can handle holding your hair."

"Ha-ha. I'm not sick. I'm not even all that drunk."

Kathy snickered. Moira might not be drunk, but she was far from sober. They got to the office, and Moira toed the door open and pulled them through. Finally she released their hands and pushed them forward, closing the door behind them. Kathy looked around to figure out what was going on.

Near the desk, Jimmy stood with Liam, his best friend

and one of Moira's brothers, and his own brother Kevin. Kathy froze as she took in the sight of him. Of course he would be here. She'd known that, done her best to mentally prepare for seeing him.

Unfortunately, no amount of preparation could ready her. It had been four years, but seeing him put her whole body on alert. There might as well have been a flashing red sign above his head. Danger!

While Moira talked with Liam, Kathy took a moment to regain control over herself and better assess the situation. Kevin looked good in jeans that were worn but neat. His sweater stretched across his biceps and chest just enough to allow her to notice he was still fit. Why couldn't he have a beer gut and suffer from male pattern baldness? Her gaze drank him in all the way up to a full head of dark hair, styled, but not overly so—like it was ready for fingers to run through it.

Everyone stood huddled around the desk. Kathy edged forward wondering what Moira was up to because the woman was always up to something.

"So here's the deal. Jimmy and I have been talking a lot about the wedding."

"Correction," Jimmy said. "She's been talking. I've been a sounding board."

Moira walked around the group to stand next to her fiancé. She rose up on tiptoe and kissed his cheek. "That's one of the many things I love about you." Then she turned to the rest of them while holding Jimmy's hand. "The thing is, we have to figure out the wedding party and we really don't want anyone to be upset or hurt because you're all so important to us."

Kathy smiled. She knew exactly where this was going.

Apparently, so did Maggie, who stepped forward and said, "I bow out."

"What?" all the guys said in unison.

Men. So clueless.

Maggie rolled her eyes. "Kathy should be your maid of honor. I appreciate you thinking of me, but your friend should do this. I've been gone for most of this romance. She was the one holding your hand when Jimmy was being an ass."

"Hey," Jimmy protested.

Moira patted his arm.

Kathy touched Maggie's shoulder. "You're her sister. I can't get in the way of that."

Maggie shrugged. With one brow lifted, and an evil grin on her face, she said, "Too bad. You do it or she won't have a maid of honor."

"Harsh," Kevin said.

His voice still held the light quality she remembered. Like he was ready to burst out in laughter at any moment. She'd always liked that about him. Being in the same room wasn't quite as hard as she'd thought. At least there were others to act as a buffer.

Maggie hugged Moira and then hugged Kathy. "Do right by her," she said to Kathy.

Kathy's stomach was still tight. She felt like an intruder in what should be a family moment.

"Ha!" Moira yelled. "And you thought I was going to have a hard time. Your turn," she said, poking Jimmy's chest.

Jimmy looked at Liam and Kevin. "Look, guys, I don't know how you want to handle this. You're both a huge part of my life."

Liam held up his hands. "I'd be honored to be your best

man, but I'll be there no matter what. I'm not going to be pissed. Kevin's your brother."

"Hell, I'll be pissed," Kevin said. Then with that wicked smile he enjoyed tossing around, he added, "Just kidding. Whatever you decide is fine."

Kathy's heart sped up and then tumbled into her stomach. She did not want to stand up to her best friend's wedding with her ex-boyfriend. Talk about uncomfortable situations. Although she'd known she wouldn't be able to escape seeing him, having to interact with him was a different thing altogether.

Jimmy continued, "I can't decide. That's why we asked you guys here."

"Flip a coin," Liam offered.

A fifty-fifty shot at freedom was better than nothing. Kathy crossed her fingers and sent up a silent prayer.

"Rock, paper, scissors," Kevin countered.

Before Jimmy could stop the game, both Kevin and Liam were waving fists. Kathy's heart stopped as they called it.

Liam was a rock—apt for him because he was as steady as they came. Kevin, on the other hand, chose paper and won. Didn't that just figure. He was a guy who got carried away on a breeze or whim.

The men congratulated each other, and Kathy forced a smile. Jimmy poured everyone a shot of whiskey and when the glasses were drained, they left the office to rejoin the party.

In the hall, Kevin stepped in front of her, startling her to a halt.

Standing close he asked, "Can I talk to you a minute?"

Although he'd phrased it as a question, his eyes said more. Her sense of fight or flight kicked in—and with her it was always flight—but she fought the urge. She didn't want to talk to him because she had nothing to say, but she nodded. Kevin O'Malley had the look of a man who'd make a ruckus if he didn't get his way. She wouldn't cause a scene at Moira's party. Or anywhere else, for that matter. Not only did she dread any negative attention, she also wouldn't risk ruining what should be a fabulous night for her best friend. Kevin stepped backward, deeper into the dim hallway. The noise from the party raged behind them.

"Moira said something to me earlier, and I wanted to clear the air." His words came out harsh and he sounded pissed.

Kathy crossed her arms. She was well aware that although Moira was often annoyed by Kevin, his relationship with Kathy had become a special point of contention between them.

"She said something about me breaking your heart. . . ."

Kathy felt sick. She didn't want to rehash anything. Especially with Kevin. "Don't worry about it. It was a long time ago."

He paused, confusion filling his face. "I'm not apologizing."

"Excuse me?" She'd figured Jimmy had put him up to this to create peace before the wedding.

"Why the hell would I apologize when you're the one who took off? No good-bye, no fuck you very much. Nothing." His gaze met hers and those brilliant, deep blue eyes held an emotion that looked eerily similar to hurt.

But Kathy knew better. His sharp comment kept her heart at a gallop as she processed his words. "What?"

"You were there in my life, then all of a sudden you weren't. We were having a great time. Then, like a ghost, you were gone." His dark eyebrows lowered.

Kathy licked her lips and took a moment to formulate her response. The audacity of this man. What had she ever seen in him? Only a pompous ass like him would try to spin the crappy way their relationship ended to place blame on her. She lowered her voice and through gritted teeth said, "I disappeared because I found out you were cheating on me. As far as I was concerned, that sent a clear message that we were over."

Her breathing sped up, but she managed to get the words out without her voice wobbling. *Go, Kathy! A first for everything.*

His eyes widened in shock. Looking down, he rubbed the back of his neck as if he regretted starting this. "It wasn't—"

His reaction gave her the fortitude to continue. She stepped closer and kept her voice low. "Do *not* lie to me now. I saw. You canceled a date with me, claiming you had to work late. I felt bad for you and wanted to surprise you. I came to your apartment just in time to see you stumble up with another woman. She was hanging all over you, and you went into your apartment together."

His eyes squinted as if he struggled to remember the night. He appeared genuinely confused. Had everything meant so little to him that he had no memory?

Waving a hand, she dismissed both her thoughts and him. "Look. It doesn't matter. It was a long time ago. Water under the bridge. Life goes on and all that."

She turned to walk away because she didn't want to continue this conversation. Her stomach was still in knots and now she'd have to explain to Ray where she'd been. At least she felt slightly vindicated at letting Kevin know how wrong he'd been about what had happened between them.

"See you around?" he asked quietly.

Not if I can help it. "Some, I guess, with the wedding." She walked out of the hallway and toward her boyfriend. Yeah, that was right. Life did go on, and she was at this party with her boyfriend. If that caused an extra cocky sway in her hips, so be it. Kevin should know what he'd been missing.

Chapter Two

Present day

Kathy walked through her apartment, gathering torn wrapping paper and empty cups. How the heck had a group of women made such a mess? If they were this bad for Moira's bridal shower, she'd hate to see what would happen at the bachelorette party. Jimmy and Moira stacked presents near the door to prepare to leave.

In a moment of sweet bliss, Jimmy pulled Moira into his embrace and kissed her. Kathy almost sighed. Envy was such an ugly thing. But she wanted that. She was glad Moira found it, even if it was with Jimmy. Kathy would never quite understand the attraction to a guy who was little more than a caveman, but somehow they made it work.

She shoved another handful of paper into the industrial-sized trash bag. Moira pushed Jimmy toward the door with a stack of presents. Then to Kathy, she said, "Let me help."

Kathy shook her head. "This was your shower. As the bride, you don't do any work." She eyed the pile by the door. "Plus, you'll need your energy to unpack all of that."

Moira laughed. "That's Jimmy's job. He has some kind of organization in his head for everything."

"How are you going to get all of that back to your house?"

Moira's gaze bounced around the room. "Don't kill me." She took a deep breath and then added, "If anyone deserves to be killed for this, it's Jimmy, but since I love him and I want to spend my life with him, don't kill him either, okay?"

Kathy ignored the bad feeling Moira's words conjured because when Moira got into full-on rambling mode, she was hilarious. "Just spill."

"Kevin's coming to help bring everything to our house." Moira closed her eyes as if to brace for impact.

Kathy froze. She'd expected this. At some point, they would have to interact. Of course, she didn't really want him in her house. She'd wanted to keep any interaction with him impersonal. Having him in her apartment was anything but impersonal. Inhaling deeply, she said, "It's fine. He's doing a good thing, best man and brotherly duty all rolled into one. Besides, if Jimmy listened to Kevin, he wouldn't think about whether this would bother me. He probably just believed what Kevin said about us."

"What's that?"

She let the trash bag slide to the floor and she plopped on the couch. She'd never mentioned her conversation with Kevin to Moira. Kathy always avoided any situation where he might show up, and Moira treated Kevin like Voldemort—he who must not be named. Plus, Kathy never wanted to cause a problem between Moira and Jimmy. "At your engagement party, he told me that you said he broke my heart—thanks for that, by the way—and he was confused. He thought I broke it off because I just slipped away."

"What? God, he's such an ass. How could he not know that you were done with him because he cheated?"

Kathy gave a half-hearted shrug. She'd asked herself that often enough, but never quite arrived at an answer. "We were young and weren't very good at communicating. He was keeping it casual, and I've never done casual. So some blame was on me." After all, she'd never even confronted him.

Moira sat next to her. "I still want to throat punch him."

Kathy laughed. She loved having such a close friend. She'd always wanted a sister, and Moira was as close as she got. "Thanks, but that might cause a rift with your new family."

"Ugh." Moira performed her best eye roll.

A thump at the door caught their attention. Jimmy came back in with his brother trailing behind. Kathy was struck by their differences. Where Jimmy was broad and muscular, Kevin was lean. They both shared the same dark hair and blue eyes, so there was no mistaking them as siblings.

Making eye contact, Kevin smiled at her and said, "Hi."

The smile still got to her. God, how she hated that it did. His smile was part wicked, part boy-next-door charm. Such a lethal mix. She nodded and pushed up from the couch to resume cleanup.

"Moira, baby, you had a party and didn't invite me?" Kevin boomed from the doorway.

"It was a bridal shower. Women only."

"Jimmy was here."

"Believe me, I wish I hadn't been." Jimmy hefted a stack of boxes and pushed them into Kevin's arms. For all his complaining, Jimmy had been a great sport. He played all the silly games and even posed with Moira's ribbon bouquet.

When the guys were gone, Moira said, "I'll stay and help."

Kathy nudged her. "Thanks for the offer, but you go home and handle things there."

"You sure?"

She nodded.

"You're the best." She threw her arms around Kathy and squeezed. "I'm glad Maggie begged off being maid of honor. I love her, but this would've been a mess with her in charge."

"Speaking of which, how did she manage to scoot out of here without doing cleanup?"

Moira shrugged. "That's Maggie for you. She drove my mom home, but as baby of the family, she's excelled at getting out of work her whole life."

"At least Norah and Carmen have wrangled the kitchen. They're dishwashers extraordinaire," Kathy said, speaking about Jimmy's sister and Liam's girlfriend. "I didn't want to be rude and ask Carmen, but did Liam pop the question yet?"

"No, the big dork. We all know he wants to. I have no idea what he's waiting for."

"Is your mom any better with Carmen?" When Liam and Carmen had first started dating, Mrs. O'Leary was rude and distant to Carmen because she wasn't a "nice Irish girl."

"Yeah. I think that once she got to know her and realized how much Liam loves her, she knew she needed to get with the program. Carmen is awesome. It's like having another sister."

"It looks like your whole life is gonna be one wedding

after another, huh? Everyone's falling in love and getting hitched." She cleared off another table and tied the bag. One more load and she should be done.

"At the rate all the O'Learys and O'Malleys are dropping, we could open our own wedding planning business. When are you joining the ranks?"

"Need a man first. The dating scene is dismal." She hadn't had a steady boyfriend since Ray, and they'd broken up not long after Moira's engagement party.

Jimmy and Kevin came back in. Jimmy said, "Hey, sweetheart, we're set. Are you ready?"

Moira looked over her shoulder, "One minute." Then she turned back to Kathy. "Jimmy knows some guys. I could—"

"No. The last time you introduced me to someone . . ." She looked pointedly at Kevin.

"First, that wasn't an introduction. You happened to be in the same place. Plus, that's all the more reason to let me set you up. I owe you."

"No, thanks. Now go before Jimmy gets cranky."

Moira walked to her fiancé and said, "Jimmy's always cranky. It's part of his charm."

The couple walked out the door and Kathy went to the kitchen to get another trash bag. On her way back to the living room, she almost crashed into Kevin.

"What are you still doing here?"

"I wanted to talk to you."

She skirted around him. "So talk." She picked up more paper plates so her hands had something to do and her eyes had a focus.

"I wanted to make plans to talk to you about the bachelor and bachelorette parties."

She straightened. "By definition, they're different parties. What's there to talk about?"

"I think we should coordinate dates."

"Why?"

He strode closer and helped clean the mess. "I love my brother, but I also know him. If we don't plan the parties for the same night, there's no way Moira will enjoy herself. Jimmy won't be able to sit at home waiting, knowing Moira is running around the city getting drunk."

"Oh." He surprised her by caring about whether Moira had a good time. That was different. Not the usual selfish attitude she'd come to associate with Kevin O'Malley.

Kathy continued to pick up cups, but her focus waned with Kevin standing so near. She despised that he could still affect her.

He shoved more trash into the bag, completely unaffected by her. The story of her life.

"I was thinking we could meet for dinner one day this week to talk about it."

Kathy yanked the bag and looked at him.

He held up his arms in defense. "You can bring your boyfriend. No funny business."

"I don't have a boyfriend," she said and turned away to clear the coffee table.

"Oh, uh . . . the last time I saw you, you were with a guy, so I thought . . ."

"It didn't work out." Ray had turned out to be a bit of a dud. The spark between them, what little of it there was, had fizzled fast.

"Well, then, I don't have to feel bad about stealing you away for dinner one night."

She rolled her eyes. Always the player.

Carmen and Norah came into the room.

"The kitchen is back to normal," Carmen said. "Anything else you need?"

To Kevin, Norah said, "What're you doing here?"

Kevin turned and said, "I'm trying to convince Kathy

that the bachelor and bachelorette parties need to happen simultaneously, or Moira won't have any peace."

Tucking her hands into her back pockets, Norah said, "As much as I hate to admit it, Kevin's right. Jimmy will pop a vein just thinking about how reckless Moira might be."

"Fine. I get it." Realizing how snippy she sounded, she took a deep breath. "Sorry. Thank you, guys, for washing everything. I really appreciate it. I can handle the rest."

"You sure?" Carmen asked as she let her long, black hair down from her ponytail.

"Yeah, I got this."

Norah grabbed her purse and said, "Give me a call if you need help planning."

They said their good-byes and let themselves out of her apartment, leaving her completely alone with Kevin. He took the bag from her and emptied his hands of the garbage he held.

"Thank you," she mumbled. "I don't want this to be weird, but it's going to be, isn't it?"

He stood silently for so long, she began to question if she actually said it aloud. The rise and fall of his chest in a sigh was the only signal she had that he was paying attention. He had that in common with Jimmy: the sigh of resignation. She'd witnessed Jimmy do it in regard to Moira on more than one occasion.

Kathy looked up into Kevin's blue eyes and prayed her face wouldn't reveal the effect he had on her.

"I don't want this to be weird either. It's up to us to not make it weird. What do you say? Let me buy you dinner. We'll talk about party plans." His smile was warm and friendly.

She'd forgotten he had the ability to do that. To just be friendly without flirting. "Any night except for Friday."

"Got a big date planned for Friday?" he asked with a tilt of an eyebrow.

She wished. "Not that it's any of your business, but no. I have a big wedding order to finish putting together and I'll be working late."

He looked almost relieved at her response. His intense gaze held her captive. When he spoke, his voice was low and seductive. "Thursday good for you?"

She nodded and gulped. To break the spell, she bent to grab the trash bag.

"Can I have your number? I'll text you details. Unless you'd like me to pick you up?"

"No." That would feel far too much like a date. For all his joking and crassness, one thing she remembered about Kevin was that he always picked her up and walked her to the door. In that respect, he was a consummate gentleman. Not like when he was sticking his dick in another woman.

Ugh. She had to keep her mind off things like that. She pulled her phone from her pocket and handed it to him. "Call yourself."

She tied a knot in the bag and set it near the door. When she turned, Kevin was in front of her again. What was with this guy invading her space?

He handed her the phone. "I added myself as a contact. I'll call you on Thursday to make sure we're still on and figure out a time and place."

"Okay."

He slipped out the door without another word, but he'd taken the trash bags with him. She sank to the couch and propped her exhausted feet on the coffee table. Then she scrolled through her phone. Sure enough, he had programmed himself in. He was listed as "Sorry-ass Kevin."

Kathy started laughing and couldn't stop. If nothing else, Kevin was definitely good at making her smile.

* * *

Kevin was freakishly happy all week at work. For over a year, he'd been kicking himself thinking about Kathy. As he watched his siblings all fall in love, he'd been feeling a little bitter and seeing Kathy last year bummed him out. He'd really liked her and missed her when she'd slipped out of his life. He didn't know why he hadn't chased her down for answers. Ultimately, he treated her like any other girl who came and went. Knowing that it was his actions that caused her to leave made him want to kick himself harder.

Back then, he and Kathy hadn't talked about exclusivity. And the time she'd referred to catching him cheating, he hadn't actually had sex with the woman. He'd run into his ex, Tina, at a bar. They'd both been drinking and pretty much passed out as soon as they cleared his front door.

But the thing was, looking back, he couldn't say that he'd been totally faithful either. He just wasn't sure. He'd been twenty-five and enjoying life. Settling down had been the farthest thing from his mind. His time away from work consisted of being at the bar every night. The only time his head had been completely clear was while he was actually at work. Or with Kathy.

However, in one alcohol-fueled conversation with Sean about women, he'd admitted to his brother and himself that Kathy was the one that got away. Now he had a fresh opportunity. She was single and so was he. And he wanted the chance to get it right. He'd spent a lot of time over the last year thinking about their brief relationship, and he couldn't remember a happier time.

He knew he had a lot to overcome to win her back, but nothing was impossible. They weren't the same people they were five years ago. He could show her that he'd changed.

She'd agreed to have dinner with him. So she didn't

quite jump at the chance, but she hadn't said no. If she truly hated him, she would've said they could figure out schedules via e-mail. She could've avoided ever laying eyes on him until the wedding. But she hadn't.

As far as he was concerned, that meant he had a shot.

As Thursday neared, he made plans. If he remembered correctly, Kathy loved pizza. Pizza would be a nice, casual dinner, nothing that could be construed as a ploy or a romantic meal. What he really wanted to do was apologize for hurting her. It didn't matter that she said it was old news and she was fine; he'd seen the look in her eyes that told him the hurt had been very real. His hurt at her leaving had been real too, but he could admit it probably didn't compare.

Normally, he'd give a woman flowers, but Kathy was a florist. Moira had bragged that Kathy owned her own shop and was doing the flowers for the wedding. Chocolate was a good backup, but he wasn't sure. Asking Moira might cost him one of his testicles, so not a good idea.

On Wednesday night, he and Jimmy met for drinks and after listening to Jimmy's complaints about a bachelor party and what he didn't want—no strippers? What the hell?—Kevin asked what he thought about Kathy.

"You need to get that out of your head right now. Moira will kill me if there's even a hint of me helping you get to Kathy. Then she'll go after you."

"I know I fucked up with Kathy. In all honesty, though, I didn't know until your engagement party when Moira told me I broke Kathy's heart. Dude, it was five years ago. I thought we were casual."

Jimmy shook his head. "I taught you better than that. Live how you want, but make sure everyone's on the same page."

"I thought we were. She took off without a word and I

was pissed. Who does that? No fight, no big breakup, she was just gone." Kevin didn't need to explain how hard it was to have someone disappear from his life. Jimmy knew. He took a swallow of beer. "I'm not looking for you to talk to her for me. I just need an idea of what to give her. The usual apology gift—flowers—is out. Chocolate seems cheap."

Jimmy grunted. "Not if you get the good shit. Look at Godiva or Frango. Not cheap."

"I wasn't talking price. I meant the sentiment behind it."

Jimmy eyed him. "Since when do you use words like 'sentiment'?"

"I'm skilled in many things. I write at work and my whole job is to make the people around me sound smarter than they are. Just because I choose to limit my words around barbarians like you doesn't mean I don't have an excellent vocabulary." He turned the bottle in his hand. "I don't know how to explain this. I really liked Kathy. I wasn't ready for anything serious back then, so I was probably willfully oblivious about her feelings. And that was shitty. I want to make it up to her."

"You just want to apologize? Not get back with her?"

Kevin swallowed hard. He couldn't lie to Jimmy; his brother would see right through him. "Yes, I want to apologize, but if doing so opens a door for me to have a second chance, I'm jumping at it."

"She's not a fling kind of girl. That much I've figured out in the time I've spent with her. Your casual shit won't fly this time either."

"I didn't say I wanted it to be casual."

Jimmy froze with his beer halfway to his mouth. He stared at Kevin for a long moment, probably to assess whether Kevin was spinning some bullshit. Kevin held his stare.

"Why her? You've dated plenty of women. No one has stood out as particularly serious."

Kevin shook his head and searched for the words. "I've been thinking about her a lot since your engagement party. I see you and Sean and even Tommy falling in love. I wasn't in any hurry for that, but your life doesn't seem all that bad. What Kathy and I had years ago could've been that. I was stupid not to hold on to her."

Jimmy drained his bottle and stood. With a pat on Kevin's shoulder, he said, "She'll like chocolate, but she'll value your words more. Don't bullshit her. Be honest. It might get you further than you think." He stepped away and then added over his shoulder, "But you didn't get that from me."

Kevin took Jimmy's advice to heart. He also spent a ton of money on the best chocolate he could find before going to the restaurant Thursday night. He and Kathy had only communicated via text, so he didn't know how she felt about their meeting. A text didn't reveal any nuance, and while he usually liked the efficiency of texting, he wished he could've spoken to her.

He waited at the hostess stand for Kathy, feeling much like a guy afraid of being stood up by a blind date. Every time the door behind him opened, he turned to look. At seven on the nose, she walked in. Her curls were piled on her head in a messy bun and her face was clear of makeup except for the gloss on her lips, making it clear that she was coming from work and didn't put in extra effort to look special for him. However, it backfired.

She was beautiful.

"Hi," he said, suddenly nervous. Normally, he'd greet a

date or a friend with a kiss on the cheek, but he feared the act wouldn't be welcome. "I'm glad you came."

Her brow crinkled. "I said I would."

He nodded, feeling more foolish. "Here." He thrust the box of chocolates at her.

"What's this for?"

He put his hands up. "I wanted to get you something, but flowers would be dumb. . . ."

She smiled and the nerves in his neck loosened. "Let's get a table and talk."

Kathy stepped in front of him and he placed a gentle hand on her lower back as they walked. She stiffened, but didn't pull away. The hostess seated them at a quiet corner booth. Kathy set the box of chocolates on the table as if to remind him that he needed to explain.

Their waitress came by to set a basket of bread between them along with glasses of water.

Kevin slid his menu to the side for a minute. Might as well get this part over with. "I feel like an ass for what happened between us."

"And you thought chocolate was going to make up for it?" Her eyes narrowed and her brows furrowed with confusion. Not quite as bad as calling him an idiot, but close.

"No. I'm not that dense. I didn't want to come empty-handed." He inhaled deeply and remembered what Jimmy had said. Kevin knew how to be honest, but he spent so much time spinning the truth and couching it in BS that being straightforward was a novelty. "I've been thinking about you ever since the engagement party. The first thing I thought of when I saw you was that we had a great time together. Followed quickly by the anger I felt when you cut out without a word."

When she opened her mouth, he held up a quick hand.

"I understand why you did what you did. More or less. Most women would've attacked, but that's not your style." He took a deep breath. "In the year since the party, I haven't been able to come up with one thing that was bad with us."

She nodded. "Things were good. That's why it was such a shock to find out that you were cheating." She snapped her jaw shut and closed her eyes for a second. "We don't need to rehash this. Like I said, life goes on."

"But I need to explain and give you an apology. You deserve one. First, I didn't think I was ready for anything serious when we were dating. I think part of me recognized that what we had was getting serious and instead of backing out or talking to you, I self-sabotaged. That night you saw me with Tina, who was an ex. We'd both been drinking and I invited her back to my apartment. It was a shitty move. You didn't deserve that."

"No, I didn't," she said quietly, her head down.

"But I didn't sleep with her."

Kathy's eyes shot back up. "What?"

"I'm not going to lie, she wanted to, but we didn't have sex."

"Oh."

"But if I'm being totally honest, I can't say for sure that I didn't cheat on you some other time. I just don't remember." He took another deep breath. "Saying that out loud makes me feel like an even bigger asshole. The thing is, except for when I was at work or with you, I was out partying, always looking for the next good time."

Her throat worked as she swallowed. "Why are you telling me this now?"

"Because you deserve the truth. And I want to start

fresh." Kevin reached across the table and laid a hand over hers. "I'm really sorry."

She stared into his eyes for a long moment. He remembered spending hours getting lost in her light brown eyes.

"Okay."

He knew that was as good as he was going to get for now, and he could live with that. He pulled his hand away and slid a menu toward her. "Did you want to take a look or just order a pizza?"

"Pizza." She said the word with reverence.

"Pizza always was your weakness."

"Is that why you chose this place?"

He nodded. "Of course. My apology was sincere, but I'm not above using every possible advantage to earn your forgiveness."

The corner of her mouth tilted up. "I'm not sure what it says about me that I can be bought with chocolate and pizza."

He laughed. "It says you have excellent taste—in food and company," he added, pointing at himself.

"I see your ego is as big as ever."

"In my world, I'd never survive without being confident. Even if I have no clue what I'm doing, I can't admit it. It would be career suicide." He waved the waitress over and ordered a large pizza with everything.

"Where are you working that's so cutthroat?" She took a sip of water.

"The mayor's office."

She started to laugh and choked on her water. He handed her his napkin with a shrug. "Chicago politics will always be Chicago politics, but I like where I am."

"What do you do for the mayor?"

"I don't work directly for the mayor. I'm one of the staff writers in the PR department."

She stared at him with narrowed eyes. "I don't see it."

"What?"

"You working in a cubicle, being an anonymous creator."

"It's what I do."

"But it goes against everything I remember about you. You always liked to be the center of attention, with everyone knowing who you are."

He drank some water and began to think a beer was in order, especially if they were going to start dissecting his life choices. "I know the value of hard work. So does the mayor. This job is a stepping-stone. The mayor has a lot of things in the works that might give me more opportunities. I have the most seniority in my department, so it's got to be my turn soon."

Kathy had no idea how she'd landed here. When she left the shop today, she'd convinced herself that she could meet Kevin for dinner, talk about bachelor/bachelorette party stuff, and move on. Never in her self-talk did she envision sharing a bottle of wine and laughing with him.

She sipped on the red now as the waitress stopped by to box up the remaining pizza. "I can't believe we ate all of that. I feel like I'm going to explode."

"Does that mean you don't want the leftovers?" he asked with a smirk.

Damn him. He knew she wanted that pizza. "I never turn away pizza. It's life's perfect food. Works for any meal or snack, day or night. I'm sure by breakfast I'll no longer feel like exploding."

He pushed the container to her side of the table. "Enjoy."

She sighed. Her cheeks hurt because she'd smiled so much. "We haven't even talked about the parties—you know, the whole reason for meeting tonight? What are you thinking about for Jimmy?"

Kevin shook his head. "Jimmy gave me a litany of don'ts for the party. Then he tried to give me a similar list to pass on to you for Moira's party."

"Uh-uh. The groom doesn't get to tell me what kind of party to throw. Who does he think he is?"

"Jimmy O'Malley, boss of everyone." Kevin drained his glass. He waved at the waitress and ordered coffee. "Would you like one too?"

Kathy shook her head. "The caffeine'll keep me up all night. I have an early morning."

When the waitress left, Kathy asked, "Do I even want to know what Jimmy demanded?"

He shook his head. Then he leaned forward and put his elbows on the table. "Jimmy thinks the whole idea is ridiculous because the concept is outdated. The bachelor party is one last night of freedom for a guy, but Jimmy feels like he's already had enough of running around. Moira's it for him."

Kathy's heart hefted a happy sigh. Bossy Jimmy had a romantic side.

"Did Moira talk about this?"

"Nope."

"Here's what I'm thinking. It's a little unorthodox, but I think they'll enjoy it." He leaned even closer and lowered his voice.

Kathy found herself pressing toward the table as if they were going to share a secret.

"What if we plan a lake cruise? We keep it a secret from the two of them until we're all on board. I know a guy who can get us a good deal. We can get a private dinner cruise."

"Are you suggesting a joint party?" Kathy's mushy

heart plunged into her stomach. Although the night had been wonderful, she wasn't looking to spend more time with Kevin.

"Yes and no. I think we let them believe that we're setting up the usual raunchy bachelor party. Jimmy doesn't want that, and if the way Moira looks at him is any indication, she's not looking for it either. The wedding and marriage thing is a formality. Their days of freedom have been over for a long time."

Kathy sat back and thought. She hated to admit it, but he was right. They weren't kids getting married before experiencing life. Moira had been in love with Jimmy since childhood. Having a naked dude shake his ass at her wasn't going to do much for Moira. Kathy smiled. It might kill Jimmy, though.

"What's that smile about?"

"I was thinking that you've made an excellent argu-ment and a cruise would probably be a good time. But part of me really wants a stripper for Moira just to drive Jimmy crazy."

Kevin chuckled. "I knew there was something about you I liked." He tapped the table. "I got it!"

She didn't like the look on his face and regretted voic-ing her opinion. "No."

"I haven't even told you the idea."

The waitress deposited a cup of coffee in front of him and he immediately drank.

"Your face tells me enough." The pizza turned to stone in her stomach as she tried to envision how Kevin would screw this up.

He suddenly raised his hands. "Whoa. I'm just talking about having fun. If we have the boat to ourselves, we can have a private room with entertainment for those people who want to enjoy a typical wild party."

Her wariness didn't fade, but she wanted to believe him. "That wasn't what the evil genius look was about."

He flashed a brilliant smile. "You think I'm a genius?"

"Did you not hear the evil part?"

His smile lessened by a fraction, but he still looked far too good. She bit her tongue before any part of that slipped past her lips. She couldn't allow the wine to talk. Surely that was all it was.

"I had a picture in my head of taking Jimmy into a room to greet a stripper and conveniently putting him in the wrong room. He'd get to enjoy the stripper meant for Moira."

She couldn't help it. She giggled. It wasn't nice, but it would be funny to see Jimmy's reaction. And it wouldn't be anything horribly offensive to ruin Moira's night. In fact, she might even get a laugh from the joke.

Pointing at Kevin she said, "Do what you want, but I'll have no part in it. I don't want to be on the receiving end of Jimmy's anger."

Kevin waved a hand in dismissal. "Nah. He won't be angry. I'll liquor him up first."

"So many ways that could end badly for you."

"Never underestimate me," he said with a wink.

Man, did this guy ever let up? She folded her napkin and set it on the table before reaching in her purse for her wallet. "How much do I owe you for dinner?"

"It's on me."

"This wasn't a date. It was more like a business meeting. I should pay at least half. I am taking all the leftovers."

"Correction. This was old friends getting together for a meal. My treat." He finished his coffee and pulled bills from his pocket. "I'll walk you to your car."

She stood and gathered the pizza and box of chocolates. "When you get actual numbers on the cost of the cruise, let me know and we'll talk. I imagine that renting out the ship for the night will be expensive."

"We'll figure it out. You like my plan though?"

She did. An intimate party with all of Jimmy and Moira's closest friends would be perfect. Even if it meant Kathy would have to spend more time with Kevin. This night hadn't been anywhere near the torture she'd imagined. "It's a good idea. It'll work for them."

As they headed out of the restaurant and toward her car, Kevin said, "Do you have any business cards on you?"

"Why?" She pressed the key fob to unlock the door. Night had fallen and it was near her bedtime, but the cool breeze made her want to stand and enjoy it for a while. She inhaled, filling her lungs with fragrant air. Summer in Chicago was her favorite time of year.

"I know a lot of people who organize functions in and around the mayor."

"I don't need some pity business because you're trying to clear your conscience. The chocolates and apology were enough."

"As a businessperson, you shouldn't care about the reason behind the work. Just be glad when some comes your way."

She set the boxes on the floor behind the driver's seat and rummaged around in her purse. Finally, in the side pocket, she found her business card holder. She handed him a few cards. "I am grateful for every customer who walks through my door. But if you start pimping my business, I'm afraid it'll come with strings attached. I don't want to owe you anything."

Standing straight, she gave herself a mental pat on the back. There was a time she'd never have had the guts to say that aloud.

He studied the card for a moment. "Love in Bloom. You really did it."

"Did what?"

"I remember lying in bed with you, talking about how much you wanted your own flower shop. I'm impressed. You did everything you set out to do."

His words shouldn't have had any effect on her, but they did. A gentle warmth spread through her belly at his praise.

He slid the cards into the pocket of his jeans and looked at her in silence for a minute. She tried not to fidget, but the intensity of all that attention on her made her want to hide.

Or curl up in his arms.

Oh, hell no. She needed to get to bed. Thoughts like that about Kevin O'Malley would only lead to heartbreak.

He finally moved, slowly stretching an arm out to brace on the car beside her. "I'll never expect anything more from you than you're willing to give."

It took her a second to figure out what he was talking about. Then she realized that he was referring to her accusing him of attaching strings. Her breathing went shallow and her heart sped up. A big part of her had expected him to try to kiss her, but a bigger part was glad he hadn't.

He spoke the truth. In a nutshell, he'd managed to express her single biggest problem. She was always willing to give a relationship everything without knowing she'd get anything in return. Kevin had been one of many men to teach her that. In recent years, she'd done everything possible to protect herself as she attempted to learn to be more assertive. Next time she fell for a guy, she planned to be able to demand what she wanted. It was a work in progress.

Kevin waited, but she had nothing to say to him. He

pushed off the car. "Good night, Kathy. I had a great time tonight."

"Me too," she admitted, which probably wasn't the smartest move.

As he stepped away, he reached and opened the door for her. When she turned and sat, he closed it. He waited until she started the engine and shifted into gear to leave.

She offered a small wave as she pulled away. In her rearview mirror, she saw Kevin standing in the near-empty parking lot, hands tucked into his pockets, staring at her.

She should've left sooner. If she'd really been thinking, she would've started the party planning conversation first thing instead of letting him lead. As she made her way home, she realized that she had, in fact, underestimated Kevin. He'd been polite and kind and funny, so she played right into his hand. She'd had dinner with him and enjoyed it.

No matter what he'd said about them being friends, she knew better. She'd gotten good at being honest with herself, even if she was still working on being blunt with those around her. In being true to herself, she had to admit that she was still attracted to Kevin. And he was attracted to her.

Which meant that she had to double her defenses when she was with him. If he wanted to pretend as if they were friends, she'd show him that she could be a friend. And nothing more.

Chapter Three

Kevin stared at the e-mail in front of him as he tapped a pen on the desktop. The mayor was contracting with an outside company to handle tourism for the city. Chicago had been outsourcing various things for years. Some of it made sense, other things didn't. He wasn't sure which category this fell under, but he knew that with the advent of this kind of push, there would be opportunities for promotions, or at least lateral moves.

The mayor was looking for ways to implement such a program. The details outlined were vague, so Kevin dug into research. He looked at how other major cities attracted tourism. He came up with a handful of companies that were currently doing the types of things the mayor wanted: a single website where business could request proposals for conferences and conventions, a searchable calendar of events, a solid marketing plan. Bottom line, the mayor didn't want another committee draining city resources without producing positive results.

Kevin wrote up a proposal for the mayor, but he saw the need for an additional player. A position for which he would be the perfect candidate. Within his proposal he included the creation of a liaison position within the mayor's office so that the mayor could be kept in the loop without having to be hands-on.

With it being July, the timing of such a program seemed odd. But if the right company got into place, they could move quickly to use the winter season to promote Chicago as a vacation spot. The city was great in the winter, especially with outdoor skating downtown and indoor winter festivals at Navy Pier. But nothing could touch summer in the city. From sunup till late at night, everyone could find something to do in the summer.

Kevin clicked over to the calendar of events and it looked bare-boned. It should've been packed. July had barely started. Then the pieces clicked into place. He'd remembered hearing some office gossip about the woman who had run the city events website. He'd never gotten the full story because he hadn't cared, but if she'd been canned—or more likely, forced to resign—that would've opened the door for the mayor's new plan.

Thoughts of summer brought him to his own plans. The highlight of the season would take place later this week, the annual block party at home. His dad's house, the block where he'd grown up. As far back as he could remember, the block party had been the defining point of his summer. Damn, probably the best part of everyone's summer. Balloon toss, relay races, and the football game against the O'Learys were staples of his childhood summers.

The block party was a place of many of his firsts. It was during one of those football games that he'd broken his first bone. It was at one of the bonfires that he'd kissed his first girlfriend. It was the place where he'd first gotten drunk.

It was also the place where he'd first met Kathy. He didn't think she'd attended a block party since. He felt bad about that but didn't even know why. She hadn't grown up in his neighborhood. But all of them had brought friends to the block party over the years. He knew without having to ask that she stayed away because of him. One more reason for Moira to hate him.

He pulled out his phone and called Jimmy.

"What do you need?"

"Does it physically hurt you to say hello when you answer the phone?" Kevin asked. "How the hell does Moira put up with you?"

"I have other charms. You only call when you want something and I'm at work, so spit it out."

"Not true. Sometimes I call to get together for drinks."

"Yeah, you *want* to get together."

Kevin sighed. Jimmy was in a mood. Maybe it would've been easier to go to Moira, even with her general pissy attitude toward him. "I want you to get Moira to invite Kathy to the block party."

Jimmy laughed. It was quiet, maybe more of a chuff, but it was there. "Don't you think if she were interested, she would've called you?"

"I think she wants to keep her distance from me, and I get that. But if I want to convince her that I'm a different man, she needs to see that in a place that's not threatening."

Now Jimmy started to laugh in earnest.

"What the hell is so funny? I'm not the same guy I was five years ago."

Jimmy coughed and then said, "I know that. But I also know that there's something about the block party that brings out your juvenile side. You fuck with Moira every year. Hell, you fuck with everyone."

"I can control myself. I promise." He sighed. "I want Kathy to think about me in a different light. We had dinner a couple of weeks ago to coordinate bachelor/bachelorette parties and we've texted since then. But I need an in, and I think the block party could be it."

He could picture Jimmy shaking his head as he debated. Jimmy came across as an asshole to most people, but what they didn't see was that if Jimmy cared about someone, he'd do anything, even risk the wrath of his fiancée. "What is it about this woman? When she disappeared years ago, you didn't seem all that affected. Why now? Why her?"

"I can't explain it. When I saw her at your engagement party, I was genuinely disappointed that she had a boyfriend. I've spent the better part of a year thinking about my time with her, and she's single. I was young and stupid, but what we had was more than fucking. With every other girl I'd been with back then, it was nothing more than a good time. Kathy was different. I felt it then and I screwed it up."

Silence met him and he thought Jimmy had hung up. "Jimmy?"

A heavy sigh. "That's what I get for asking. My damn woman is ruining me."

Kevin knew that Moira had softened Jimmy, not that Kevin would ever say that out loud to his big brother. Hearing Jimmy admit it, though, made him smile and gave him hope. "Does that mean you'll get Kathy there?"

"How the hell am I supposed to convince Moira to invite her? She'll never believe me if I tell her that you want another chance."

"Hell, no. You can't tell Moira."

"I'm not lying to her."

"I'm not asking you to lie. Just tell her to invite Kathy because the rest of the wedding party will be there. She'll have fun."

"I'll see what I can do." Then he hung up.

Kevin didn't care that Jimmy couldn't be bothered to

say good-bye any more than he could say hello, because if Jimmy said he'd try, it was as good as done.

He turned back to his computer to address the next press release he had to improve. He spent hours every day cleaning up communication from people in the mayor's office. He couldn't say it was from the mayor because he knew the man had other people writing most things, but really, they sucked.

Just as the document opened, one of his coworkers stopped by his desk. Deb plopped in the chair he had in his cubicle for nonexistent guests.

"I owe you a beer," she announced.

"Yeah?" he asked with one eye still on his screen. *Don't these people use spell-check?* "For what?"

"The florist you recommended was amazing. She managed to pull together centerpieces for the banquet in a day's time. She totally saved my ass."

Kevin slid back from the desk and spun to look at Deb. When he'd heard one of the interns calling florists to get prices, he'd given her one of Kathy's cards.

"Instead of buying me a beer, do me a favor and use her again."

"That's not doing you a favor. That's a given. She deserves the work after pulling that off. Plus she didn't even overcharge." She leaned an elbow on the desk. "You should probably have a talk with her and let her know how much we usually spend on these things. It wouldn't look good for me to tell her, but as her friend . . ."

Kevin smiled. "I doubt she'd raise her prices just because she's doing something for city hall. She's a straight shooter."

When Deb left, Kevin looked at his phone. He wanted to call Kathy, at least text her to see how she thought the banquet went. He knew that Deb could sing someone's praises behind their backs, but rarely to their faces. When he'd given her Kathy's card, he'd told her to be nice, but he wasn't sure Deb knew how to be nice. In Deb's eyes Kathy was a godsend, but Kathy might very well be cursing his name for handing out her card.

He sent a text: I hope Deb was nice to you. I know she was in a pinch, and she just told me you saved her ass.

He went back to fix the messy memo on his computer. His phone sat near the keyboard taunting him. Kathy might be busy with customers and couldn't text, but the teenage boy in him wanted an immediate response. By the time he rewrote most of the press release and sent it back, Kathy still hadn't responded.

Just when he'd about given up, the phone buzzed.

Glad it all worked out for her. She was demanding, but not unbearable. Thanks for thinking of me.

I should be thanking you. You made her look good, which makes me look good because I passed on your card.

His fingers itched to say more. He wanted to ask her out again, spend time with her, but knew he'd get shot down. But he also knew that if he didn't make some moves soon, he'd probably never see her again after Jimmy's wedding. Then he decided he would set the groundwork for Moira and Jimmy and plant the seed of the block party.

Our annual block party is this week. You remember that, right? You should come. It's a blast.

Her response came immediately. Of course I remember. It's where we met.

Kevin didn't know what came over him. He saw an opening and asked even though he'd already asked Jimmy to handle it. Stop by. I'll be on my best behavior.

Ha! Moira has told me too many stories for me to believe that. But maybe.

He swallowed a groan. Damn Moira was screwing this up without trying. But at least he'd gotten a maybe out of her. He'd prove to Kathy and Moira that he was a better man.

Kathy stepped back from the cooler and leaned against the case. Five more minutes until closing. She wanted nothing more than to twist the lock early, but she couldn't. Her hours said she was open until six, so six it was.

When the jingle of the bell above the door alerted her to another customer, she wanted to kick herself for being such a rule follower. Even her own darn rules. Sometimes being the owner sucked. She pushed off the cooler and smiled as she went to the front of the shop.

Her smile widened when she saw it wasn't a customer, but Moira standing at the counter. "Hey, you. What's up?"

"I figured since it was closing time, we could catch up." Moira held up two cups. "I brought chocolate shakes."

Kathy glanced at the clock, saw that it was six, and locked the door. "If you'd called, I could've met you somewhere."

"I wanted to catch you off guard."

"Why?" she asked as she reached for a shake. She sipped, or at least tried to, but the drink was too thick to be pulled into the straw easily.

Moira hopped onto the battered but sturdy counter and crossed her legs. "I had an interesting conversation with Jimmy today."

"Yeah?"

"He asked if I had invited you to the block party. I told him that I hadn't exactly invited you, but that you know you're always welcome to join us. I didn't think I needed to extend a formal invitation. Besides, you've begged off ever since the mess with Kevin."

Kathy waited. While Moira would never run out of energy for talking, she would eventually run out of breath.

When Moira stopped, Kathy waited some more before asking, "And?"

"And the whole conversation was weird because first, Jimmy rarely invites anyone to the party, so why would he think of inviting *my* friend. Second, the reason Jimmy doesn't like to invite extra people is because that gives him more people to keep an eye on, and because you're my friend, he would feel the need to make sure you're okay. So then I started to wonder more about *why* Jimmy brought this up."

Kathy swallowed a lump of chocolate shake. "Why not just ask him?"

Moira snorted. "Getting information out of Jimmy is harder than getting my mom to talk about her feelings." She swirled her straw through her shake. "I think Kevin put him up to it."

Kathy absorbed the statement, knowing in her gut that Moira would get to this point. But she didn't have anything to say. She hadn't talked to Kevin. Not since his text yesterday.

Although Kevin's text had surprised her, it had also made her smile. She'd worked her ass off most of the night to make the centerpieces for Deb Hanover. It wasn't until the flowers were out the door that Kathy had the time to find out who the woman actually was. When Deb placed the order, she'd only told Kathy that it was a banquet for city officials. After the delivery, Kathy found that Deb was pretty high up in the city's food chain. Her name was attached to almost every high-profile event sponsored by the mayor's office.

"That! That look!" Moira yelled, and pointed at her. "What's going on with Kevin?"

"What do you mean?"

Moira's mouth tightened and she arched a brow.

"We've been in touch to plan the bachelor/bachelorette parties on the same night. Then he gave my card to some woman he works with and got me a huge order."

Moira slid from the counter and stood in front of her. She was so short that she barely passed Kathy's shoulders. Moira tilted her face up. "So you're talking to him."

Kathy couldn't tell if Moira felt betrayed or intrigued.

"Kind of. Mostly we text." She set her cup down. "We had dinner together to talk wedding parties."

"I knew it. I knew he'd try to weasel his way back into your life."

"What?"

"When he got a glimpse of you at the engagement party last year, he looked like a wolf homing in on his prey. I cut him off, but I honestly didn't think he'd listen. Seems like I was right."

"I don't think that's it. He's been friendly and laid back. He hasn't done anything nefarious." Kathy knew better than to lay any of her suspicions out for Moira to grab on to. What she said was the truth; Kevin had been nothing but nice.

"That's not like Kevin. What could he be up to?"

"Don't you have anything better to obsess about? Like your wedding?"

"My wedding is planned. Kevin is the only wild card. I have no idea what to expect from him as best man. I'm afraid he'll take Jimmy to Vegas for the bachelor party and marry him off to some stripper,"

Kathy laughed. *Obsessed* was too kind a word for this. "Even if Kevin had some evil plan, there is no way in hell Jimmy would fall for it. Jimmy would never marry someone else, no matter how drunk he was."

"Yeah," Moira acquiesced, "but what about the toast at the wedding? Kevin has known me his whole life. What if he gets up in front of everyone and tells embarrassing stories?"

"He probably will tell stories. About Jimmy. Why do you let Kevin make you crazy?"

Moira slumped. "I don't know. He's made me nuts for as long as I can remember. It's like his sole purpose in life is to make me miserable."

Kathy put her arm around Moira's shoulders. "Kevin isn't going to do anything to ruin your wedding. Even if he thought he was being funny, I'm pretty sure Jimmy would kick his ass." As she spoke, she knew that Moira's fears were really shaking her up. She sighed and added, "Do you want me to talk to him?"

"I can't ask you to do that. Jimmy said the same thing. Kevin won't do anything bad. I just don't trust him. He made me so miserable as a kid."

"This is going to sound stupid, but have you ever said this to him?"

Moira pulled away and reclaimed her seat on the counter.

"He does it intentionally. What good would it do me to point out how effective it is?"

Kathy saw where Moira was coming from but something made her think that Kevin didn't truly realize the effect his teasing had on Moira. "Maybe if you explained it to him like you are to me. He is a guy after all. They're not too bright when it comes to understanding women."

Moira slurped her shake. "Wouldn't matter to Kevin." Another loud slurp. "I'm probably being melodramatic. You're right. Jimmy will keep him in line."

She spoke without her usual enthusiasm or conviction. Kathy hated seeing her friend like this. It was too out of character.

Moira abruptly changed the subject. "So tell me what's going on with you."

"I've been working, getting ready for my best friend's wedding. That's it." She sank onto the stool she kept behind the register. She rarely used it because once she sat down, she usually didn't want to get back up. Right now her feet were screaming.

"Come on, Kath, give me something. A distraction from my stress."

"Sorry to disappoint. You're the one with the glamorous life. You should tell me about all the fancy parties you're going to."

For the next hour, Kathy listened to Moira chatter, and it was like old times. By the time their cups were drained, Kathy was rejuvenated. Her body was still tired, but her mind had spun around thinking about Kevin. For a man who had been out of her life for years, he'd certainly been taking up quite a bit of space as of late, and she didn't know what to do about that.

But seeing Moira so stressed about the possibility of

Kevin wreaking havoc at the wedding, Kathy decided it was her duty as maid of honor to prevent that from happening. She just needed a plan.

The neighborhood block party seemed like the perfect venue.

Chapter Four

Kevin parked around the corner from his childhood home. The street was already blocked off by wooden horses and some families were assembling card tables and canopies to provide shade for the day ahead. The area hadn't changed much over the years. Sure, some people died or moved away and younger families took their places, but the traditions remained the same. The families who had planted roots here decades ago passed the torch to the younger generation.

Many of his childhood friends came back for this party every year. They always had. In college, it had been a way to reconnect with high school buddies. Now they came with families of their own, and Kevin felt out of place in the crowd. Even his own damn brothers were falling in love and getting married.

He hefted the bags of groceries from the back of his SUV and walked around the corner. He glanced over at the O'Leary house. He'd spent his entire childhood jealous of that family. They were much like his, six children to the O'Malley five, but Kevin had no doubt that had his mother, Siobhan, lived, she would've had more children.

The lack of a mother was what separated the families.

Jimmy and Liam had remained best friends and Kevin and Moira had been in the same elementary school class every year. But once Siobhan had been killed, the O'Learys had stayed away. Climbing the concrete steps to the house, Kevin admitted that it had probably been the occupants of this house that had kept the O'Learys away. His dad had become distant, and Jimmy took care of everyone in his stead. The O'Malley boys had always been a little out of control.

He set a bag down and shoved the ancient door open. Whenever he got around to buying a house, he wanted a door like this one. It had taken a beating from all of the O'Malleys. It had been slammed countless times, had hockey pucks smashed into it, had baseballs thrown against it, and it still functioned. Scarred and battered, but working.

A lot like the man sitting on the couch.

"Hey, Dad," Kevin called as he took the groceries into the kitchen.

"You bring burgers?"

"I brought meat to make burgers."

Seamus huffed.

"What are you moaning about? All I have to do is plop that meat in front of Liam O'Leary and he works his magic. Best burgers you've ever had and you know it." Kevin unloaded the food into the refrigerator, which had actually been stocked. Weird, since Norah had moved out last month.

Then Kevin remembered Tommy's new wife, Deirdre. Another O'Leary. "Tommy and Sean around?"

"Tommy's upstairs. Make sure you call out. Deirdre's home."

Kevin paused before getting to the steps. His dad not

only gave a thoughtful warning, but something in his voice sounded odd. He looked at his dad, whose focus remained on the TV screen. "Yo, Tommy. Time to get ready."

A few minutes later, Tommy pounced down the steps wearing nothing but a pair of jeans. "Since when do you show up this early?"

"Since it shouldn't be Jimmy's job to get food for all of us and do all the work. He's getting married in a couple of weeks. Don't you think it's time we picked up the slack?"

Tommy crossed his arms and stared. "Who are you and what have you done with my brother?"

"Funny. Go make sure the grill is clean."

"It's clean. We cooked dinner on it two days ago."

"We?"

"I'm a married man, now. I have a wife who wants to eat at home."

Tommy had just married the O'Learys' cousin who had been visiting from Ireland. They were all still getting used to the idea that Tommy had been the first to tie the knot. And in secret. "So your wife is the reason there's actually decent food in the house?"

"I go grocery shopping. Been doing it for a while. If you were around more, you'd know that."

His siblings were always making little digs like that. As if he was never supposed to grow up and move out. At some point, each of them had cycled back around and moved in with Dad again. Not him. He liked having his own place.

Softer footsteps sounded on the stairs. Deirdre entered the dining room wearing shorts and one of Tommy's old T-shirts tied at the waist. Her red hair was pulled into a high ponytail and for a moment, Kevin was struck by how much she looked like a younger version of Moira.

"Hi," he said.

"Hi," she replied with a small nod of her head. She turned to Tommy. "Will this do?"

"With that much skin showing, Cupcake, you better invest in some sunscreen. July in Chicago isn't something a white girl like you can play with."

"You speak as though you're some golden Adonis," she shot back playfully.

Kevin felt like an intruder even here. He cleared his throat. "When's Jimmy getting here?"

"Probably any minute."

Deirdre took Tommy's hand. "What do we need to do? I'm excited for this party."

"I brought food. It's in the fridge. I'm going over to the O'Learys' to see if they need help with the keg or anything."

He grabbed the ground beef, left the house, and crossed the street. A few people called out to him, and he waved a greeting. Michael O'Leary stood at the corner of the house setting down a keg in a barrel.

"Hey, man. Good to see you," Kevin called. "How'd you get off from the firehouse this year?"

"I worked the Fourth. Long-ass night of stupid people. I'll take the neighborhood stupid shit over people blowing themselves up any day of the week."

"Liam here yet?"

"Yeah. He's in the kitchen. Door's unlocked. Go on in."

For as long as he'd known the O'Learys, he'd never just walked into their house. In fact, he'd only gone into the building when he'd been tagging along with Jimmy and Liam. He knocked and twisted the knob. No one was in the living room, so he walked through toward the kitchen. "Liam?"

"Yeah."

The layout was the same as his dad's house, but it

somehow felt foreign. In the kitchen, he said, "Hey, man. Wanted to see if you needed help with anything."

Liam turned with a confused look on his face. "Jimmy okay?"

"Don't see why not. He's not here yet. I brought some ground beef since we always con you into making our food." He set the bag on the counter where Liam was making patties.

"Thanks."

"Thank *you*. You feed us every year." Kevin leaned against the counter while Liam dug his hands back into the meat. "I also wanted to make sure you're really okay with me being best man."

Liam lifted a shoulder. "He's your brother. I get it. No hard feelings." He paused, leveled a stare at Kevin, and then added, "Just don't fuck it up."

He'd been hearing some version of that his whole life. While it had been warranted when he was a teen, he'd had his life together for a long time; unfortunately, no one seemed to notice. "I won't."

Liam nodded. As much as Liam and Moira looked alike, his personality was nothing like his little sister's. Liam was fine working in silence.

Straightening, Kevin said, "I'll be across the street. Holler if you need anything."

As he walked back out into the stifling air of summer heat, a motorcycle rumbled down the street. Sean and his girlfriend, Emma, rode up and parked in front of the house. They dismounted and took off helmets with a smile.

Even though he was envious of what his brothers had found—and so much earlier than he had—his heart swelled with pride. They had grown into good men. Their mom would be proud.

"Hey," Sean yelled. "What're you doing here so early?"

Kevin crossed the street. "Figured I'd help set up. Don't know why everyone is so surprised. I was here early last year."

He'd shown up early last year to help because he'd hoped Moira had invited Kathy. He was like a lovesick kid. This year, however, he knew what to do. He had an approach. If he won Moira over, Kathy would give him another chance. Their chemistry still clicked, so he only had to jump over the hurdle of his past stupid actions.

In his gut he knew that if Kathy gave him another shot, he'd have the chance to have what his brothers did.

Kathy sat in her car and stared at her phone. Moira had texted her at least three times this morning telling her she didn't really have to come unless she wanted to. She shouldn't feel pressured.

But Kathy did feel an obligation to Moira. When they had met in college, Moira had broken through all of Kathy's carefully constructed walls and taught her how to be a friend. To be part of a real friendship with ups and downs.

It had been Moira who suggested Kathy go see a therapist. Moira had seen past the face of calm and peace Kathy projected to the world. And without that little shove from Moira, Kathy wouldn't be in the relatively sane place she was now. Until she had started talking to a therapist, she hadn't even really understood that her childhood had been traumatic. Not the kind laced with violence and physical abuse or addiction, but one of passive-aggressive barbs and hurled insults. The kind of place that taught her that if she could keep the peace, everything would be okay.

Except it never was.

And her learned behaviors created an obstacle for her in establishing healthy relationships.

So, yeah, she owed Moira. And spending time with Kevin wasn't torture. She could put those walls back up to protect herself in order to help a friend.

Grabbing the container of cookies she'd bought, she tucked her phone into the pocket of her shorts and walked toward Moira's mom's house. From down the block she heard kids yelling and laughing. At the corner, she took in the scene in front of her. A group of adults huddled in front of the O'Leary house, so Kathy waited until she saw Moira's red hair.

Nearing the group, she heard Moira's brother Ryan say, "Who else is playing? We're pretty even splitting up by family."

Jimmy stepped forward. "Moira's with us."

Moira laughed. "I'm still an O'Leary, babe. For the next two weeks anyway."

"That's not even right," Jimmy grumbled.

Moira caught sight of Kathy and squealed. "You made it. You'll play, right? We get Kathy."

Before she even knew what was happening, Kathy found herself thrust toward the crowd of O'Learys and someone took her cookies. "What am I playing?"

"Football. Annual game."

"Well, if Moira stays with you, I guess we get Cupcake. She's an O'Malley," Tommy O'Malley said.

Moira lifted her chin. "Fine. But Shane's ours."

Kathy had no idea who Shane was, but the man was big. Then she remembered Moira talking about Maggie's boyfriend. He moved to the O'Leary side. Definitely the kind of guy you wanted protecting you in a football game.

"We get Kai. He's mine," Norah said from the O'Malley

camp. She held on to the arm of a man who was the size of a wall. So much for having Shane on their team.

"Hey, O'Malley," another woman said. She was much shorter than Jimmy, who was the only O'Malley to turn to look. She pointed at the woman across from her. "You sure it's okay for me and Carmen to play?"

"Why wouldn't it be?"

"We're adding a bit of color to this group. All this white is kind of blinding."

Moira's brother Liam started laughing. Carmen stared at the ground, a hint of pink filling her cheeks. Kathy had only met her a couple of times, but Carmen was always a little shy.

"What's so funny?" Moira asked, giving her brother a shove.

Liam straightened. "Carmen and her cousin used to call me Wonder Bread." He lifted his shirt. "I came by the nickname honestly." Pointing at Moira, he added, "Like you."

Everyone joined in the laughter because with the exception of their red hair, Liam and Moira were white enough to disappear in a snowstorm.

In truth, Kathy didn't quite fit in the mix either, but no one called any attention to her.

"You should play on our team, Gabby," Carmen said.

Jimmy held Gabby's arm. "No way. For all the years Griffin Walker played, you claimed him as an O'Leary. Gabby's my partner, she plays with the O'Malleys. Plus, she makes us even."

With Jimmy's comment, Kathy finally connected that Gabby was a police detective and Jimmy's partner at work. Kathy hadn't met her, but Moira talked about her often.

There were a few stragglers on the outskirts of the group. Kathy nudged Moira. "What about them?"

Moira smiled. "They want to watch. Everyone's welcome to play, but the first game of the day is O'Learys versus O'Malleys. It's the way it's always been."

"I'm neither."

"Today, you're an honorary O'Leary because you're here as my guest." She started walking away as did everyone else.

As a mob, they crossed the street kitty-corner to the open field behind a school. Kevin strode next to her. "Glad you made it."

"Why?" she asked.

"I want to spend time with you. I had fun at dinner. Although I take some issue with you being on Moira's team since I invited you first."

"But I'm Moira's friend."

"We're friends."

Kathy looked at him from the corner of her eye. "I'm not sure what we are, but like Moira said, today my allegiance goes to the O'Learys."

The O'Learys huddled to come up with a plan.

"Can someone explain the rules for those of us who are new to this?" Kathy asked.

Ryan looked at her. "Mostly we play tag football. Sometimes it gets a little rough, but no one gets hurt. If someone passes the ball to you, run with it. Don't get tagged by an O'Malley."

"Sounds easy enough."

Moira clasped her hands. "I'll go down field. Kath, you stay near the middle."

"Why?" Ryan asked.

"I'll be a distraction. I always am because they'll assume you'll throw to me. Get it to Kathy and she'll score."

Kathy shook her head. "I don't know about that."

"You ran track in high school. Hell, you still run because you like it. Trust me, you can outrun them. They won't see it coming."

"Little sister, I like the way you think," Ryan said. He turned to the other brothers. "You guys make a path for her."

Shane stepped closer. "And me?"

"You cover Jimmy. He's the best they have. He played football. The rest of them are hockey all the way."

Carmen and Maggie crossed their arms. Maggie said, "Are we just supposed to stand there and look pretty?"

Shane turned to Maggie. "You are good at that."

She shoved his shoulder. "We can play."

"We'll need you after this. We'll only be able to pull this play once. Then they'll be all over Kathy."

That didn't sound fun at all.

"Let's go." Ryan clapped and they all spread out to their respective positions. Maggie jumped on Shane's back, and he gave her a piggyback ride to midfield.

Kathy swallowed hard as she realized Kevin was guarding her. Knowing him, he'd volunteered for this spot.

Jimmy let out a sharp whistle and then nodded to Ryan.

Carmen snapped the ball to Ryan and all the O'Learys scrambled. If she hadn't known their plan, she would guess they didn't have one. Before she knew it, the ball was hurtling toward her. Conscious of Kevin standing beside her, she snatched the ball and turned.

He barely made a step in her direction when she'd taken off. She had a clear path all the way down. Kevin chased, but even with his slightly longer legs, he couldn't catch her.

In the end zone, she spiked the ball and jumped up and down. Kevin bent over at the waist, out of breath.

"What. The. Hell. Was. That?" he huffed out.

"That was a touchdown," she said with a broad smile.

The rest of her team came over and cheered. Jimmy grabbed the ball and shot a dirty look at Kevin.

"Like to see you catch her," he said.

Kathy patted his shoulder. "Don't feel bad. I ran track in high school."

"Shit. I forgot about that."

Had she ever told him?

"You went to state three years in a row. Fuck me. I never had a chance." He raised a hand. "You brought in a ringer. If Jimmy can't be quarterback, Kathy can't be running back."

"I'm not a running back. I've never even played football."

"Sweetheart, you just ran harder and faster than any amateur player I've seen."

"If it's any consolation, they know we won't be able to do that twice, so I don't think you'll have to worry about me."

"That's what they all say."

"Then maybe you should have the big guy keep an eye on me. Or Tommy or Sean."

"They're all too busy looking at their girlfriends. You're stuck with me."

That's what she'd been hoping he'd say. The more he focused on her, the less time he'd have to bother Moira. The problem was that his words made her almost as warm as the sun beating down on them.

Kevin was having more fun at the football game than he'd had in a long time. They played every year and the teams were slightly different each time. Although they all tried to be home for the block party, and this game in particular, there was always some shifting, especially as girlfriends and boyfriends entered the picture.

He'd planned on guarding Moira during the game, but Jimmy shot that down, so Kevin was with Kathy, not that he minded. In between plays, they chatted about work and families, mostly him filling her in on all the new players on the field.

One of the best things about the game, though, was that his dad and Mrs. O'Leary sat in lawn chairs on the sidelines and cheered for all of them. *Cheering* wasn't really the right word because his dad yelled at them when things didn't go their way, and he could almost hear Mrs. O'Leary cluck her tongue at them all. But as their kids all left the field, both parents were smiling.

Kevin wasn't sure what had been happening with his dad, but ever since Deirdre had joined their brood as Tommy's wife, Dad had been spending a lot of time with Mrs. O'Leary. She was good for him, though, because she forced him to get off his ass and do things. Even if it was to go to church, it was better than his permanent location on the couch.

The O'Learys won the game by a touchdown and Kevin clenched his teeth when Moira came over to gloat. He would *not* engage in anything that would make him feel better. He would earn a chance with Kathy by winning Moira over, even if it killed him in the process.

"You had an all-star runner and a football player on your team," he rebutted with a nod toward Shane.

"You guys had Jimmy."

"Jimmy's getting old. I bet Shane could take him."

Jimmy glared. "I'm not old. The teams were evenly matched. They won."

For the first time ever, Kevin saw that it didn't bother

Jimmy to lose. With the exception of the dirty look at Kevin, Jimmy was smiling. Moira made him deliriously happy.

Kevin looked at Kathy and wondered if she'd ever look at him like that.

"Time for water balloon toss," Moira called.

Jimmy said, "Liam and I will start cooking. Any special requests?"

Kevin pointed at his brother. "Don't you mean Liam will cook and you'll stand around barking orders?"

Everyone snickered.

"We all have our talents," Jimmy responded.

Kevin bumped Moira's shoulder. "What the hell did you do to my big brother? He's a big softy now. Nothing riles him up."

"It's amazing what the love of a good woman can do." She froze in her tracks. "Holy crap. That's it. You're such an insufferable ass because you haven't found a woman who can put up with you."

"Are you going to fix that?"

"Hell no. I couldn't do that to some unsuspecting woman."

Maggie and Shane came down the steps of the house carrying buckets filled with water balloons.

"Let's be partners," Kevin said before Moira walked away.

"Yeah, sure. I'm gonna give you the opportunity to turn this into a wet T-shirt contest." Then she added, "Again," in reference to him soaking her a couple of years ago.

"I'm trying to redeem myself here. I'm not going to pull anything."

On his side, a soft hand slipped into his. "Partners?" Kathy asked.

He looked at her hand in his, and she promptly dropped

it. Damn. Now he was caught. How could he prove to Moira that he was a good guy if she wouldn't give him a chance? Then again, maybe he just needed to prove it to Kathy.

"Sure," he said.

They lined up and Colin, the oldest O'Leary, blew a whistle. Moira and Norah partnered up next to him and Kathy, Moira warily beside him. With every blow of the whistle, the partners each took another step apart. Moira deftly tossed the balloon and Norah caught it.

"I wasn't playing a game by suggesting we partner up," he said to Moira.

"Yeah, sure."

"Seriously."

"Wish I could believe that, but after a lifetime of misery, I know better."

The balloon came at him and he cradled it. Moira's words hit him hard and they rattled him as he tossed the balloon back, arching it high in the air.

Kathy squealed and ran forward to catch it, but she grabbed it too hard, and it exploded in her hands, splashing water all over her.

"I'm so sorry," he said as he met her in the middle.

But she wasn't mad. She was laughing as water dripped down her legs. She was absolutely beautiful with her head thrown back, the springy curls in her ponytail whipping around. "I'll get even. That was the lamest throw ever."

The light brown of her eyes sparked with her laughter and Kevin would've done anything to freeze that moment.

"Come on. I'll buy you a beer."

"Big spender today?"

"Of course. The O'Learys provide the kegs. Free beer."

"That was a fun game. While it lasted anyway."

"We'd never beat Moira. She wins every year, no matter

who her partner is. I thought this year might be my chance, but she turned me down."

Kathy wiped ineffectively at the water on her arms and followed him toward the keg at the O'Learys'.

"You want me to get you a towel?"

"Nah. I'm fine. It won't take long to dry in the sun." She walked at his side. "So what were you and Moira talking about?"

"I was trying to convince her that I didn't have ulterior motives by offering to be her partner for the toss." He cleared his throat at the twisted half-truth. "She didn't believe me."

"Not surprising. She's not part of the Kevin O'Malley fan club."

"There's a fan club? Why didn't anyone tell me?"

Kathy laughed again. That sound alone was enough to make him want more time with her.

At the keg, he pumped and poured drinks for both of them. Jimmy and Maggie were setting food out on the tables. Plates filled with burgers and hot dogs sat alongside bowls of salad and fruit and chips. The O'Learys might have their flaws but putting together a party wasn't one. Years ago, Jimmy had finally given up on trying to get his siblings to do the work, and they all just chipped in and gave the O'Learys money toward the food and beer and both families ate together.

"You want to eat, or wait awhile?"

"I can wait," she answered.

"Come on then. I'll take you on a tour of the neighborhood." This being-honest-and-laying-your-heart-out-there shit was tough. Kevin had never approached any relationship like this. Not that he was a constant liar or anything, but there was a customary dance between a man and a woman. It allowed for some flexibility in what he wanted to reveal at any given time. But he'd taken Jimmy's advice and played it differently.

She hadn't run away screaming when he asked her to hang out with him. He took that as a decent sign. And now, she was walking with him through his childhood neighborhood.

He'd never brought a girl home before. Sure, he'd introduced a few to his family. Hard not to when he spent so much time with them, but this was different. He wanted Kathy to know where he came from.

Pointing at the tree on the corner, he said, "That was where I fell the second time I broke my arm."

"Second time?" she asked.

"I suffered a few broken bones in childhood. Broke both arms—different times."

"How did you fall out of the tree?"

"I was dumb. I did something to piss Jimmy off, and he was way bigger than me. Still is. I'd climbed the tree to get away from him. I went too high and then fell." They got to the tree, and he looked up into the branches. "It sucked because I ended up missing half of hockey season. The upside was that Jimmy felt so guilty that he did anything I wanted the whole time I wore that cast."

Kathy shook her head, making her curls bounce. With a smile, she said, "You started the trouble and then took advantage of his guilt. And Jimmy says Moira's the menace."

"How about you? Were you trouble growing up?"

With her lips pressed together, she shook her head again. "No one to get into trouble with."

He knew she was an only child. Every time he thought about it, it seemed so lonely. Bringing up her childhood took the smile from her face, so he changed the subject again. He pointed at the house they were in front of.

"Danny Lynch lived here. He was my partner in crime for most of my childhood. He was the one who told me to climb the tree to get away from Jimmy."

"Does he still live here?"

"No. His was one of the few families that actually left this neighborhood."

"Is the neighborhood that fabulous or do people stay because it's what they know?"

"I never thought much about it. I guess a little of both. It's a tight-knit community in a huge city. Not too many people in Chicago can say they know all their neighbors. This is like a small town. We take care of our own here. But it's the people who make it that way, not the location itself."

"I never had that. We moved around when I was a kid, so I sampled a lot of neighborhoods. Some were good, some not, but we never lived in a place like this." She tucked her free hand into the pocket of her shorts as they crossed to walk in the middle of the street. "Do you miss it?"

"Yeah. But I don't regret moving out. I needed to get away, become my own person, away from Jimmy. But one day, I want to buy a house in a neighborhood like this. I want my kids to have a childhood like I had."

"You want kids?"

She said it like he'd just announced that he wanted to have an orgy in the street.

"Yeah." Then he thought maybe her question was less about him and more about her. "Don't you?"

"Maybe. I'm still working on me, so I'm not ready to try to teach someone else how to live."

He took a few steps in front of her and walked backward as he talked. Eyeing her up and down, he said, "Working on what? You look damn fine."

"I'm working on the inside stuff. Nothing you can see."

"Anything I can help with?"

She shot him a glare, but couldn't hold it and smiled.

He moved beside her again and put an arm around her shoulders. "Just tell me this. Am I the cause of any of the things you need to work on?"

He hated the thought that his careless attitude five years ago caused ongoing damage to her.

"You didn't cause anything. But being with you taught me about myself and what I need to work on."

"You want to tell me about it?"

"Not today. Today is about having fun."

She didn't shut him down completely. In fact, she left the door open for the conversation to happen at some point in the future.

"Tell me about the rest of the people here," she said.

Leaving his arm around her, he pointed with the hand holding his beer. "That's the Doyles' house. They were the only family that could give the O'Malleys a run for our money. Half of them got kicked out of school at one point or another. If the gossip is true, one even did some jail time."

"Sounds like a rough bunch."

"Rough, yeah, but not bad. Their mom was raising them alone. Seven kids. Six boys and one girl. One day, the dad just up and left. Rumors ran wild then. Some say he had a girlfriend who lured him away from his family. Others say he was into the mob for gambling and they made him disappear."

"So much intrigue. Do you have a theory?" She kept her voice low, as if she was afraid someone might overhear.

"For as gossipy as this neighborhood is, and make no mistake—Moira is always in the thick of it—that's one thing that isn't talked about much. The boys never mention their dad. Personally, I don't buy the girlfriend thing. Michael Doyle loved his boys." Kevin couldn't imagine ever abandoning family, especially your kids. He'd hung out with Ronan Doyle growing up, even though Ronan was a few years older. They had never become really close, but they'd been friendly—friendly enough to get into trouble together. Kids with only one parent in a neighborhood like this shared that bond. Kids like the O'Learys didn't understand what it was like.

Kevin stopped two doors down. "This is where the McCarthys live. They are everything the Doyles aren't. Two girls, two boys, all of them straight A's through school, captain of whatever sports they joined, leaders of everything. I bet they never needed to go to confession. The priests probably just blessed them for being so perfect."

Kathy burst out laughing. "No one is perfect, even if they look like it from the outside."

To prove his point, he walked closer to where the McCarthys had tables set up and a white canopy to block the sun. Spread across the table was every variety of cookie imaginable. Off to the side sat a box of random toys that kids would come by and help themselves to.

"Kevin O'Malley as I live and breathe. It's not like you to travel to this end of the block."

Kevin turned to see Chloe McCarthy standing with her hands on her hips. Chloe had been a year behind him in school, but the McCarthys befriended everyone.

"Hi, Chloe. This is Kathy. I was just giving her a tour of the neighborhood."

Chloe stepped forward and shook Kathy's hand. Leaning closer, she said, "Don't let him take you on a tour of the alleys."

Releasing Chloe's hand, Kathy shot him a questioning look.

"I'm not fourteen anymore. I have better places to

make out with a girl." He winked at Chloe and led Kathy away before Chloe gave Kathy more ammunition to use against him.

"So did you ever take Chloe to the alley?" Kathy asked.

"Hell, no. Everyone knew the McCarthy sisters gripped tight to their V-cards. We half expected them to join a convent."

"You are awful."

"I *was* awful. Turned over a new leaf. I didn't even steal any of their cookies. As a kid, I would've taken a whole tray and then sold them for a quarter each on the next block."

Kathy laughed until she had tears filling her eyes. As far as non-dates went, Kevin considered this one a win.

Chapter Five

Kevin led Kathy to the table. They piled food on their plates and sat at the curb, leaving the folding chairs for older people and pregnant women, of which there seemed to be a growing number. Looked like the O'Learys were breeding the next generation of football players.

"Eat up. Relay races are starting soon. This time, I don't care what Moira says, you're on my team. I deserve to win at least once today."

"The adults run relay races?"

"Some. I'll beat a bunch of kids. I don't care."

Kathy laughed because she knew he was joking. "That's just wrong."

He bumped her shoulder with his and tilted his chin across the street. "See that kid? I bet I could take him."

He was looking at the toddler who was obviously still mastering the ability to walk.

She smiled and shook her head. "Setting the bar kind of low." She glanced down the block. "How about them?"

They turned to see a group of gangly teens squirting one another with giant water guns.

"I'll wait until they exhaust each other, then I'll be able to win."

"You always have a scheme, huh?"

"Scheme sounds evil."

"You're the one who relished being called an evil genius."

"I plan the best way to have fun while winning. That part is just genius. Nothing evil about it." He quieted again for a few seconds as he ate. "What do you do for fun?"

She shrugged. It was one of those questions she always hated on a date because she knew she sounded like a little old lady.

"Come on. Tell me."

"I like to run. I go at least three or four times a week. The shop takes a lot of my time. Being a business owner is no simple task. I love it, but I'm not in a place where I have a lot of breathing room, you know? By the time I get home at night, I flop on the couch and watch TV." As they talked through easy conversation, her appetite had returned and she continued to eat.

"I can relate. I'm trying to get in on a new project at work, so there are a lot of long hours. I'm lucky if I manage to get my tie off before I collapse."

"I never have that problem. The first thing I do when I walk in the door is strip."

Kevin coughed and choked on his beer.

"You okay?"

"You could warn a guy if you're gonna fill his head with images like that." He took another drink of beer.

It took a second for her brain to catch up. "Jeez, you have a dirty mind. I don't walk around naked. I change into comfy clothes."

"Too late. I already have a picture of you sprawled all over your couch totally nude. Wild hair fanning out, eyes half-closed, the beginning of a smile on your lips. Can't undo that."

How he managed to spin a totally innocent conversation into a sexual one, she didn't know, but she pushed past it. "Did you say *tie*? You actually wear a suit every day?"

"Yep. Kind of a requirement."

"I can't picture it." In her head, he was always relaxed Kevin, like he was today. Casual.

"I'll send you a selfie on Monday." He set his plate on the ground. "Unless suits are a turnoff. Then we can pretend they don't exist."

She smiled again. "Even women who don't like suits can appreciate a man who looks good in one."

"Better watch out. That sounded almost like a compliment."

"I didn't say *you'd* look good in a suit, just that I like a man who does."

"I don't remember you being so quick with the barbs."

He was right. That kind of joking was something reserved for people who were close to her, like Moira. People who she knew wouldn't be offended, where no fight would be stirred or feelings hurt.

"Can I get something out in the open?" Kathy asked him with her plate carefully balanced on her knees.

"Shoot," he answered before putting his plate on his lap and digging into his burger.

"I have an ulterior motive for being here."

He said nothing, so she set her plate on the curb and twisted to fully face him. "I planned on playing this close to the vest, but I'm no good at being duplicitous."

"That's one of the many things I like about you."

As much as she wanted to bask in his words, she focused on her goal. "I'm here to keep you away from Moira."

Confusion filled his face. "Why?"

Kathy inhaled deeply and Kevin's gaze dropped to the rise and fall of her chest.

"She's worried about you. No—not about you. About what you might do. She's afraid you'll do something to ruin the wedding."

"I would never do that."

She smiled as she looked into his blue eyes. "I'm starting to see that. I've watched you all day and I don't see what she does."

"What do you see?"

"A man trying to make amends."

His face brightened with her admission.

"What was your duplicitous plan?"

"To distract you and keep you with me and away from her. To spend enough time with you between now and the wedding that I could make sure you had no nefarious schemes."

"Hmmm. I like that plan. Let's go with it."

"What?" she asked, leaning back.

He cocked an eyebrow. "You never know. Maybe I have an evil genius plot already in motion. You, Kathy Hendricks, might be her only hope."

She relaxed and picked up her food again. "That's part of the problem. You don't take anything seriously. That's what scares Moira."

He put his plate down and shifted closer to her. "If we're being completely honest, I have an ulterior motive for being nice to Moira."

Kathy's breath hitched and she frowned.

"You were my ulterior motive. My plan was to prove to Moira that I'm not the same man I was five years ago. If I could sway her, I might have another chance with you."

He waited a moment, then leaned closer still and her pulse quickened. She was afraid he was going to try to kiss her. Instead, he whispered, "That is something I take very seriously. If this plan doesn't work, I'll come up with another. And another still, until I convince you."

Kathy's heart throbbed in her chest and neck and spread all over until she was one giant heartbeat. She nervously held her plate of food and focused on it. She didn't have any words to respond to Kevin. In the time they'd dated and in their few meetings since, she'd never seen him so serious. It was unnerving.

She liked the playful side of him. That kept her off balance in a good way. But his declaration that he would work to get another chance with her scared the crap out of her. Rather than trying to figure out a plan, she gave her attention to the awesome food and watched the kids running around with water guns.

"I'm not sure how to interpret your silence," Kevin said.

She didn't want him to interpret it. She wasn't even sure what it meant. Gripping her plate on her lap, she turned to him again. "I don't know what to say. I'm only here today as a favor to Moira. She's genuinely worried about you and your antics. I never had any intention of . . . God, I don't know . . . starting anything with you again."

His expression turned stony. "Moira has nothing to worry about." He reached over and laid a hand on her arm. "I'll make sure she understands it too."

Kathy bit her lip. "Thank you."

He moved his hand and shifted closer. "Now, about us."

"There is no us."

"There could be."

"Not likely." Her pulse kicked up another notch.

"If we're being honest, and I think we should be, I'm still very much attracted to you, and I think you are to me."

"So what? You're attracted to many people. That's what

ended us, remember?" She spoke in a low whisper so she didn't draw attention.

"I know how to be monogamous, Kathy. I fucked up. I didn't really get it until last year, but I do now. I'll make this right."

"You can't make this right. You can't erase the past." The food on her plate lost all of its appeal. She couldn't keep doing this. He'd turn her into an emotional wreck if the conversation continued.

"I understand that too." His gentle hand came up to her jaw, nudging her to look at him again. "I'm asking—no, begging—for a second chance. You don't need to decide right now. Take some time and think about it. I'm going to prove to you that we can be good again." His thumb stroked her cheekbone and then he pulled away. "But that's enough seriousness for one day. This is a party. Finish up. We have more games to play."

She had never been so grateful for a break in conversation. She couldn't decide if he really wanted her to have time to think or if she looked like she was about to have a panic attack. Swallowing hard, she looked across the street and down the block. Moira's siblings had some blankets spread on the grass and toddlers played with toys and food while their mothers chatted and laughed.

Jimmy stood near the corner where Liam was cooking, but his attention was on the people in the street. Always watching out for those around him. Kathy figured it was part of being a cop. He looked at Kathy and raised his eyebrows in question. She nodded at him to let him know she was okay. It was kind of amazing how quickly Moira's family, both old and new, had brought her into the fold.

* * *

Kathy understood why Moira always asked her to come to the block party. She couldn't imagine anyone not having a great time. There was a little bit of everything for everyone. As things wound down and the sun set, the adults gathered around a small bonfire in the middle of the street. Couples paired off, leaving the singles to meander through the group to settle into a spot.

She was a single and so was Kevin, but he continued to act as though they were a couple. She wanted to be near the fire so her shirt would dry—the shirt that was currently soaked because she got caught in the crossfire when both Moira and Kevin had gotten their hands on the super-shooting water guns. They had apologized in that lame, giggling way kids would, and she had to laugh along. After all, it was only water.

Being shot incessantly with a squirt gun was just another of those things she hadn't experienced as a kid. Now she was getting ready to make s'mores. The group around the fire passed a bottle of whiskey but she stuck with her beer. Even that wouldn't go well with chocolate and marshmallow.

Kevin sat at her side.

Moira jumped up from Jimmy's lap and said, "Time for a game. Truth or dare."

Jimmy groaned and stood.

Moira eyed him. "Sit. You're playing. You survived last year."

He moved back to his lawn chair.

"What's that about?" Kathy asked Kevin.

"Moira always tried to trap him with this game. In case you didn't know, Jimmy doesn't like to be challenged."

Kathy laughed. "And yet, he's marrying Moira."

"Go figure."

"Who's going to start?" Moira asked.

She looked around the group, the firelight making shadows dance across their faces. Kathy thought about her move. She had no idea what kind of dares they asked of each other, but she could use truth to her advantage. If she asked Kevin the right questions, she might be able to set Moira's mind at ease.

It had nothing to do with him proving anything to her about the possibilities for them. Nope. Not at all.

Maggie stood. "I'll go."

Moira returned to Jimmy's side and held his hand. Maggie lurked around the fire studying everyone. She turned to a man Kathy hadn't been introduced to.

"Ronan." She stopped and crossed her arms.

"Who's that?" Kathy whispered.

"One of the Doyle boys. Ronan and I got into our share of trouble too."

"Is there anyone in this neighborhood you haven't gotten into trouble with?"

"Not many."

"Truth or dare?" Maggie asked Ronan.

"Not fair," someone called out. "Everyone knows the Doyles will do anything. A dare won't scare him."

"Especially a dare created by Maggie," he said with a smirk. "But I'll take truth."

A few people moaned, obviously hoping for a good dare.

"Hmmm . . ." Maggie stroked her chin as if deep in thought. "What's the worst thing you've ever done to anyone in this neighborhood?"

Several people laughed, including Ronan. His voice was deep and dark, fitting for a man like Kevin had described.

"Hey, Jimmy, what's the statute of limitations on grand theft auto?" Ronan asked.

"That's my cue to bow out. I'll be back. Anyone need a refill?" he asked, holding up his cup.

"Where's he going?" Kathy asked.

Kevin watched his brother leave. "If Ronan admits to breaking the law, Jimmy would arrest him. Just the way he is."

"So he's leaving so he won't have to. He's a loyal man, isn't he?"

"Yep. The best."

Ronan leaned his elbows on his knees and stared at Maggie and Moira. "When I was fourteen, I stole your father's car. Crashed it into the liquor store so I could get some more beer. Needless to say, I was already drunk."

Moira stared open-mouthed at Ronan.

"Your dad was cool about it. Pissed, but cool. Didn't call the cops or tell my old man. He just made me work off the cost of the repairs." He raised his cup of beer. "To Patrick O'Leary."

After everyone took a drink for the toast, Moira asked, "Why did you steal his car?"

"The only other car that I had a chance of stealing was Seamus O'Malley's. Even drunk, I knew it was stupid to steal a cop's car."

Kevin laughed. "He would've hauled you in for sure."

"I don't doubt it."

"I can't believe you stole my dad's car," Maggie said.

"I do," Moira responded. "Your turn, Ronan."

Leaning forward once again, he looked around at the crowd. "Chloe."

Kathy turned to look at the cute woman she'd met down the block.

"Oh, this'll be good," Kevin said.

They definitely had Kathy's rapt attention.

"Dare," Chloe said with a steely look in her eye.

"Oooo," rumbled through the group.

"Didn't expect that," Kevin said.

Based on the look on Ronan's face, he hadn't expected it either. He rubbed a hand over his scruffy jaw. "I dare you to let me do a body shot off you."

"Who's got the tequila?"

Michael O'Leary passed a bottle. Someone Kathy didn't know ran to the curb and returned with a bowl of limes and a salt shaker. With a cocky expression, Chloe lay on the street in front of the fire. She lifted her shirt and placed a lime between her teeth. Ronan sprinkled salt on her abdomen and slowly licked it off. Then he downed the shot and sucked the lime from her mouth. Even as an outsider, Kathy knew heat when she saw it.

Before she had a chance to ask Kevin about it, Chloe turned and studied the crowd. "Kevin."

"Truth."

Kathy couldn't believe it. He was a dare kind of guy.

"Why didn't you ever ask me out when we were younger?" As Chloe asked the question, her gaze bounced from Kevin to Kathy.

"You were a good girl."

"So?"

Ronan burst out laughing, and Kevin shot him a look. "When we were younger, I was only after one thing, and you weren't about to give it up."

She pursed her lips.

Kevin immediately turned to Kathy. "Kathy."

Her heart sped. She didn't know if she could handle a dare that Kevin dished out, but truth might be worse. She licked her lips.

"Truth or dare?" he asked quietly, like they were the only two people there.

Panic was setting in. She hated being in the spotlight and right now all eyes were on her.

Kevin saw the panic in Kathy's eyes, but he couldn't figure out what he'd done wrong. It was only a silly game. To try to put her at ease, he winked. He wouldn't do anything to embarrass her.

"Truth," she croaked out.

"Hmmm . . . What was your favorite part of this day?"

She released a breath and her shoulders relaxed. "Easy—outrunning you for the first touchdown of the game."

A round of laughter made its way through the neighbors. "Go ahead and laugh it up. I'd like to see any of you catch her. She's a track star."

"Was," Kathy corrected.

"Based on how you ran today, I'd say you still are." His hand brushed hers. "Your turn."

"Can I ask you, or is that against the rules?"

He shrugged. "Moira, she wants to know if she can toss it back at me."

Moira looked at her friend and back at him. "Shoot, if she wants to waste a turn on you, let her."

"Truth or dare?"

Although he wasn't afraid of any dare she might come up with, he knew what she was looking for. "Truth."

She looked back at Moira and then asked, "Why have you always harassed Moira?"

He laughed. "Because she makes it fun."

Everyone else joined in his laughter. When Moira and Kathy shot him dirty looks, he continued. "When we were young, I pulled your ponytail because I liked you. It's one of the stupid things little boys do. As we got older, you were such a fireball when you got mad, it became a game. You're hot when you're pissed."

"Watch it," Jimmy warned.

"I'm not saying anything new. Every guy in the neighborhood thought it." Directly to Moira, he said, "You never gave me the time of day, so pissing you off was the best I could get."

The look on Moira's face softened.

"So you tease her because you like her?" Kathy asked. "That makes no sense."

"Well, now that she's marrying my brother, I get to tease her because she's family. It's how we show love." The whole game was getting too personal at this point. In the past, it never bothered him because someone else was being grilled. He didn't much like it when he was on the hot seat. "I'm getting a refill. Moira, you can have my turn."

"Cool."

He asked Kathy if she wanted more beer.

"I'll come with you." She followed him toward the O'Leary house. "I'm sorry about that. I just wanted Moira to hear your side of things."

"It's fine. I needed a break. Things were getting too serious. I don't care that you asked me questions. I'll tell you anything you want to know."

He pumped the keg and poured her beer, then refilled his own. Instead of going back to the fire, he sat on the curb again. She sat beside him, her bare thigh dangerously close to his. "I'm really glad you came today," he said.

"So am I." She drank from her cup. "What would you have made me do if I said dare?"

"I don't know. If I were smart, I'd have taken a page out of Moira's book and dared you to kiss me. That had been her plan with Jimmy a couple of years ago, except, being Jimmy, he went for truth."

Kathy gulped more beer and he watched her throat work as she tilted her head back. Springy curls had escaped her rubber band a long time ago and he wanted to play with them.

"I wouldn't have done it though," he added as she pulled her cup back. "You looked scared when I called your name. I wouldn't force you to do anything. When I kiss you again, it won't be because I dared you to, but because you want it as much as I do."

"I wasn't scared. A little nervous maybe. I don't like to be the center of attention and that game forced it. I definitely wouldn't want Ronan doing a body shot off me." She chuckled nervously.

Kevin laid a hand on her thigh. "I wouldn't let him touch you."

She twisted, causing his hand to shift to the inside of her leg too close for him not to think about where he wanted to go. "What would you have done to stop him?"

"I wouldn't have had to do anything. Just tell him to back off." How could he explain the unwritten code they all lived by? You don't fuck with another man's woman. It just wasn't done.

With a sigh, she lay down on the grass and stretched out her legs, so he lost contact with her thigh. He lay next to her. "Are you drunk?"

"Nope," she said. "Buzzed pretty good though. Weird, since I don't like beer much. Beautiful night." She pointed up at the starry sky.

As she looked at the stars, he stared at her. She was so beautiful and relaxed, he wanted to kiss her, but he'd keep true to his word. It couldn't happen until she was ready.

The crappy part was that he had no clue what effect those words were having on her.

"About what you said earlier," she began. She turned her head to face him. "I don't know what to think or say."

He waited. As much as he wanted to fill the silence with a joke, he waited.

"I really liked you. Part of me must still, but you hurt me. Whether you meant to or not doesn't matter all that much. I felt betrayed by someone I cared about." She blinked slowly. "Someone I was falling for and thought I had a future with."

Kevin rolled to his side to fully see her face. "I was a dumb fuck for not seeing what I had."

He stroked the inside of her arm. Her eyes fluttered closed and she whispered, "I'm scared."

"It's okay to be scared. I'm sorry I caused that. Like I said before. Take your time and think about it, but know that I'm not going to give up." He rolled onto his back and took her hand. She didn't pull from his grasp, but interlocked her fingers with his.

"Do you want to go back to the game?" she asked.

"Nope. I'm good."

Maybe Jimmy did know a thing or two about how to get a woman.

Chapter Six

Kevin felt like he was losing his mind. It had been two days since the block party and he hadn't heard from Kathy. Of course, he shouldn't have been expecting a call since he'd told her to take her time and think about it. Him. That was it. He'd wanted her to think about him and them. When he'd said good-bye two nights ago, he'd had little doubt that she would give him another chance, but now he began to think that maybe his brothers had been right this whole time. Maybe his ego was too damn big.

The mayor had asked to see him and when he got to the office, Deb was already there waiting.

"What are you doing here?" she asked.

He shrugged. "He called. I came. That's the way it works."

"I was told this was about the banquet later this week."

"What banquet?"

She shook her head at him. "You wrote the damn invite. Thursday night, the mayor is having a party for all of the competitors for the tourism partnership."

Damn. How had he forgotten about that? Probably because he had Kathy on the brain. "I wrote the invitation, but if I recall, you were playing with dates."

While Deb rattled on about why she needed to pick a certain date, Kevin's brain went into high gear. If the meeting was this week, that meant the mayor was close to making a decision. The fact that Kevin was being brought back in was a good sign. He had his chance to show the mayor exactly what he could get done.

The door behind them opened and the mayor welcomed them in. Mayor Park had been in office for a few years. Jimmy had worked closely with him the same summer Moira had gotten tangled up in a story that interfered with Jimmy's case. Although the mayor had made note of Kevin sharing Jimmy's last name, it hadn't gotten him any perks. At least not until now.

"Have a seat," Park said.

Kevin waited for Deb to sit and then he joined her. Park stood and leaned against the edge of his desk.

"Are we set for Thursday?" Park asked Deb.

"Yes. Everyone has accepted the invitation, although most were puzzled about the format. I don't think I'm clear on how you expect them to present their proposals."

Park waved a hand. "God, no. I don't want to sit through any more presentations. If I have to look at one more slide show, I think I'll be sick. Don't these people have any other way to share information?"

He shook his head, realizing he was going off course. Kevin had seen him do this often.

Park crossed his arms. "I'm going old school on this. Tourism is about more than pretty pictures. It's word of mouth and a sense of personalization and community. If these people can't sell my own city to me over a few drinks at a cocktail party, I don't need to waste my time with them."

Kevin liked the idea. "Excuse me, sir, but why am I here? I don't plan parties. That's completely Deb's domain."

"I read the proposal you put together and I think you're on the right track. I don't think the tourism board should be totally farmed out, but I don't want to waste valuable taxpayer money to convince everyone else in the world that Chicago is great."

This was it. This was what Kevin had been hoping for. If he were given the opportunity to be in a position where he could showcase his ability to make things happen, his career would be moving. "What do you need from me?"

"I expect you to be at the party on Thursday. Help me vet these groups. It's not an interview, so don't treat it like one. The businesses vying for this contract have no idea who else will be there, so they should be looking to impress everyone they talk to. Help me find the bullshitters."

Kevin smiled. Being a bullshit artist himself made him a bit of an expert at spotting one. He turned to Deb. "Is this black tie?"

"Not formal. Cocktail attire is fine."

He continued to stare at her.

She sighed. "What you're wearing is fine."

"Thank you."

Park began to move back behind his desk. "And bring a date, Kevin. This is supposed to be a party. If they see you walking solo, they'll peg you as someone to suck up to."

"I might like people sucking up to me for a change."

Park laughed. "You'll have plenty of time for that later."

Kevin wouldn't press the issue of a new position right now—not in front of Deb. First, he'd work the party and find the right people to work with and then he'd talk to Park about appointing him to be the liaison.

As he left Park's office, he didn't have to think about who to bring for his date. He was dialing Kathy's number before he got back to his desk.

"Good afternoon, Love in Bloom. How may I help you?"

His blood pounded at the sound of her offering her services. "Hi, Kathy. It's Kevin. Do you have time to talk for a few minutes?"

"Um, sure."

He heard her moving around and waited a second for her to get settled. "I know I said I'd give you time to think, but I was wondering if you might be free Thursday night."

"Why?"

"I have a cocktail party I have to go to for work. The mayor specifically told me to bring a date, and I immediately thought of you." So many thoughts of her raced through his head, but he pushed them back.

"I don't know if that's a good idea."

"It's not a date. Unless of course, you want it to be." He realized he was rushing, so he took a deep breath. As much as he wanted to see her, he knew this would also be a good opportunity for her. "This cocktail party is going to be filled with businesses who coordinate events throughout the city. Between you and me, they're trying to land a partnership deal with the city to handle tourism. This will be an excellent networking opportunity for you."

When she stayed silent, he added, "We could finalize details for the bachelor party. It'll be efficient. You might make connections that lead to new customers, and we'll get party stuff done." He wanted to add that he really wanted to spend time with her, but he didn't know if that would give her a push in the right direction.

"Okay. What time?"

"I'll pick you up at six-thirty."

"I can drive myself."

"The mayor asked me to bring a date. It might look suspicious if we don't arrive together."

She sighed. "Fine. I assume I'll need to wear a cocktail dress."

"That would be perfect." On every level.

"See you Thursday."

They hung up and Kevin was excited. Not only had the mayor liked his ideas, but he was also bringing Kevin on board to help develop the partnership. On top of it, Kathy would be spending the evening with him as his date.

On Thursday night, as Kathy slipped into her only little black dress, she wondered how she could determine if she had, in fact, lost her mind. She was getting ready for her date with Kevin.

The word sank like a rock in her stomach. Not a date, she reminded herself. It was a networking opportunity to increase business. That was all.

Her fingers trembled as she attempted to apply eyeliner. She never had been a very good liar, even to herself. She inhaled slowly and deeply. Kevin had offered her an excellent opportunity, and it wasn't like she hadn't enjoyed their time together at the block party.

He'd said she should take time and think about the fact that he wanted another chance with her. All she'd been doing outside of work was think about him. The whole thing was crazy. Sure, they'd been good together when they dated, but they were different people now.

What if they didn't mesh well anymore?

Her hormones answered with all of the ways she'd like to mesh with Kevin. The sexual attraction was still there, more than she ever wanted to admit. But they couldn't base their relationship on sex, no matter how good it might be.

He scared her because she wanted to give him the chance

he asked for. Spending the day with him had reminded her of all of his good qualities. He loved his family. He was playful and fun. He cared about those around him. He was a more mature version of the man she'd fallen for years ago. And physically, he spoke to every nerve in her body.

Her heart, however, wouldn't listen. It spoke to her in quiet words of warning. He'd hurt her. She'd given him love, and he'd tossed it aside. What would happen if he did that again?

But what if he didn't?

She tossed her eyeliner in the sink in frustration. Her mind had been stuck on an endless loop for days. *Give him a chance. No, he can't be trusted.* Back and forth so many times, she suffered from a mental case of vertigo.

Shoving the inner voices in a closet in the back of her brain, she resumed putting on her makeup. The argument could continue after she rubbed elbows with wealthy, powerful businesspeople. Kevin was simply her avenue to make that happen.

She could handle this. And she was fine until her doorbell rang at six twenty-five. "Come in," she said into her intercom, and hit the buzzer. Then she swiped on a quick coat of lip gloss and stepped into a pair of heels. Closing her eyes, she said a silent wish that Kevin would look rundown and crappy tonight.

Swinging the door open, she was disappointed that her wish hadn't come true. Kevin stood in the hallway looking damn fine in a dark gray suit and navy tie. He was sporting a couple days' worth of scruff, but it was neat.

"Hi. I'm almost ready." She left the door open for him to come in. Grabbing her small black clutch, she filled it with her cell phone and a stack of business cards. It took a moment for her to realize that Kevin still stood in the hall. "Is there a problem?" she asked.

"Uh, no. You look amazing."

"Thank you. Is this appropriate for a cocktail party for people trying to woo the mayor?"

"That is appropriate for just about anything." His gaze traveled down her body and back up.

Her skin heated under his praise and attention. With her purse in hand, she said, "All set."

He stepped away from the door to allow her to leave and lock up. When she turned to put her keys in her purse, he was standing close, too close for someone who was just a business associate. He fingered her curls.

"I forgot how sexy these curls are when you leave your hair down."

She never thought of her curls as sexy. They'd been an annoyance most of her life. Now she at least liked them. Once her keys were tucked away, she looked into his eyes and forgot everything.

A shade darker than her favorite faded blue jeans, the pupils were dilated, and there was no mistaking the look of lust.

He released her hair and stepped back. "Thank you for agreeing to come with me tonight."

"It's just drinks and conversation, right? No big deal." They headed down the hall to leave.

"It's a slightly bigger deal for me. Mayor Park asked me to work this party to help him figure out who might have the best way to handle tourism for the city. If things work out tonight, I could get a promotion out of this."

"Wow. But no pressure, huh?"

He smiled and led her out of the building. "No pressure for you. You can mingle and talk about flowers, pass out business cards, stand around looking pretty, and have a good time. The pressure is squarely on my shoulders."

For the first time probably ever, she saw Kevin O'Malley

look unsure of himself. "I'm sure you'll be fine. What are you looking for?"

"That's just it. We're not even sure." He unlocked his car and opened the door for her. "We're hoping we'll know it when we hear it."

"That's a tough order to fill." She slid onto the cool leather seat, and he closed the door for her.

On the way into downtown, they chatted about work and Kevin's family. He steered far from the topic of them and being a couple, for which she was grateful. At the restaurant, he used the valet and walked around to her side of the car to let her out. They walked to the door together, where he flashed his credentials at the doorman.

"Why is this being hosted at a restaurant? Why not just use space at city hall?"

"Mayor Park wanted something different. He was afraid that if he invited everyone to city hall, he'd be stuck listening to formal proposals all night. Basically, he's sick of looking at slide shows."

"Interesting." She knew very little about the mayor. It wasn't like she ran in those circles. Inside, Kevin led her straight to the mayor, who was flanked by three very large men.

"Good evening, Mayor," Kevin said.

"Kevin, glad you're here."

Kevin pressed slightly on Kathy's back to nudge her forward. "This is my date, Kathy Hendricks."

"Mayor," she said with a small nod, and extended her hand.

"Nice to meet you, Miss Hendricks. How long have you and Kevin been dating?"

Kevin flinched beside her. He obviously hadn't thought the mayor would get personal. "Kevin and I go way back," she started. She looked over her shoulder at him and smiled. "But this is relatively new."

She felt his tension slip away.

"Well, I'm glad you're here tonight. Help yourself to a drink and mingle. I hope you won't be offended if I occasionally need to steal your date away."

"Not at all. This is a working cocktail party, right?"

"That it is." With a nod to Kevin, he said, "I'm going to greet guests as they enter. Before you leave tonight, I want to touch base to debrief."

"Yes, sir."

Kathy swallowed a giggle. Hearing Kevin call anyone sir went against everything she thought she knew about him.

"I need a drink. How about you?" he asked.

"Sure." Although she wasn't thirsty, she wanted to have something in her hand as she mingled. At the bar, she ordered a white wine and Kevin ordered a whiskey. "Kind of strong for a business meeting," she said.

"I'll make it last. Probably. But I know a lot of these blowhards are gonna bore me out of my mind."

They stood near a high-top table, and Kevin waited until the first wave of guests wandered past them to get to the bar. When drinks were in hand, it was time to start talking.

"Kevin O'Malley. And this is Kathy Hendricks," Kevin said to introduce them to a guy who said he was the head of an event planning company.

"And what's your specialty?" the guy asked.

Kevin took that moment to drink and eye Kathy. Weird, but she could take a hint. "I'm a florist."

"Interesting."

"Kathy is excellent at her job. I happen to know that the mayor was very pleased with the last job she did for city hall."

"Really? I'd love to hear some more about the work you did. What makes you stand out compared to any other florist?"

"I don't know that I do anything particularly special. I listen to what my customers want and what price point they're looking for, and then I deliver."

"Don't let her fool you, Tom." Kevin said. "She has an excellent eye for detail and anticipating what a client wants before they do."

"Did you do the work here?" Tom asked.

Kathy glanced at the centerpiece near her elbow, one that they had shifted back and forth numerous times because it interfered with seeing across the table. "Oh, no," she said, and then realized that it came across as condescending. "What I mean is—"

"You don't need to apologize. They're hideous."

She grinned.

"What would you have done instead?"

Kathy took a moment to review the entire space before speaking. "First, I would've used a smaller setting completely. Something this tall inhibits people from talking across the table. And given that each table also has a candle, I would've gone simple, something that would play against the firelight."

"Not bad for an off-the-cuff response. Here's my card." He slid a card onto the table. "Send me your information and we'll add you to our database of vendors."

"Thank you. It was nice to meet you."

Tom walked away and began chatting up the next table. Kathy stood and stared at the card. She hadn't even been trying to network that time. She'd thought Kevin would want to ask some questions, but he never did.

"You're good," Kevin said.

"Not as good as you. Throwing out compliments left

and right about things you know nothing about." She sipped her wine.

"I don't need to know about flowers."

"I was talking about me. You have no idea if I'm any good or if I have an eye for detail."

He shifted closer and set his glass on the table. "That was no bullshit. I didn't need to see the centerpieces you made for Deb. I know Deb. She's hard to please and she was singing your praises. And I know enough about you that you would do right by anyone who was counting on you. That's just who you are."

Suddenly she didn't feel like they were talking about flowers anymore. "Thank you," she whispered. She wasn't used to having someone believe in her unwaveringly like that. Her mom and Moira, of course, but other than that, she'd mostly just depended on herself.

"Will you be okay on your own for a while? I need to go talk to people and if I stand here, they'll be distracted by your beauty."

Kathy rolled her eyes. That was the Kevin she was used to. "A cheesy compliment like that will get you nowhere."

"I'm well aware. I'm saving my sincerity for when we don't have an audience." He winked and walked away, leaving Kathy feeling warm in all the wrong places.

Kathy spent the next hour and a half talking with local businesspeople, some of whom might've considered using her services, others not at all, but she was still grateful for the connections. She'd been able to talk marketing with one person and tax incentives with another. During some conversations she felt completely out of her depths, but no one treated her like an imposter.

Kevin had mostly disappeared for the night. So much

for thinking he'd been trying to wrangle a date. He came by twice after their initial conversation: once to deposit a fresh glass of wine on the table and again to hand her a glass of water. As guests began leaving, she searched for him, but saw him nowhere.

She didn't know how she felt about the evening. It had been the great networking experience that Kevin had promised, but part of her had expected more from him. Which she was aware was totally unfair to him. He'd offered her space and then gave it to her. He was being thoughtful, but she felt a little neglected.

And there went the endless loop again. She was worse than a lovesick thirteen-year-old.

As her gaze wandered across the room, Kevin turned a corner in the back, shoulder to shoulder with the mayor. They were in deep conversation, but as if he felt her staring, Kevin looked up. When their eyes met, he smiled, and whatever chemistry they shared zipped through the room.

Kevin and the mayor shook hands and parted. As Kevin made his way to her, she noticed how tired he looked. She was suddenly painfully aware of how much she wanted to get out of her heels.

"How'd it go?" she asked.

"Long. I should've asked Moira to be my date tonight. She's the only person I know who can talk as much as these people."

Ignoring the ping of irritation at him talking about dating her friend because she knew it was ridiculous, she asked, "Did you get the information you wanted at least?"

"I think. We were able to narrow the field of prospects. I'm sorry I abandoned you. Park told me to bring a date, so it would be more social. I don't think either of us expected this."

"It's fine. I talked with a lot of people. It was interesting.

You know, running a business tends to be kind of solitary. I do my thing to keep everything going. Sometimes I forget to step back and connect with other people who get it. Thank you for inviting me." She picked up her purse, which was still filled with business cards, but this time with those of people she'd met. "Ready to go?"

"Like you wouldn't believe." With a hand on her lower back, he led them through the room, waving at stragglers. "I'm fucking starving. You want to get something to eat?"

While they waited for the valet to bring his car around, she shifted from foot to foot. "Food sounds fabulous, but my feet are killing me. I'm not used to standing in heels for hours."

Kevin opened the car door for her and handed the valet a tip. When she sat, her entire body sighed, but her legs wept.

"We could pick something up and eat at your place." He pulled into traffic. "Pizza?"

Her stomach rumbled. Pizza sounded so good. But did she want to invite Kevin into her house? She took a quick breath. She was being silly. They'd had a good night. They could share a meal. Plus, they hadn't yet talked about the final details for the bachelor/bachelorette party for this weekend. "Sure. I'll call and it'll be delivered right around when we get back."

She called and placed the order. The rest of the ride to her apartment was quiet. After an evening of nonstop talking, they both needed some peace. When the car was parked and Kathy pushed the door open, her leg muscles protested. Swinging her legs out of the car, she bent and pulled off the heels. Kevin stood on the curb and watched.

"Not very glamorous, huh?" She wiggled her toes and then pushed herself out of the car.

Kevin closed the door behind her. "Those things look like torture, but as someone who only has to enjoy the view they create, I have to say—and I think I speak for all of mankind on this—we appreciate what you do to look good for us."

As they walked into her building, she realized the difference in their height. With her shoes on, she was nearly eye to eye with Kevin. Now her eyes were at his mouth. Thoughts of his mouth being on hers slipped into her mind. She must've been really tired to go there.

Inside her apartment, she tossed her shoes near the closet and pulled some cash from her purse. "Do you mind grabbing the pizza when it comes? I really want a hot shower."

Kevin stared at her for what felt like a full minute before clearing his throat. "Sure."

Kathy went to her bedroom and grabbed some comfy pajamas and carried them to the bathroom. Normally, she'd walk through the apartment naked or in a towel, but she wasn't silly enough to attempt that with Kevin standing in her living room. Regardless of whether she thought she could give him another chance, she couldn't deny the attraction they shared.

Even if her hormones wanted to act on it, she wasn't ready to give in to that attraction until her heart and mind agreed.

She stood under the hot spray until her tense muscles relaxed again. Then she dressed and went back to the living room. Kevin had removed his jacket and loosened his tie. He'd made himself comfortable, sprawled on her couch with his feet up on the table, looking like he was at home.

Memories flooded her brain of the times they'd hung out just like this, watching a Blackhawks game and eating pizza. She'd lie on him and pretend to understand hockey simply because she'd liked the feeling of his body close to hers, his arms wrapped around her. When the game had ended, they'd spent the night together.

There were no walks of shame or sneaking out in the middle of the night like they were hooking up. They'd been in a relationship. It hadn't been her imagination.

Kevin turned and looked over his shoulder. "Feel better?"

"Much."

He waved at the TV. "I didn't know if you wanted to watch something, so feel free to change it."

Moving his feet back to the floor, he leaned forward and opened the pizza box. He'd already grabbed napkins from her kitchen and had a beer open for himself.

By the time she sat, she knew she needed answers before she could think about taking this anywhere with him. She needed something to get her off the merry-go-round in her head.

She sat in the corner of the couch and curled her legs up on the cushion. "You know, as I walked into the room, I was struck by how comfortable you made yourself."

He looked sheepish for a minute. "Sorry. I figured it was okay since you were in the shower and we planned to eat together."

"No." She held up a hand. "That's not it. I don't mind. It reminded me of when we were dating. And yeah, we were dating. We hung out and spent the night together. We weren't just friends with benefits or whatever. We were in a relationship." Her skin warmed as her anger and frustration rose again.

Kevin hung his head. "Yeah, we were. I never meant to imply we weren't."

"Then what did I do wrong?" As soon as she said the

words, she wanted to pull them back. They were needy and weak. She knew she'd done nothing wrong.

"Nothing."

"I know that. I'm not being clear." She swallowed and closed her eyes to gather her thoughts. "What I meant was, what did I do to make you think it was acceptable to sleep with other people?"

"Again, you did nothing. I really liked what we had going, but we never talked about it. We didn't have *the* talk." He shifted on the couch, putting himself closer to her. "What I said before was true. I knew we were getting serious, and it freaked me out. I wasn't ready. I had no fucking clue what I wanted. Part of me thought playing the field was it."

"And I made it easy by disappearing from your life without a fight." She had to admit he impressed her. Kevin took responsibility for the crappy way things went, even though it wasn't all his fault. Sure, he could've figured out that she wasn't looking for an open relationship, but back then she didn't have the backbone to stand up and tell him he was being an asshole. "Okay. Let's eat. I'm starving."

He pulled a slice of pizza and handed it to her. "For the record, I know now."

"Know what?" she asked as she sank her teeth into the gooey cheese.

"I know what I want. I've been focused on my career for the last few years. I'm not exactly where I want to be, but I'm on the right path. I'm ready to settle down. I've always known that one day I'd want to get married and have a family. I'm ready."

She swallowed the pizza in her mouth, but it wasn't moving down her throat. What the heck? First Kevin tells her he wants another chance with her, but she can take her time to think about it. Now he's talking marriage and babies.

He burst out laughing. "Right now, you look like I imagine I would've five years ago if you'd mentioned settling down. I'm not expecting to get you pregnant anytime soon. I'm just letting you know that I'm in a different place in my life. I'd like you to be part of it."

Then he sat back and returned his attention to the TV and the baseball game that he'd turned on. He ate his dinner like he hadn't just dropped a bomb on her. She was adept at listening and although he'd said he wasn't looking for a baby right now, she also heard what he left out. He didn't say he wasn't looking to marry her, or that he wanted to test the waters of monogamy; he simply said he wasn't quite ready to impregnate her. Her—not just anyone.

So much for clearing her mind. Kevin had just given her even more to think about. And for the first time, she really wanted to consider it. It was more than lust or chemistry. She found that the more time she spent with Kevin, the more she liked who he'd become. She just wasn't sure she was ready to trust him.

Chapter Seven

Kevin's week had been exhausting but productive. He'd been working closely with the mayor to get the new tourism initiative off the ground. Thursday night's party had only been a blip on the radar for everything he'd accomplished.

And he was dying because Kathy hadn't contacted him once. He reminded himself that it had only been two days. They shared a brief e-mail exchange about the bachelor party, but that was it. When they'd talked after the mayor's cocktail party, he'd thought he'd made headway with her. He'd been sure she was at least considering giving him a chance.

He wondered if her silence was her answer. After all, that was what she'd done last time. As irritating as that thought was, he pushed it aside. He'd promised her time to think, and he'd give it to her, but he had no intention of sitting idly by forever.

He got ready for a night on the lake, free-flowing drinks, and half-naked women and men to torment Jimmy. His big brother only had eyes for Moira, so he wouldn't want to look at a stripper, but he might pop a vein if he thought Moira wanted to watch a striptease. As best man, he couldn't in good conscience not have hired a stripper at all. The guests would expect it, so he delivered.

The show he had planned would put all others to shame. This might go down in history as the best bachelor party ever.

He and Kathy planned to arrive early so they were there to greet everyone as they boarded the boat. It wasn't often that he used his city hall contacts to his advantage, but to give Jimmy a night to remember, it was worth it. They'd gotten the cruise for a steal and what was better was that they had it all to themselves. The only people on the ship were those invited for the party.

After parking at a nearby lot, he walked to the dock. Kathy was already there, talking with someone from the crew. The sight of her had his mouth watering. She wore a bright yellow dress that hit mid-thigh and because it had thin straps, she showed plenty of golden skin. Her hair was down, spiral curls blowing in the lake breeze.

When he joined them, Kevin introduced himself to John from the crew and got the plans. He and Kathy would wait on the dock to greet everyone and make sure they didn't leave anyone behind. Once the cruise started, they'd get out on the lake and within the hour, dinner would be served. Then there would be dancing with music provided by the DJ.

John left them and Kevin turned to Kathy. "You look amazing."

"Thank you. Not so bad yourself." She swiped at her hair that flung into her face. "I swear, I don't know what I was thinking leaving this mess down."

"It's not a mess. I love your hair."

"Trust me, by the time we actually get moving, it'll probably look like a bird's nest."

"I doubt that."

Maggie and Shane arrived, and Kathy let them know that Moira and Jimmy were already on board in separate rooms. The rest of the O'Learys came shortly after. His brothers, of course, were later. Friends and relatives started arriving in mass numbers, so he and Kathy couldn't talk much. When the entertainment for the night came up to him, they caught Kathy's attention.

"I thought you told Jimmy no strippers."

"Jimmy said no strippers. I never agreed. Every man in this place might look for blood if I didn't provide some entertainment."

"Two women? That's *some* entertainment?"

"Don't underestimate me. That's two women and one man. They perform together."

He waited for his words to sink in. Kathy's eyes widened. She stepped closer and lowered her voice. "They do three-some stuff?"

"They're gonna do something."

"Something that'll probably give Jimmy a coronary. You might want to warn the guy not to touch Moira. Jimmy will break his arm."

"They all know hands off. Jimmy's not the only one with a protective streak." Sean would definitely go off if a stripper touched Emma. Tommy wouldn't be much better. Kevin thought briefly of what his reaction would be if it were Kathy being touched. Although he had no right to be jealous or protective, he was.

They waited outside in the warm summer air until the only people milling around were those enjoying a night at Navy Pier. Kevin looked up at the Ferris wheel and thought about taking a ride with Kathy. Too bad he didn't know the operator so he could call in a favor and get them trapped at the top.

"I think that's everyone," Kathy said. "There are only a couple of people on my list who haven't shown, but I told them all we would be leaving at eight."

"Sounds good. I wasn't keeping track, but off the top of my head, I think we're good. All the important people are here anyway."

Kathy bent and grabbed the tote bag at her feet.

"Hell of a purse."

She rolled her eyes. "It's not my purse. It's supplies."

"Everything is included in the cruise."

"I have a bride-to-be sash for Moira to wear, and little gifts for the bridal party. Games to play. Stuff like that."

"Shit. Was I supposed to come up with stuff? I thought my job ended with making sure the party was planned."

"I've got you covered."

"The least I can do is carry this then." He took the bag from her shoulder, his fingers grazing the soft skin.

If he wasn't imagining things, her breath hitched at his touch. "So, have you had time to think about us?"

Her stride caught and she blinked rapidly a few times. "Really? You want to talk now?"

"Now is perfect. I've got you captive for the next four hours."

She laughed. "I've been doing nothing but thinking. But I don't have an answer for you. My head is a mess. Just zipping back and forth. I don't know if I should follow my heart or my head."

"That's easy. Follow whichever one says I should get another chance. We'll get the other on board."

"You're impossible."

"It's one of my finer qualities."

They walked aboard the ship and Maggie met them.

"I'm so sorry. We tried to keep it a secret, but you know

Jimmy. He refused to stay in that room you put him in," Maggie said.

Kathy's shoulders sagged. "Oh, man. I really wanted to get pictures of their faces when they realized it was a joint party."

"Don't worry about that. As soon as I heard Jimmy coming, I had my phone out. They are immortalized."

Kevin smiled. "How'd they take it?"

"Seemed okay to me, but they're looking for you."

The first thing Kevin did was grab a drink for him and Kathy. Kathy might've been disappointed at missing out on the surprise, but Kevin knew how little Jimmy enjoyed surprises. Then he went to find Jimmy and Moira. They had drinks in hand and Moira was already wearing the satin sash Kathy had brought. Jimmy wore a crown.

Kevin pointed at his brother. "That's fitting. You've always acted like king of the world."

"I'll get you for this."

"I had nothing to do with playing dress-up. That was all Kathy. Take it up with her."

"I think it's cute," Moira said.

"Just what I've always wanted. To be cute."

Moira turned to Kevin. "Kathy said this was all your idea. Thank you. It's awesome. Having my fiancé here kind of ruins the whole last-night-of-being-single thing, but the rest is amazing."

Kevin stared for a minute. "Is Mouthy Moira really paying me a compliment? No way. I think I've entered an alternate universe. Aunty Em, Aunty Em . . ."

Moira playfully smacked his arm while she laughed. Then she did the one thing he'd never thought possible: she hugged him. Willingly.

He awkwardly wrapped his arms around her to accept the hug.

"All jokes aside," she said, "I appreciate you taking this seriously."

"I'd do anything for him."

"That's good. So would I."

Kathy came up and said, "Are you starting already?"

Moira stepped back and Kevin asked, "What?"

"You're not even drunk yet and you're bugging Moira?"

"Ha! Shows what you know. She threw herself into my arms."

Moira answered with her patented eye roll. "He wasn't bothering me. I was thanking him for this amazing party."

"Oh." She handed Kevin a beer. "I figured you'd need this."

He smiled. "Great minds," he said, and showed her the drinks he'd grabbed for them. "Guess we need to drink fast."

"They're seating us for dinner now. They have a huge table set up for the bridal party."

Kevin grabbed two beer bottles by the neck in one hand. His other hand rested on Kathy's back. "After you."

Kathy held tight to her glass of wine. While she had no intention of getting drunk, she'd need the alcohol to get through the night at Kevin's side. Every time they were together, it was getting harder and harder to know why she didn't want to give him another chance. Dinner was delicious, but went by too quickly. The DJ started playing dance music, and Kathy was shocked to see how many of the guests were already paired off.

No wonder Moira was fine with having a joint party. While many of them weren't married, these people were far from single.

Unlike her.

And Kevin.

She looked at Kevin, who was currently dancing with a woman who was laughing at whatever he was saying. There was a respectful distance between them, and he'd done nothing to flirt with her.

The Kevin in her memory had flirted with everyone, even if he wasn't interested. Kathy had assumed that was just his personality. When the song ended, he waved at his partner and beelined for Kathy's position.

"Can I have this dance?"

"Sure." She took his hand and as soon as they got to the dance floor, the rhythm shifted to a slow song. "Did you plan this?" she asked as he pulled her against his body.

"Nope. I'm just lucky like that."

They didn't talk during the song. Their bodies were pressed together in a way that was more intimate than she'd consider with a stranger, yet it felt good. It had been a long time since she'd had a steady boyfriend. She'd dated some since Ray, but she was experiencing a relationship drought. Maybe that's why Kevin was so appealing.

"You're thinking too loud. Can't you just enjoy the dance?"

"I am. Too much, I'm afraid."

She felt his chuckle more than heard it. A deep vibration through his chest sent more wild thoughts through her. She couldn't decide if she needed more alcohol to be able to ignore those thoughts or if they would just get worse.

She did what she could to block out her hormones and enjoy the dance, and the two that followed. They took a break to get a drink, and Kevin surprised her by ordering a water for himself.

When she stared at the glass, he said, "I'm designated everything tonight. No way will Jimmy relax if no one is sober to keep people safe. I have to make sure no one fights, falls overboard, or drives home drunk."

Kathy had never thought about how sexy responsibility was, but Kevin had certainly introduced the idea. He guzzled his water, slammed the glass back on the bar, and said, "I gotta go. Time for entertainment. You coming?"

"Nah. Not my idea of entertainment, but thanks for asking. You go have fun. I think I'm going to go for a walk out on deck. Tell Moira to text me if she needs anything."

Kevin made a quick announcement to the partygoers and then led a large group to a private room. From where she stood at the bar, she could see Jimmy grumbling and giving Kevin dirty looks. Moira, on the other hand, threatened that if there was nothing for her to enjoy, he was in trouble. Jimmy grabbed her ass and whispered something in her ear that made her pale skin go red.

Although the crowd around the bar and on the dance floor had thinned, there were still a lot of people. Kathy needed a break from all of them. The cruise would be over soon. They'd already taken their turn to circle back, so she wanted to go outside to enjoy the fresh air and the view of the city from the lake.

She walked out and leaned into the rail, closing her eyes and raising her face to the wind off the lake. When she reopened her eyes, she looked up at the moon and sighed.

"Couldn't imagine a more beautiful sight."

She spun at Kevin's voice. "I thought you were doing the entertainment." She cringed. "That sounded bad, but you know what I meant."

"I had to get the entertainment started, but a moonlight walk alone with you sounded much more appealing."

She licked her lips. For as much as she'd thought she wanted to be alone, she liked the idea of being with him. "There's not far to walk."

"We can do a circuit or two of the deck." He reached

for her hand, and they walked in silence toward the back of the boat.

When they got there, they were alone in the shadows, the only sound the sloshing of the water against the boat. The scene was perfectly romantic, and Kathy's heart thundered in her ears.

"Heart and mind still at odds?"

"More than ever."

"I know I said I'd give you time, but I'm an impatient man. So unless you tell me not to, I'm going to kiss you now." He released her hand and moved it to her cheek, using his thumb to tilt her chin upward. Staring into her eyes, he waited a beat, cocking one eyebrow in question.

She should stop him, but she wanted to feel his mouth on hers, so she said nothing.

He moved in slowly, using his other hand to shift her body and pull her flush against him. He kept his eyes open and on hers as his lips met hers softly, a gentle stroke. He parted his lips, and she felt his breath whisper across her mouth before their lips reconnected.

Kathy wrapped her arms around his back, anchoring him to her, as she closed her eyes and angled her head, inviting more from him.

He took the cue and stroked his tongue into her mouth, a quick sweep that left her seeking more. She darted her tongue out to meet his, so he would feel how much she wanted this. And for long moments then, the gentle sway of the ship rocked their bodies together. Pressed together, they became reacquainted, sharing breath, sighs, and moans.

They were so close, Kathy couldn't feel where she ended and he began. Yet Kevin's hands hadn't moved other than to stroke her cheek, her neck, tug at her hair. The hand at her hip did nothing more than flex and hold her.

The kiss spoke of intimacy they no longer had, but there was comfort mixed with the desire.

When he finally pulled away, a chill ran through her. She attributed it to the cool breeze and not the absence of his warm mouth on hers. Leaning his forehead against hers, he breathed slowly. She opened her eyes to find him staring again.

"Wow," he whispered.

"I remember you being really good at that. Glad to see that hasn't changed."

"You're fucking amazing. I'm harder from one kiss with you than I would've been watching three strippers get it on."

She halfheartedly rolled her eyes.

"I'm serious." To prove his point he yanked her body close, grinding her hips to his.

There was no mistaking the hard ridge prodding her. As if she hadn't already been turned on enough. The feel of him being hard for her made her want more. Her body thrust even closer to him and he groaned. His fingers gripped her hips hard enough to leave fingerprints.

She moaned and lifted her mouth to his again, but he stepped back.

"I can't do what I want to do. Certainly not here. And not until you've decided to take a chance on me." His hand found hers again and linked his fingers in hers. "Just know I want this."

Her body screamed at her to do this. Tell him yes and go back to his apartment with him, but her mind prevailed and she inhaled slowly, filling her lungs with lake air.

"I think we should tour the other side of the deck now before I have to go back to the party and embarrass myself," he said.

A laugh bubbled up and Kathy's whole body shook.

"I don't think it's that funny."

"It's only fair that you suffer a little too. My mind has been dancing in circles tormenting me for over a week."

"I can handle a little discomfort as long as I know you've been thinking about me."

She nudged him with her shoulder as they turned the corner and headed back to the party. "Always making it about yourself."

"Uh-uh. This discomfort is *all* about you."

Kathy found herself laughing yet again as they rejoined the party and all of their guests. The boat was getting ready to dock and Kathy was sad to know the evening was coming to an end. Even though this still wasn't a date with Kevin, she felt closer to him. Like maybe she should give him a chance. It wasn't like they were getting married. They could date and see how it went.

For the first time in days, she felt optimistic about her life. Kevin stepped away to say good-bye and get people safe rides home if necessary. They had a week until the wedding. She could use these days to cool off and make sure her decision was not solely a lust-fueled one, but that she really wanted to date Kevin.

Her heart and mind settled.

Her body, on the other hand, rioted.

Chapter Eight

Kathy's week blew by in a blur. Between a couple of big orders that came in and getting ready for Moira's wedding, which included talking her friend down from the ledge a few times, Kathy hadn't had time to breathe much less talk to Kevin.

After the haze of lust faded, she still wanted to give him the chance he sought. They'd sent a few texts throughout the week. He'd flirted incessantly with her, but she wasn't going to tell him via text that she wanted to go out with him. That was definitely a face-to-face conversation. Mostly because it might not stop at talking, and she was looking forward to that.

But today was the day—not only for Moira and Jimmy's wedding, but also for Kathy and Kevin to figure things out. Moira and Jimmy had made it to the church on time and everything ran as smoothly as possible for a long Catholic church wedding—mass included to make Mrs. O'Leary happy.

They made it through the wedding ceremony, and Kathy only needed to dry her eyes a couple of times. When she walked down the aisle of the church to leave with Kevin at her side, she smiled at him as she looped her arm through his. "You did a very good job as best man."

"Easiest job I ever had."

"Jimmy wasn't nervous?"

"Nothing rattles him. He doesn't make a move until he's sure about what he wants. He never had any doubt. Not about Moira."

At the back of the church, they were separated again to line up and take more pictures. Kathy's face ached from all of the smiling. And they'd been genuine smiles because Kevin kept everyone laughing with stories about his brothers.

By the time they made it to the reception hall, the entire wedding party wanted a drink. Moira, or more likely, her older brother Ryan, thought ahead and made sure the bar was open early. Bottles of beer and glasses of wine were set out waiting for them. Moira and Jimmy thanked them all for being part of their wedding. They had a brief break, enough to finish their drinks, before it was back to work for Kathy. She stood beside Moira and collected gifts and cards while her friend greeted her guests.

Kathy's stomach grumbled and when they finally lined up for the introductions before dinner, all she could think about was food. She and Kevin strolled in together and he held her chair at the head table. When she sat, he lowered his mouth to her ear and said, "In case I haven't told you, you are absolutely stunning in that dress."

She'd been lucky that Moira hadn't been a bridezilla. The bridesmaids' dresses were beautiful short, strapless numbers that looked good on all of them. Unlike so many bridesmaids' dresses, this one could be worn again to a fancy cocktail party—like the ones Kevin went to. Smoothing her hand over the dark blue satin, she said, "Thank you. You look pretty good in a tux."

He sat beside her and food was served. She didn't taste a darn thing because Kevin kept giving her heated looks. When servers came to remove their plates, Kevin leaned close and said, "I can't think about anything but kissing you again."

"As tempting as that is, you better get your head on straight. Don't you have to make a toast?"

"Damn it." He turned and clinked his fork against his water glass and stood. Everyone quieted. He cleared his throat, and Moira stiffened. Kathy reached over and patted her friend's hand.

"As best man, I'm expected to make this special toast. I know Moira assumes I'll say something to embarrass her." He paused. "And I probably could, but I won't. Moira and I have known each other since first grade. We spent more years in the same homeroom than not, and since teachers prefer alphabetical seating charts, I spent my childhood looking at the back of her head."

A few people chuckled.

"Moira was the bane of my existence. She was always smarter, definitely prettier, and she wouldn't give me the time of day. She thinks I tormented her because I hated her, but the truth is, I bugged her because I liked her and I could never beat her. It drove me crazy." He turned to Jimmy. "And now, she gets to drive you crazy."

More people laughed.

Kevin tucked a hand into his pocket before continuing. His face was serious. "Most of you know that the O'Malleys had a tough time. Our mom died when we were all young. My dad was a cop and worked crazy hours. At ten years old, Jimmy managed to hold our family together. He took care of us, taught us everything we needed to know, and kept us mostly in line. Part of that he enjoyed because he's a bossy control freak."

The O'Malley siblings all laughed, but Kathy didn't. Kevin threw in the line to be a smart-ass, but she'd never seen him so serious.

"But no ten-year-old should've had to carry that weight. And Lord knows, we didn't make it easy for you. There is no way for us to ever thank you enough or repay you. I'm glad you found Moira. No one deserves happiness more than you."

He choked a little on those last words, and Kathy's eyes filled. If she hadn't already decided to give him another chance, that speech would've done it. She'd never heard anyone speak so clearly from the heart.

Jimmy stood and pulled him into a tight hug, thumping him on the back. They exchanged words too quiet for anyone to hear.

When Jimmy stepped back, Kevin brought the microphone back to his mouth. "Moira, baby, welcome to the family."

The crowd erupted in cheers and Moira stood to hug him. He whispered something to her too, and she looked up at him with a huge smile. With his arm still around her shoulders, into the microphone, he said, "All I had to do to finally get a hug was give a speech. Who knew?"

When he sat, he handed Kathy the microphone. "You better go now before any of the rest of the family grabs it. You'll never get a chance then."

She took it and stood. "Whew. I knew I should've gone first. Tough act to follow." She licked her lips. She'd prepared a speech, but it seemed too simple and generic now. So taking Kevin's lead, she spoke from her heart.

"Moira and I met in college. She was my first friend." Kathy paused. "Not my first college friend, my first real friend. She's more of a sister than a pal. She taught me about living and taking chances. And in all honesty, I thought she was crazy for liking Jimmy. He's bossy, and she doesn't like to be told what to do. The man barely speaks, and Moira loves to talk."

"That's why they're a match made in heaven," Kevin announced. The crowd laughed.

"I never held much stock in fairy-tale endings, but seeing Jimmy and Moira together is magical. Moira taught me that true love is possible." Kathy picked up her glass and held it high. "To a long and happy life together."

She took a sip and set the microphone down so she could give Moira a hug. While in her arms, Kathy said, "I told you you could trust Kevin."

"Yeah, yeah. The night's still young."

But when she pulled back, Moira was smiling.

After Kathy sat, Moira's brother Ryan took the microphone. Kathy was just relieved to be done with her speech.

Kevin leaned close and although Kathy tried to pay attention to Ryan's words, Kevin's nearness distracted her.

"You don't believe in happy endings?"

Tilting her chin toward the bride and groom, she said, "They make me believe it exists. For everyone? That I'm not so sure about."

"I never pegged you as a pessimist. You're a florist. It's your job to sell happiness."

That was exactly why she'd become a florist. Flowers made people happy. "Yeah, I sell it. It doesn't just happen because you want it to."

"Hmmm. That's a sad view on life."

She angled her head and looked into his eyes. "My view seems to be evolving."

He reached over to her lap and took her hand. Then they both returned their attention to the speeches.

* * *

Kevin tapped his foot impatiently as the DJ started the first song for Jimmy and Moira to dance. At the halfway point, the rest of the wedding party was supposed to join in. That's why he was impatient. Other than holding Kathy's hand during the speeches—for once he was grateful for long-winded people—he'd had no reason to touch Kathy. It had been torture sitting beside her in that dress, her hair down over bare shoulders, makeup done perfectly.

But now, she would be in his arms for at least a couple of minutes. If he played it right, he'd talk her into another dance. Their duties as best man and maid of honor were mostly done at this point. There was still the bouquet and garter thing, but they were otherwise free to enjoy their night.

And Kevin wanted to enjoy every possible moment with Kathy.

"The bride and groom would like the bridal party to join them now," the DJ announced.

Kathy was standing at his side, so he took her hand and walked her out onto the floor. He kept his hands in respectable places, one held hers, and the other rested on her hip. She curled her arm around him and brought her chin near his shoulder.

"I've been looking forward to this."

His feet stumbled. "You have?"

She nodded. "I'm done thinking. I wanted to talk to you, but I thought it should be in person."

Kevin tried to play it cool. A million thoughts scattered through his head, but his stomach filled with dread. If her answer was no, she would've sent it in a text, right? Then again, she might've been worried that if she shot him down before the wedding he'd do something to piss off Moira.

"My answer is yes."

"Yes? As in you'll give me another chance?"

Another soft nod against his shoulder.

"It was the speech, right? I wore you down with my fabulous best man speech."

"In all honesty, if I hadn't already decided, the speech would've sealed it. Instead, it was icing on the cake. It was a damn good speech. But my decision was based on everything. The way you've approached the entire situation, the way you talk to me, the fabulous kiss last week. I never really had a chance, you know."

"Yeah, I do." He slid his hand across her lower back and pulled her closer. "This is turning out to be a better night than I'd hoped."

He held her through the rest of the song and instead of talking her into another, he pulled her off the dance floor. She'd agreed to give him another chance, and he wanted it to start now.

"Where are we going?"

"To grab a couple of drinks and then find a quiet spot." He didn't really have a plan, but he knew he wanted to have her to himself. At the bar, he asked, "Wine?"

"Cosmo, please." She still gave him a puzzled look.

He ordered, stuffed a five into the tip jar, and handed her the glass. Still holding Kathy's hand as if she might run away, he led them around the perimeter of the banquet hall. He looked in the lobby where there were a few people milling around, but there was an unoccupied bench tucked in the corner near the bathrooms. Not the most romantic setting, but they'd be alone.

When they sat, he said, "To a fresh start." He clinked his bottle against her drink.

They both drank. Then she asked, "Why did you drag me out here?"

"I wanted be alone with you. You just gave me the best news I've had all week. Maybe all year."

"It's probably a good thing that we talk. I've never been in this kind of situation before."

"What do you mean?"

"The whole second chance scenario." She waved a hand between them. "Usually when something's over, it's over. I never consider looking back. I don't know how we're supposed to proceed."

He lifted a shoulder. He didn't have a fucking clue if there were rules or guidelines for this. "Why would it be any different than starting a new relationship?"

"Because this isn't new. We already know each other. What are we supposed to talk about on our first date? What do you do for a living?"

The sarcasm was new. "You're right. Because of our past, we get to skip the mundane get-to-know-you shit. But I think there's still a lot to learn about each other. We're not the same people we were five years ago. You didn't own your flower shop five years ago. I didn't have a career path at all. While you know my whole family, I don't remember you ever telling me about yours. I know who you are, but I don't know silly things like your favorite color or your favorite dessert. What you do when you're pissed off or sad or lonely."

He took her hand again. "I want to learn all those things."

She inhaled deeply and the swell of her breasts rising over the top of her strapless dress drew his attention. "Crap. You've gotten too good with words. I'm going to have to watch myself."

"Not just words, Kathy. I might talk a lot of bullshit to a lot of people, but everything I've said to you is real. I'm done with games. I'm thirty years old. I want the next phase of my life to start."

Her eyes widened again. "But no pressure, right?"

"Look, I don't know if we're like Jimmy and Moira, but I want us to have that shot. That's all I'm asking for."

"I'm willing to give you that chance, but it's not like I can forget the past."

"Fair enough. If I do something that bothers you, or makes you want to step back, tell me. Don't run away."

She took a sip of her drink. "No one else."

"Done."

"And I'm not jumping into bed with you right away just because we know it'll be hotter than hell."

An image of her lying naked on his bed flashed in his head. He nodded.

"I want to make sure we're good together before we have sex."

Although he'd been fantasizing about having her again, he continued to agree. He hadn't been joking when he'd told her he'd do anything to get another chance. "Okay. I can kiss you, though, right? You'll at least give me that?"

"Kissing is okay."

"It's more than okay." He brushed her hair off her shoulder and allowed his fingers to caress the smooth skin there. "Can you give me a ballpark on how long we're waiting?"

"I don't know."

"You have an idea in your head. You must've thought something before bringing it up."

She wiped at condensation on her glass. "If we were totally new to each other, I'd go out at least four or five times before sleeping with you."

She waited as if she was asking for some extraordinary thing. Five fucking dates? He could do that without even trying. "Okay."

She lifted her head again and looked at him with disbelief. "No argument? No trying to change my mind?"

"Silly thing to argue about. I'll jump through whatever hoops you need. I know I'm asking a lot. Five dates? I'll handle it." He scooted closer on the bench until their thighs touched. "Just tell me this. Does today count as the first date?"

She laughed and her whole face brightened. "We'll see."

He stood and held a hand out to her. "Then we better get back to the reception before I lose my head. Let's go dance."

Kevin was totally content to wait to have Kathy in his bed. He knew it would happen, and tonight she was in his arms.

Chapter Nine

Kevin growled as he let himself into his apartment at nine o'clock. He'd just gotten home from work and Kathy was already in bed. So much for thinking getting to five dates would be easy. They'd talked every day since the wedding, but their schedules didn't match. Frustration gnawed at him. He'd never had a problem like this. In fact, he'd never had to plan much when it came to his social life. Things just happened.

He sat on his couch and turned on the TV. He thought about past girlfriends and dating and realized that he never had this problem because he never put in effort before. If his schedule didn't work with his date's, he found someone else to hang out with. He hadn't worried about making time for someone or changing his life to make room for her.

None of them had mattered the way Kathy did, and it wasn't just because he wanted to sleep with her. The thought should've unsettled him, but didn't. With every conversation they had, he liked Kathy more. She made him smile and brightened his day through simple things. He wouldn't call it love, but he acknowledged the possibility.

Picking up his phone, he texted Kathy, hoping that she hadn't fallen asleep yet. He knew she had an early morning, like four a.m. early, so he didn't want to wake her.

Are you still awake?

He laid his phone on his chest and leaned into the couch, resting his head on the back, and stared at the ceiling. Mayor Park still hadn't offered him the liaison position, even though he listened to everything Kevin had said about the businesses that attended the cocktail party. Kevin had put more hours into cultivating this partnership than anyone else. Certainly, more than any other staff writer.

His phone vibrated on his chest.

Just reading before sleep. What's up?

Instead of texting, he turned off the TV and called her. He stood and stripped on his way to the bedroom. He was down to his boxers by the time she answered.

"Hello," she said quietly.

"Hey."

"What's up?"

"I miss hearing your voice. Miss seeing you more."

She sighed. "Work gets in the way of life. Not much to do about that."

"Other people figure it out. We will too. I can't believe I haven't seen you since the wedding." He lay down on his bed on top of the messy blanket because if he crawled under, he would fall asleep, and he wanted a shower first. "What does the rest of your week look like?"

"Crazy. I have three weddings next weekend, so I have a ton of orders to put together."

"Mine's probably not any better. I never know. I can usually count on regular hours, but working with Park on this new initiative is time-consuming. If he gives the position to someone else after all this, I'm gonna be pissed."

"He wouldn't do that, would he?"

"Who knows? It's Chicago politics."

"Well, if he does that, he'll lose my vote in the next election. And if you add in all of the O'Malleys and O'Learys, he might lose half of the city." She chuckled at her own joke, and Kevin couldn't help but join in.

"What time do you get to the store in the morning?"

"Usually around four-thirty. Deliveries start coming in at five."

A sudden thought struck him. Kathy worked alone most of the time. "You're all alone accepting deliveries at five in the morning? That's not safe."

"It's fine. I've been doing it for years. My drivers know me and the neighborhood is already waking up by then. The bakery down the street opens at five, and there are regular joggers and walkers that go by."

He'd bet that in the middle of winter, when it was still dark out and the temperature struggled to get above zero, there was no one on the street. "How about breakfast tomorrow?"

"Anna doesn't come in until ten, so I can't leave before then, and that's a little late for breakfast. After being awake and working for six hours, I'm ready for lunch."

"Okay. It's a date."

"Really? Don't you have to be at work?"

"Don't worry about me. I'll see you in the morning."

"I'm looking forward to it."

"Me too." When he disconnected, he set his alarm for four o'clock and did a quick search for diners near her shop. He wanted to see what her morning was like, hang out with her, and make sure it was as safe as she seemed to believe it was.

He wasn't nearly as overprotective as Jimmy was, but having their mom taken from them when she'd been coming home from working a night shift was something that stayed with them. Probably not Sean, Tommy, and Norah because they had been so young, but Jimmy and Kevin had understood what had happened.

So he took a quick shower and crawled into bed with thoughts of Kathy's lips on his mind.

Kathy stood in her cooler rearranging pots of flowers to maximize her space. She knew her mind wasn't on flowers when she put a pot of carnations on the rose shelf. She hadn't been able to sleep after talking with Kevin. She loved that he was considerate enough to ask if she was up before calling. He didn't nag her about not being able to go out late because she had to be at the shop so early.

He was a guy who got it. Which was weird because Kevin had always been about partying all night wherever with whomever.

But his life didn't seem any more exciting that hers with his work schedule.

She was kind of sad because she was ready to move their relationship forward and while they connected most days, it wasn't the same as being together. She was looking forward to seeing him for brunch.

Walking out of the cooler, she heard someone banging on the front door. Customers never came in this early, and all of her regular delivery guys knew to come around back. She eased around the corner to see who was banging.

There was Kevin with a hand shading his eyes to see into the shop. What the heck?

She walked to the door and unlocked it. "What the hell are you doing here at five o'clock? I told you I can't leave until Anna gets here."

"True. But I also know that you don't officially open until nine, so with the exception of whatever deliveries still come in, I have you all to myself." He lifted the shopping bag in his hand. "I brought breakfast."

She inhaled and caught the scent of eggs and bacon and coffee. "Mmm . . . I don't remember the last time I ate a proper breakfast. I think this might be your best idea yet."

Tugging him through the darkened shop, she led him to her office, where she moved invoices and files to a pile on the cabinet beside the desk. She took a moment to check him out in his suit, looking all businesslike and professional.

Kevin set the bag down and closed in on her. "Before we eat, this can't wait." He wrapped his hand around her nape and pulled her close.

He lowered his mouth to hers and she opened to welcome him in. His tongue slicked along hers and her blood raced. He took his time exploring her mouth as one hand coasted down the side of her body to her hip, anchoring her in place. Her nipples, which were already hard from being in the cooler, tightened and begged for attention.

She moaned into his mouth. She didn't know if it was because she hadn't had a steady boyfriend for a while or if it was simply Kevin's talented tongue, but she wanted more. More of him. More of this.

His hand skated under her T-shirt and he palmed her breast. When he squeezed her nipple, her hips bucked in response, grinding against his leg, which was almost in the perfect position. He pulled away from her mouth and kissed his way across her jaw and then to her neck. Nipping and lightly sucking, he had her melting into a puddle of lust in seconds. Seconds that he drew out to minutes until her panties were damp, and she needed to be touched.

"We need to stop," she gasped as he shifted and moved to her other nipple.

"Not yet," he whispered against her neck.

Was he trying to push this until she stripped? She was stronger than that.

He worked his way back up to her mouth. He peppered her with kisses. "Let me touch you."

It didn't matter that his hand was up her shirt or that his lips had traveled all over her neck, she knew he wanted a more intimate touch. Part of her was ready to beg for it. "Five dates."

She shifted to pull out of his embrace, but the hand on her hip pulled her tight to him. "No sex. I just want to touch you. I want to make you come. Right here, right now. Just stand there and enjoy it."

His words were as intoxicating as the look in his eyes. She should say no, but she didn't respond.

Kevin kissed her again, thrusting his tongue in and out of her mouth in an erotic dance. When the hand on her hip moved to the button of her jeans, he paused and looked in her eyes, waiting for confirmation. "I'll stay fully clothed. Just you," he murmured against her lips.

When she didn't protest, his fingers flicked the button open and the hiss of her zipper being lowered matched the one from her mouth as his fingers skimmed the soft skin of her stomach. Kevin returned to assaulting her mouth as his hand found its way past her waistband and into her panties.

She was wet and when his fingers first made contact, he groaned. "So wet. For me." Another kiss. "So fucking hot."

He stroked, caressing her and barely touching her clit. Clever man. He wasn't going to make this fast or easy. She should've remembered that about him. He liked to keep her close until she was crazy with need. She should've backed out. She should've known better, but this felt too good.

He felt too good.

Every touch, every lick, every pinch. It was his way of reminding her that he would decide what happened next. That would be a problem to dissect later.

Right now, all she cared about was getting off.

She rocked her hips against his hand, using his palm to send rockets of pleasure through her body. He pushed one finger and then two into her, thrusting to the rhythm she created.

Kevin stepped forward, pushing her back until her ass bumped the edge of the desk. She leaned against it, which allowed her to open her thighs more, giving Kevin more room to do his magic.

He had her gasping and moaning quickly. Wrapping her arms around his neck, she let her forehead hit his shoulder. "Please," she said. "More."

She was so close.

"That's my girl."

His words sent a warm flush through her entire body. He pinched her nipple and pressed against her clit all while thrusting. Her whole being clenched and spiraled out of control. Stars, fireworks, a whole freaking light show exploded behind her closed eyes. Kathy had her face buried in the crook of his neck, warm and safe.

As she came down from that incredible high, Kevin held her. His fingers were still inside her, feeling every pulse of her body, but his other hand was on her back, holding her to his body. When she finally stilled, he pulled out, brushing her clit one last time, sending little sparks of aftershock through her. She trembled.

Being the gentleman, he refastened her pants and tugged her shirt in place. He brushed a hand over her hair, and his thumb stroked her cheek. He waited until she opened her eyes and looked at him. "I really hope you're okay with that. It was the hottest fucking thing I've done in a while."

She chuckled. She might fall for a lot of things about him, but those words didn't come close. "I highly doubt that. But I'm okay."

"Wasn't my plan when I came here today. You believe that, right?"

"You mean breakfast wasn't just a ploy?"

"No ploys." He pressed against her lips quickly and then asked, "Do you have a washroom I could use?"

"Yeah, right around the corner."

He stepped away but didn't turn his back to her until he reached the door. She probably should've felt some remorse for the funny way he was walking, but she didn't. He'd initiated that entire scene. And while she thoroughly enjoyed it, she wasn't ready to commit to doing more. Not until she was sure about Kevin.

Kevin stepped into the bathroom, flicked on the light, and leaned against the door. He'd never had to show such self-control and he hoped to God he never had to again. He shifted his hard cock in his pants. The thought of jerking off right here in the bathroom occurred to him but he couldn't. He was seriously fucked in the head.

All he'd wanted was a nice breakfast date with Kathy. But when he saw her come to the door in the dim light, her nipples already poking through her shirt, his interest stirred. Putting his mouth on hers sealed it. He'd needed to touch her and once he did, he wanted to see her fall apart. He wanted to be the one to do it. Even if he got nothing for his efforts. Yet.

He wanted Kathy to know he wasn't the same self-centered prick she'd known five years ago. Running his hand through his hair brought her scent back to him. He went to the small sink and turned the faucet handle. While he washed, he looked at himself in the mirror.

Frustration filled his face, and he needed to get rid of that. He didn't want Kathy to think he'd lied. He just hadn't counted on watching her come being such a turn-on. Drying his hands on the paper towel, he finger-combed his hair one more time to fix it for work.

Back in her office, Kathy had the food spread out on the desk. She looked up at him from where she was inhaling food.

"Sorry. I was going to wait, but it smelled so good." She swallowed. "Do you have time to stay?"

The fact that she wanted him to stay meant a lot. Maybe not as much as an orgasm of his own, but still a big deal. "I have plenty of time until I have to be in the office. The sun was barely up when I got here."

"Don't exaggerate. It's July. It was bright and cheery by the time you got here. Now in the dead of winter, five a.m. might as well be midnight."

He dragged a chair from one side of the desk so he could sit next to her, and then he picked up his own Styrofoam container. "I guess I was lucky that a delivery guy didn't come strolling in on us, huh?"

She choked on her food. He patted her back. Wiping her mouth, she said, "Why would you care? I'm the one who has to see them every week. And, yeah, that would be mortifying."

"But worth it?"

She smiled so brightly it shot straight into his chest. "So worth it," she admitted.

They ate in silence for a few minutes. When he was done poking at lukewarm eggs, he set the container back on the desk. "This counts as a date, right? I brought you food, we shared a meal."

"I came all over your hand," she added without missing a beat.

Her comment had him choking on his coffee. He hadn't expected that. Kathy had been wild in bed, but really quiet and inhibited out of it.

Setting her near-empty box beside his, she reached for his hand. "This was sweet. It was completely unexpected and I appreciate it. The orgasm was a nice bonus. Even without that, this would count as a date." She stroked her thumb over his knuckles. "I know five is an arbitrary number. It sits in the back of my head as I'm getting to know a guy. But we have history. We kind of know each other."

"I remember a lot about you, but you're different now."

"Different good or different bad?"

"Just different. I haven't figured out the details yet, but I'm looking forward to it."

"I like this." She pointed between them. "The sex had always been good and what happened here is a blatant example that hasn't changed. But I want to be sure. About you. About us."

"I know. I'm not trying to push."

"You're pretty pushy."

"It's a family trait. All in the genes."

A bell rang and she squeezed his hand. "That'll be my last delivery."

"I should get going anyway."

They stood and he took the chance to kiss her again. Their tongues barely touched when the bell buzzed again.

"I gotta go," she murmured against his lips.

"Then get outta here." He swatted her ass as she walked away. He cleaned up their breakfast mess while she dealt with her delivery. The whole time he thought about what he could do to prove to her that he'd changed. Earning her trust became his most important goal.

When the containers were tossed in the trash, he walked out of the office to say one last good-bye. He stopped in the hall while Kathy chatted with her delivery guy. Why he'd imagined some pot-bellied middle-aged dude with a hairy back and plumber's crack, he didn't know. Probably wishful thinking. The guy leaning on the cooler door beside Kathy had muscles bulging where Kevin hadn't known muscles existed.

Worse, Muscle Head was making Kathy smile. He was obviously putting some moves on her, and she just chatted away about some flower. The man's eyes kept wandering to Kathy's tits.

"Hey, babe," Kevin said as he neared and put a hand around Kathy's hip. "Did you need any help with the delivery before I head to work?"

She gave him a confused look, but the delivery guy got the message clear.

"I better get going. See you next week?"

"Yep," she said cheerfully.

When the guy had gone out the back door, she asked, "What was that about? Since when do you call me babe?"

"Does it bother you?"

She angled her face and took a moment to consider it. "I guess not. But it came out of nowhere. Or do you just assume that because your hand was in my pants, you can call me whatever you want?"

"I wanted to make it clear to your delivery boy that you're taken."

"What?"

Kevin pointed at the now-closed back door. "The guy was hitting on you."

"No he wasn't. We were talking."

"You were talking. He was staring at your tits."

She crossed her arms over her chest self-consciously. "He was not."

He took her arms and moved them away from her body. "They're great tits to look at. But they're for me, not him."

"Possessive much?"

"Hey, I'm playing by your rules. You said no one else. I like that idea. It means that this"—he allowed his gaze and then his hands to slide over her body—"is all mine."

She shivered and closed her eyes. "I wasn't giving him anything."

"I know." He waited until she looked up again. "I know you wouldn't. You should make it clear to guys like him that they don't have a chance."

Placing a hand on her cocked hip, she asked, "And are you doing the same? Announcing to the world that you're taken?"

"Yep."

"You are not."

"I tell anyone who'll listen that I convinced the prettiest girl to give me another chance even though I don't deserve it. You want more proof?" He stomped to the back door and flung it open. To the empty alley, he yelled, "Kevin O'Malley is officially off the market!"

Kathy grabbed at his arm. "What are you doing? I have to work in this neighborhood."

"I want you to know that I'm not kidding."

"I got it."

He smirked. "Okay. I'll call you later."

"Maybe we can have dinner?"

"I'd love to, but I'm not sure how late I'll be at the office." He flipped through his mental calendar, but couldn't recall anything that would cause him to be at the office late. Then again, he'd thought that yesterday too. He closed the back door and locked it. "Walk me out, so you can relock the front door."

"Yes, sir," she said cockily.

"Hmmm . . . I like the sound of that. Maybe you can try *master* next."

Kathy burst into laughter. "That's never gonna happen, but you keep dreaming."

He pulled her close at the front door and kissed his way from her mouth down her neck. "I bet I can make you say it."

"You play dirty."

"That's the only way to play." He stepped back and pulled his keys from his pocket. "Lock up behind me."

"Talk to you later. Have a good day at work."

"You too." He walked reluctantly out the door and waited to hear her lock it. He wished he could take the day to play hooky. He couldn't remember the last time he just took a day to have fun. His career had been his main focus for the last few years, but having Kathy back in his life had made him start to reevaluate his priorities. His career was still important, but now he wanted to make time for her.

* * *

Later that day, Kathy fussed with her hair and makeup. Kevin had managed to get out of the office early enough to go to dinner at a decent hour. She wanted to look good for him. She told herself it had nothing to do with the orgasm he'd given her this morning. The fact of the matter was she hadn't put in effort for him. With the exception of the wedding and bachelorette party, she hadn't even dressed nicely. So this time, she was out to impress.

He texted to say that he was running a few minutes late. She recognized that as being new for him. In the past, he would've just shown up whenever and expected her to be waiting. Part of her knew she needed to stop thinking about the past, but she feared overlooking obvious warning signs like she had before.

Was she really giving him a second chance if she was constantly comparing Kevin today to Kevin from five years ago? She didn't know. But she knew that she was nervous for their date tonight. He kept saying that he'd play by her rules, but he pushed.

This morning was the perfect example. She was a total pushover. She'd told him five dates and then she completely caved. And now she was primping for him. Lust and sex were making her lose focus.

She wanted to call Moira, but her best friend was still on her honeymoon. Kathy didn't know what to think.

Her doorbell rang, leaving her exactly no time to consider anything. She buzzed Kevin in and waited by the front door. He strode through the hall in jeans and a T-shirt, making her feel overdressed in her sundress.

"Hey," he said as he entered. "You look great." Leaning in, he kissed her cheek. "Where do you want to go?"

Before she could answer, his phone vibrated in his pocket.

"I'm hungry, so dinner would be great," she said.

The buzzing started again. He groaned. "Sorry. Let me check this."

While he swiped at the screen, she packed her purse. When she turned back, his face was still staring at the phone. His eyebrows were drawn and his lips tugged into a frown. "Fuck."

"Everything okay?"

He glanced up. "It's work. The mayor wants a new draft of something I did for him."

"And he's calling you now?" She glanced at the clock. Seven in the evening.

He sighed.

"You have to go, don't you?"

He nodded. "You could come with me."

"That doesn't make much sense."

"I can probably get this done within a half hour. Then we can grab something downtown."

He was trying. She'd give him that. "It's okay. We'll try for another day."

"No. I told you we'd go out tonight. I don't want to put it off again. A half hour, I promise."

She smiled. He seemed so sure of himself. And she hadn't been downtown in a while, other than driving through to get to Navy Pier for the party. "Okay."

If nothing else, they could talk on the ride there. Plus, she'd get to see where he worked. She wanted to see the other side of Kevin O'Malley. The side that worked at city hall and networked with politicians.

"You're an awesome girlfriend, you know that?"

Her heart jumped at him calling her his girlfriend. Silly thing. "I am quite the catch."

"You are."

Where she had been flippant, he spoke seriously. As she locked up, her neighbor Mrs. Thomas walked down the hall.

"Hi, Mrs. Thomas."

"Hello, Kathy. My, you're looking pretty tonight. And who is this?" she asked, looking at Kevin.

"Kevin O'Malley, ma'am. I'm officially off the market because Kathy is my girlfriend."

Mrs. Thomas laughed. "Good to know."

Kathy took Kevin's hand. "Are you going to keep doing that?"

"What?"

"Announcing that we're together and you're off the market."

"Yep."

"That's ridiculous."

He led them to his car. "You seem to be under some illusion that I'm fighting women off day in and day out. If I have to make constant announcements to let you and everyone else know that I'm with you, I can live with that."

She sat down in the car and waited for him to get in. "It's over the top and you know it."

"It might be. But I expect you to tell a man who's hitting on you that you're not interested because you're taken. I'm willing to do the same."

Listening to him created more questions in her head. "Did you think I was sleeping with other guys before?"

He pulled out into traffic to head to downtown and said, "Hmm?"

"When we were dating, did you think I was sleeping with other people?"

He was quiet for a minute. "I didn't think much about it. If I'd considered it, it would've made me crazy, but I also knew that I had no claim on you because I hadn't offered monogamy. I thought we were casual."

She didn't know what answer she'd been expecting or hoping for, but that one didn't sit right with her. Irritation danced along her neck and she turned her head to try to get rid of it. She was supposed to be moving past all that and she didn't even know why his answer bothered her. He was being honest, which was what she'd asked for.

Kevin reached across the seat and grabbed her hand. "You okay?"

"Yeah." It wasn't a lie, but it wasn't entirely true either.

They drove in silence, listening to the radio. When they reached downtown, Kevin pulled into an underground parking lot. As they walked together, he put his arm around her shoulders.

"I'm sorry our night got screwed up again."

"It's okay. You'll finish your work and then we'll eat."

They rode the elevator up, and Kathy was intrigued to see where he worked. The space had some cubicle-like areas divided, but there were more open spaces with tables together. Overall, she couldn't imagine more than ten people working here at a time though. Office doors were closed along one wall.

No one else appeared to be around. Kevin grabbed a chair and wheeled it behind him to one of the cubicles. "You can sit here."

He took his own seat in front of his computer and booted it up. Kathy sat and crossed her legs. She pulled out her phone and scrolled through Facebook. Kevin started to mumble at his screen. When his office line rang, she stood to give him privacy.

"Yes, Mayor Park," he said.

Kathy waved at him and wandered into a conference room, which offered a beautiful scene of the city. Twenty minutes later, Kevin was still talking and typing and her stomach growled, announcing how empty it was. Since they came in his car, she couldn't just leave. That would be a crappy thing to do anyway.

Then she had a brilliant idea. Kevin had delivered breakfast to her this morning, so she'd have dinner brought to them. Hopping back on her phone, she placed an order for Chinese food and then went downstairs to meet the delivery guy. On her way down, she hoped she wouldn't need any special pass to get back up.

In the lobby, a security guard stood by the door and one manned a desk. She approached the desk. "Hi. I'm upstairs working with Kevin O'Malley. I just ordered dinner to be delivered."

The guard eyed her up and down and she fought the cringe. She knew she looked like she was on a date.

She took a deep breath. "Should I stay down here to wait for the delivery, or can you send him up?"

"We can send him up."

"Do I need an ID or anything to get back up in the elevator?"

"The bank on the left will get you where you need to be."

"Thank you."

She took the elevator back up and when it dinged, she saw Kevin stand at his desk to see who was coming in. His desk phone was still at his ear, and he gave her such a pitiful look that she felt sorry for him.

When she got back to the desk, he mouthed, "I'm sorry."

"It's fine. Is there a vending machine where I can get us some drinks?"

"Can you hold on one minute, Mayor?"

Kathy's eyes popped wide. Who told the mayor to hang on? That seemed kind of ballsy. Then Kevin set the phone on the desk and pulled her close. "You're the best girlfriend ever." He planted a quick kiss on her lips and handed her a wad of cash. "The vending machines are in the staff lounge down the hall on the right."

Then he picked up the phone again and began talking. By the time she got a couple cans of pop from the machine, the elevator dinged again and their dinner arrived.

Kathy paid the delivery guy and carried the food and drinks to the conference room. Once she had everything spread out, she hoped Kevin might really be done.

"Kathy?" he called.

"In your fancy conference room."

A minute later, he stood at the door. "What's this?"

"You were working so hard, I ordered food. It seemed like your quick fix wasn't happening."

He sighed and hung his head. "I'm almost done. The mayor really likes to talk." He came into the room and sat at the table. "I think I can take a break for dinner."

They spent time eating and laughing. Kevin told her about what the mayor had him working on. Their evening hit a smooth stride again, and she enjoyed their time together. After they finished eating, she told him to go back to work and she'd clean up.

Taking care of the mess, she thought about their odd dates. So far, she and Kevin had attended a wedding together because they were both part of the wedding party, enjoyed breakfast at her shop, and had dinner in his office. She laughed. When she thought about being won over by a man, this wasn't what came to mind.

But it worked. If nothing else, she'd get one hell of a kiss good night.

Chapter Ten

A week later, Kevin questioned his sanity in trying to land the new liaison position with the mayor. He'd been scrambling to do anything the mayor needed, including offering to handle the lackluster city events calendar. And he had no fucking clue what he was doing. Against his better judgment, he went to Moira. If anyone understood a social calendar, it was her.

When the door opened, she stood in her shorts and tank top, staring at him. "Jimmy's at work."

"Okay. I'm here to see you."

Her pink forehead wrinkled. "Why?"

Holding up the paper file in his arms, he said, "Can I come in and explain it?"

She opened the door wider and walked barefoot into the living room. Their house was a little smaller than his dad's but not by much. He knew Jimmy was looking forward to starting a family of his own. Papers spilled across the top of the dining room table all around her laptop. "Looks like you got some sun while on the honeymoon."

She and Jimmy had gone to Disney World.

"Go figure. Florida in the summer," she answered.

"I didn't think Jimmy would let you leave the bedroom."

"I'm not discussing my sex life with you." Gathering some papers into a pile, she said, "Have a seat."

He pulled out his own laptop and set the file on the table.

"What do you have going on that you think I can help with?" she asked as she sat in a chair, pulling her feet up on the edge.

"You know I work in the mayor's office, right?"

She nodded.

"He's heading up a new initiative to outsource the tourism board. We've got the field of companies to work with narrowed down, and he's going to announce soon."

"What does this have to do with you? Or me?"

"He's going to need to appoint a liaison for this. I want it. So to prove how much I want it and how good I'll be at the job, I've been bending over backward to do anything he asks. This is the latest task." He shoved the file folder closer to her.

She flipped the folder open. "What the hell is this?"

"Stupid-ass notes from the woman who was in charge of the city calendar. Can you believe this was what she worked from? For years. I don't know where to begin."

"Dump the paper first." She scanned through the stack, much as he'd done when it was delivered to his desk. "You need to automate."

"How the fuck do I do that?"

She sighed. "Talk to whoever is in charge of the city website. Have them add a plug-in or whatever so there's a form to fill in. Items can just be plopped onto the calendar automatically. Well, maybe you want to have to approve things first. Otherwise who knows what you'll get."

"Just like that? Create a form for a shared calendar?"

"Why not?"

"How will people know to use it?"

She shrugged. "Use your big mouth to spread the word."

He shook his head. Her idea was perfect, but he needed people to use it.

"How did people used to get in touch with this woman?"

"Phone. E-mail. Carrier pigeon?" He inhaled and tried to calm down. Even if he failed at this, he'd already done so much to prove to Park what he could do. No. Failure was not an option. He didn't want the mayor to have any reason to look elsewhere.

Moira was suspiciously quiet. He looked over to see her reading through the pages of notes. "You have access to an intern?"

"Maybe. There's usually a couple floating around."

"Hand it off. Get one of them to make the calls to event coordinators to notify them of the new system. Well, obviously get the new calendar in place first. Nothing will piss people off faster than another broken city idea." She closed the folder and slid it back. "Why come to me?"

"You've spent the last few years doing nothing but going to parties throughout the city."

She glared at him.

"You know what I mean. I wasn't implying you don't work. I figured if anyone knew how to make things better than the old system, it'd be you." He smiled. "And I was right."

She rolled her eyes, but then shifted, dropping her feet to the floor and leaning her arms on the table. "What's going on with you and Kathy?"

He knew this conversation had to happen sooner or later, but he had no intention of rushing it. "What do you know?"

"Kathy mentioned that you're seeing each other again."

"We are. In case she asks, you can tell her I made it clear that she's my girlfriend."

"Huh?"

"Just . . ." He remembered Kathy pointing out how over the top his declarations were. Saying it to Moira was beyond over the top. "Nothing."

"Why are you doing this? You can find someone else."

"I don't want anyone else." He knew the response wouldn't satisfy her. Moira was a talker, and she needed thorough answers. "When I saw her at your engagement party, it wasn't pretty. We both viewed how things had ended between us differently. There'd been some major miscommunication back then. Mostly on my part, but some on hers. And yeah, I get that I hurt her. I never meant to. And in the time since we spoke at your party, I haven't been able to get her out of my head."

"So?"

"We were good together back then, but I wasn't ready for anything serious. I wasn't ready for her." His mouth went dry. Why did he feel the need to defend himself to Moira of all people? It wasn't like she was Kathy's mom.

"And you are now?"

"Yes."

She snorted.

"What?"

"You're not the settling down type."

"Five years ago, I wasn't. Now I am."

"Like anyone believes that." She stood and left the room toward the kitchen.

Kevin clenched his teeth. While he didn't need Moira's approval, he also knew that as Kathy's best friend, she had influence. When Moira returned, she handed him a bottle of cold water and opened one for herself.

"I get you think I'm a fuckup. But I've proven to Kathy that I deserve a second chance. I'm not going to hurt her."

"We'll see." She gulped water. "Keep in mind that Jimmy's on my side now. I'll have him kick your ass if you do."

"Sweetheart, I'm pretty sure you could handle that on your own." He chugged his own water and stood. "But we won't have to test that theory. Thanks for the help. I have to figure out who I need to talk to."

She rose to walk him to the door. "She's guarded, you know, but soft. It won't take much to damage her once she lets you in."

Kevin turned to look into Moira's bright blue eyes. "I'm not going to hurt her. I want this. I can't remember ever feeling about a woman the way I do about her. I missed it the first time because I was young and dumb."

"That's definitely an O'Malley family trait."

He smiled. "Tell me about it. Thanks again for the help. Tell Jimmy to give me a call later."

As he walked back to his car, he considered what Moira had said about Kathy. The guardedness he'd witnessed, but getting to the rest, he'd only caught glimpses. He'd prove to Kathy that he could take care of her.

And then he'd rub it in Moira's pretty little face.

Three more days passed without seeing Kathy. And he felt like shit because of it. Not just the lack of contact, kissing and touching her, but because he'd acted like getting to five dates would be simple. He woke every morning and sent her a text because he knew she was already at the shop. By the time he took a break to eat in the afternoon, he couldn't not think of her, so he called. She always answered, which made him feel even guiltier because it felt like she was waiting on him. If she was busier, she wouldn't have time to answer and he wouldn't feel like such an ass.

He lay in bed staring at the time on his phone. Ten o'clock. He knew she was in bed, but he wanted to hear her voice, so he called.

"Hey, you're calling late. Did you just get in?" She didn't sound like she'd been sleeping.

"Did I wake you?"

"No. I was working up some new designs for a wedding next week. What are you doing?"

"I just crawled into bed and wanted to catch you before you fell asleep. Now I feel like a slacker because you're probably still fully clothed sitting at your desk working even though you got up hours before me this morning."

She laughed and the light sound lifted his spirit.

"I'm actually sitting in bed surrounded by scraps of crumpled paper." A heavy sigh followed before she said, "I've been thinking a lot. Maybe this isn't a good time for us to be starting something."

"What?"

"You're really busy with the mayor. I get it. I'm not mad, and I'm not disappearing. I just think maybe we should step back."

"No." He sat up in bed. Rubbing a hand over his head, he tried to think of the right words. "I know things have been crazy, but I promise they'll calm down. My work life has never been this packed. It won't stay like this for long."

"You need to focus on your job. I don't want to be a distraction that costs you the position you want."

"You're not."

"As much as I like talking to you, I need more in a boyfriend. I need to be able to see you and touch you. I don't need fancy dates, but I do need to be with you. Right now I feel like that's an unfair demand to make."

"It's not," he whispered.

"It is. When I opened my shop, I didn't date for pretty much a whole year. I didn't have a social life at all, come to think of it. My business needed my attention more."

He swung his legs over the edge of the bed knowing that sleep wouldn't be coming anytime soon. His brain scrambled for the words to convince her this could work. "We said we were gonna take this slow, and I know this is slower than either of us thought, but I don't want you to walk away again."

"I'm not walking away. I'm afraid that we're both going to end up resentful. I don't want that to happen. I like you."

"I like you too. That's why I believe we can figure this out. If that means I have to drag my ass out of bed every day at five a.m. to have breakfast with you, I will." Even though the thought of early mornings made him cringe, the chance to see her and kiss her every day before work was appealing.

"You're thinking about having sex in my office, aren't you?"

Her voice was low and seductive, so while he hadn't been thinking that, now he was. Her comment definitely lightened the conversation, so he went with it. Scooting back on his bed, he asked, "What did you say you're wearing again?"

She chuckled. "You're such a guy. I didn't say."

"I'm visual. If I can't be with you, I want to be able to picture it."

"I'm wearing a navy blue tank top with Wonder Woman on the front. Black panties. Hold on."

Since he'd never been in her bedroom, he imagined

her sitting next to him in his bed. "Hair up or down?" he asked.

"Check your phone."

He pulled the phone away from his face to see that she'd texted him pictures. His cock grew hard at the sight of her kneeling on her mattress so he could see her whole outfit. It was better than seeing her in some lacy lingerie. She was cute and playful and comfortable.

"You trying to kill me?"

"You asked. I delivered. Plus, I want you to know what you're missing."

"I am."

"You are what?"

"Missing you."

Another pause. "You, Kevin O'Malley, are pretty damn good with words."

"I'm good with a lot of things. I'm going to figure this out. What does your weekend look like?"

"I have back-to-back wedding deliveries on Saturday and Sunday."

"How about I tag along? Then you can come here to hang out and spend the night."

"It's not a date if I'm working."

"I didn't say you should come over so I could have sex with you. I want to spend time with you alone, without any distractions."

"You work crazy hours all week. How about I just come over when I'm done?"

"I don't mind extra work. I want to spend time with you."

"You won't have any fun delivering flowers. Plus, this way, you'll have time to clean up your man cave to impress me."

Kevin glanced around his dimly lit room at the laundry

scattered on the floor. "Point taken. We'll order in Saturday night and watch a movie. I'll even give you a foot rub."

She moaned. "Now you're just bribing me."

"I'm willing to offer much more than a foot rub."

Her gentle sigh whispered in his ear. "I know. We'll talk tomorrow. Good night."

"Good night. This will get easier. It has to."

"I hope."

He disconnected. While settling in to fall asleep, he stared at the photos she'd sent to his phone, wishing she were there with him.

Kathy was used to being busy in the summertime because of weddings. She worked long hours and took every job she could fit in because it made up for the slower months with no holidays demanding flowers. But this summer had suddenly exploded with other jobs, ones that she felt Kevin was behind. Deb had used her two more times, and during the last event, Kathy found out that either Kevin or Deb had gotten Love in Bloom on a preferred vendors list for the city, so she was fielding more calls than usual.

Her long hours almost matched Kevin's. She knew he was striving to get a promotion, or at least a job shift, but because of that, they were having a hard time connecting. He usually called when he took a break for lunch and they talked at night before going to bed, but she needed more time with him.

She hated to admit it, but neither of them seemed to be putting in much effort to make this relationship work. He'd been so apologetic when he called late last night that she felt bad for even suggesting that they weren't in a good place to start a new relationship. He hadn't called her on her lack of effort, so it was a little unfair to blame his job for everything.

This morning she decided that she wasn't going down without trying. When she finished a set of arrangements for a luncheon, it was about eight-thirty, so she knew Kevin would be awake. Sitting at her desk in the office, she called him.

"Hey, beautiful, what's up?"

"I want to have lunch together today. What time will you be free?"

"Uhh . . . I don't usually plan lunch. I take it whenever I get a chance. Name the time and I'll meet you."

She thought about her afternoon and decided earlier would be better. "Can you do eleven-thirty?"

"Hang on."

She heard some rustling on his end.

"I have a meeting on the Gold Coast at ten-thirty. How about I come to you?"

She loved the sound of that and before she could reconsider, she blurted, "Excellent. Come to my apartment as soon as you're done."

"Want me to bring lunch?"

"Nope. I have it covered."

"See you in a few hours then."

She disconnected and butterflies took flight in her gut. She just demanded Kevin come to her apartment for lunch. Although they still hadn't had five dates, they'd had three solid ones, if you counted the wedding. And a ton of substantial conversations. She believed Kevin was committed to their relationship, but they were both failing at making it happen.

They needed a physical connection. If nothing else, they would each have something to carry them through until the next time they could be together. She hadn't been able to stop thinking about the fantastic orgasm he'd given her with just his hands the other day. She wanted more of everything with him.

She sped through the rest of her morning, making sure Anna had everything she needed so Kathy could get away for a while. She left Anna alone often, but Kathy was never out of touch. Today, she wanted to be unreachable.

"You're sure you can hold down the fort?" she asked Anna again before heading out to pick up lunch.

"For the fourth time, yes. Go. Have a great lunch." Anna winked and grinned. "And whatever else you have planned. Like maybe a much-needed dessert."

Kathy's cheeks flushed. She considered Anna a friend, but they normally didn't get into personal details. "Thanks. I might just indulge in some dessert today."

Anna clapped her hands. "Excellent. Get out of here."

"I'm going. Call if there's an emergency."

"Has there ever been an emergency?"

"Well, no, but you never know."

Anna came around the counter and began pushing Kathy toward the door. "Take the rest of the day off."

Kathy shot her a look.

"Well, I don't want to see you again before two o'clock."

"I don't think lunch will take that long."

"Then take a nap. You've been working too much lately. You need a break." She opened the door and shoved Kathy through.

With a deep breath, Kathy went to her car. Anna was right. Although she'd always been available, Anna never called. She was a great employee who knew what she was doing. Kathy stopped at the sandwich shop on the corner and ordered food to go. She wanted something that she could stick in the refrigerator in case she and Kevin were busy doing other things.

She definitely wanted to be busy doing other things.

As soon as she got into her apartment, she put lunch in the fridge and then got antsy. She never had free time in the middle of the day. Her phone buzzed with a text and her stomach sank. She was afraid to look in case Kevin was calling to cancel.

On my way. Be there in ten.

I'm waiting. She responded, trying not to sound too eager. She debated changing into something sexy, but then decided not to. What if he didn't have a lot of time for lunch and all he really wanted to do was eat? He didn't run his own business. He had to answer to people. She would feel foolish standing there in a nightie if he had to leave in thirty minutes.

She didn't expect hours-long sex, but their first time—again—shouldn't be a quickie. Even if it was a nooner. Her head was spinning out, so she plopped on the couch to wait. It made no sense to make herself crazy. Kevin would be here soon and they'd figure it out.

Together.

She liked the thought of that. For the first time in a long time, she actually felt like she was part of something. It might not be the easiest or smoothest-running thing, but she enjoyed it. Her bell rang and she buzzed Kevin in. She opened the door to see him standing in her hallway in a suit, looking downright sinful.

"Hey," he said.

"Hey," she said a little breathlessly before grabbing his

hand and pulling him into her apartment. "I'm really glad you made it."

"Uh-huh." His eyes stared intently into hers as he closed the door behind him. Then he spun her back against the door and lowered his mouth to hers. His hips pinned hers in place as their tongues tangled.

She wrapped her arms around his neck and ran her fingers through the soft short hair at the back of his head.

He came up for air and studied her face. "Hello."

"Hi. When do you have to be back at work?"

"Whenever I get there."

Thank God. She moved against his mouth again and loosened his tie. His fingers skimmed along her waist, pushing her shirt up a few inches, just enough to reveal some skin.

He pulled away again and Kathy almost groaned. "We should probably stop if we're gonna get to lunch," he whispered.

"I planned ahead. Lunch is in the fridge. Sandwiches." She continued to kiss his stubbly jaw and down his neck. She unknotted the tie and began to unbutton his shirt. "Let's go to the bedroom."

"What?" He froze and took her hands to stop her.

She swallowed hard and looked up.

"Are you saying what I think you are?" he asked. Lust burned in his eyes and she already felt the hard-on in his neatly pressed pants.

"I'm saying we should go to my bedroom for some much-needed sexual relief."

"But . . ."

She didn't wait for him to finish. She cupped him and ran her tongue on his neck.

Grabbing her hands again, he said, "We haven't had five dates."

"Close enough," she answered against his warm skin.

"Kathy." He waited and then stepped away from her, this time putting an arm's length between them, still holding her hands.

She lifted an eyebrow and waited.

"Are you sure about this?"

"Have I ever struck you as the kind of person to do something unless I'm sure?"

"No. But you wanted slow. This isn't exactly slow."

She took a step but made no attempt to touch him, other than where their hands connected. "I wanted time to get reacquainted. Even with our crazy schedules, I think we've been doing a pretty good job. We need this. The talking and texting is great, but we need the physical part too. It'll give us something for when we're not together. Don't you think?"

"Who am I to argue with logic?" He released her hands and began undressing. "Where's the bed?"

She laughed and stepped around him. "You might want to hang up your clothes so they're not all wrinkled. Everyone will know what you did on your lunch break."

"Let them all be jealous that I spent my lunch buried in the most beautiful woman around."

His words caused more desire to stir through her, and she couldn't get to the bed fast enough. She walked into her bedroom and opened the curtains to let the sun stream in so they could leave the lights off. She wanted to see him, but wanted the quiet of a dimly lit room. When she turned, he was down to his boxer briefs, a sizable hard-on making its presence known.

She pulled off her T-shirt and flicked the button on her jeans. He moaned as she lowered the zipper. He tugged her hand, bringing her close, and pushed her jeans over her hips. His hands skimmed her thighs, and he kissed her stomach along the waistband of her panties, which were already damp.

When he had her jeans at her ankles, he lifted each foot and moved the pants out of the way. Then he pulled her toward the bed. She sat and reached behind her to unclasp her bra. She barely got the straps off her arms before his mouth was on one breast while his fingers toyed with her other nipple.

"You feel so good," she said, throwing her head back and thrusting her chest into his touch.

With an arm around her waist, he angled her more fully onto the mattress. "Lie back," he whispered, his breath causing goose bumps to rise on her skin. The pillows cradled her head and she watched him kiss his way down her torso. When he reached her panties, he glanced up at her. The look in his eyes was halfway asking permission, halfway warning her she was about to have a great time. That wicked glint got her every time.

He yanked her underwear off and settled his shoulders between her legs. "I've been dying to do this. Still the fastest way for you to come?" He didn't wait for an answer, licking her once. "I want you to come hard and fast." Another lick. "The first time."

His words were as seductive as his tongue on her sensitive flesh. That he remembered what she enjoyed in bed meant something. Maybe she hadn't been just a notch on his bedpost.

He sucked and nibbled on her, driving her insane. "Taste so good," he murmured against her thigh.

She bent her legs and widened the space between for him to get comfortable. She was on the edge and he knew it. He used his tongue and lips and then added his hands to make her writhe. Digging her fingers into his hair, against his scalp, she held him in place and thrust her hips to meet his movements.

Then she was spiraling out. Every muscle tensed and tightened as blinding white lights flashed behind her squeezed-tight eyelids. Her muscles relaxed as she came down, panting, heart still racing. She realized she still had a tight grip on Kevin's hair.

Releasing her fingers, she smoothed his hair. "Sorry," she said on a pant.

"I'm not. You're fucking hot when you come." He crawled up her body, his hard dick prodding her thigh. "All I have to say is this is the best lunch ever."

She laughed, even though his self-satisfied grin should've irritated her. She reached between them and wrapped her fingers around his dick. His hips flexed and thrust into her grip. She pumped a couple of times, then said, "I can return the favor with my mouth, or would you rather come in my pussy?"

"Everything. I want it all."

She rose up, kissing him as he backed away, tasting herself on his lips. Their positions reversed, with him leaning back on his elbows. He was hard and throbbing against her lips. She loved knowing she had done this to him. She hadn't even touched him yet, and he was this turned on for her. He made her feel sexy and wanted.

She licked up and down his shaft and cupped his balls. Then she took him deep. His fist wound in her hair, much like she had done to him, but she knew he wanted to see. He liked watching her take him in.

"Fuck yeah," he said. His thighs were bunched muscles of tension as he held tight to his control.

She had only managed to bob up and down a few times before he released her hair and grabbed her shoulders. Kevin wasn't a huge guy, but he had the ability to move her entire body like she was nothing. Before she blinked she was splayed out on her back again with his body covering her.

"I'll get more of that next time."

She smiled. Every time he mentioned the future, she wanted to believe him. Wanted to believe this time was different. "Condom's in the drawer." She pointed at the bedside table.

He opened the drawer and ripped open the wrapper. She watched him roll it on and slowly licked her lips.

"You'll pay for that."

"What?" she asked innocently.

"You know what." He settled between her legs and bent to take a nipple into his mouth. He bit down harder than she anticipated. She sucked in a sharp breath, and he thrust inside her.

Chapter Eleven

Kevin knew he wouldn't last long. He'd been doing nothing but jacking off to mental images of Kathy for weeks. And now he had her naked in his arms.

He sank deep inside her and buried his face in the crook of her neck. She smelled good. Sweet like her flowers. He thought he could die right here, and it would be the perfect way to go.

But his body demanded that he move, that he pump into her, make her come again, tight on his cock. Propping himself up on one elbow, he hooked the other under her knee, opening her wider so he could go deeper.

He pumped his hips slowly at first, long strokes to feel every inch of her on him. Her fingers glided along his shoulders in a lazy motion. He wanted her frantic and wild again, so he picked up the pace and kissed her. His tongue mimicked the movement of his cock, sliding in and out. He sucked on her tongue and nibbled on her lips.

Releasing her leg, he lay so their pelvises touched. His thrusts were shallower, but with each pump, he pressed against her clit. She began chasing him with her hips, seeking release again. He rested his forehead against hers.

Her brandy-colored eyes looked into his, pleading to make her come, but she didn't say it. His heart raced because she remembered this game they'd played. It was a cat-and-mouse game of who could outlast the other. He smirked and pressed deep inside of her, grinding a slow circle against her clit with his hips. Her eyes widened, pupils taking over her irises, and she bit her lower lip.

"All you have to do is say it." He twisted his hips again.

Her palm slapped his ass, and she dug her fingers in. "God, yes, fine. You win. Fuck me and make me come already."

He chuckled and kissed her. He almost always won this game, but it was so much fun. Then he gave her everything he had until her body clamped down around him and pulled him deep. She bowed and arched under him, pulsing all around his cock, pulling his release from him.

Her body milked him through a few more thrusts that were punctuated by tender kisses. He held her close, still inside her body, their chests rising and falling in a unison of gasping breaths.

They lay like that until he could see straight. He rose to dispose of the condom and then returned to her side and wrapped his arms around her.

She turned her head to face him. "I agree. Best lunch ever."

He laughed and kissed her shoulder. If he had any doubts about whether he would fall completely for this woman, it ended here. "You're sure you're okay with this?"

"Except for the fact that you still want me to beg to be able to come, yeah."

His heart did that weird thump again. "The first orgasm

was a freebie." He sank his teeth into the spot on her shoulder he'd kissed. "Actually, the first *two* orgasms, if you count the one from the other morning."

"So this was payback?"

He levered himself above her. "No payback. When I'm buried deep inside you, I want you to be fully aware of who's making you come."

"As if I could forget."

He cradled her jaw, allowing his thumb to caress her cheek. "I know I'm not the only man to ever share your bed. But when you're wild with need, I want my name to be the one you're screaming."

"And you kind of like to be in control," she said, a little cocky in her assuredness.

"Something wrong with that?"

"Not if you're into that sort of thing."

"Are you?" he asked.

She blinked slowly. She'd never complained before, but they were different people now. If she didn't like what he'd done, she needed to let him know now. His thumb brushed her lower lip and she bit him.

"Never before you. Never since."

Her teeth on his thumb distracted him, and he blinked to refocus. What was she talking about? His brain rewound to his question. Then the pieces fell together. She'd only enjoyed this with him. That weird thump of his heart was replaced by a full stillness he couldn't explain.

As if reading his momentary confusion, she added, "Relinquishing control in bed? Only with you."

He kissed her tenderly then, stealing her breath because his lungs hadn't worked on their own. Lying beside her again, he pulled her to his side.

"Don't you have to get back to work?" she asked.

"I have time. How about you?"

"Anna isn't expecting me until at least two."

They lay in silence for a few minutes. He stroked her arm and thought about them. And her. When he'd gotten to her apartment today, she'd said they had gotten reacquainted, but for all he knew about who she was, there were still many gaps.

"Why don't you ever talk about your family?" he asked. She stiffened under his touch, and he had the feeling that he'd just ruined their perfect lunch.

"Not much to tell."

"I know absolutely nothing about them. We talk about mine all the time. You've met my entire family. All I know is that you're an only child. I know nothing about your parents, where they are, if they're still alive, why they didn't have more kids."

Her fingers brushed his chest hair and then she settled her chin on his chest to look at him. "I'm not sure they planned to have me, so I never asked why I don't have siblings."

"Are you not close to your parents? Is that why you never talk about them?"

She shrugged, and he knew she wanted to get out of this conversation, but that told him it was one they needed to have.

"I talk to them. They're divorced now, so I touch base with each of them every few weeks to check in."

Every few weeks? Damn. He spent time with his family at least every week. If he wasn't with them, he definitely spoke to them.

"When did they get divorced?"

"Not until after I went to college. It should've been a whole lot sooner." She turned her head until her cheek was against him. "My childhood wasn't happy. It wasn't horrible either. I wasn't abused or neglected. But I'm also hard-pressed to come up with truly happy memories."

He stroked her hair and hoped she'd continue. This was a whole new side to her he never knew existed.

"My parents didn't belong together. I love them individually. But together, they were a mess. I wish they would've gotten divorced earlier. We all would've been better off." She swallowed, and he felt her throat work. "They stayed together for me, but in doing so they had no idea the damage that caused."

"If you don't want to talk about it, you don't have to."

"It's okay. Years of therapy later, thanks to Moira, I should be able to tell you about it. They were miserable together. They were constantly at odds. Argued about everything, but not in a vicious, nasty way. They both excelled at passive-aggressive jabs. As a young kid, I felt the tension, but I didn't get it. By the time I was older, I just avoided them altogether. I did everything right, exactly what I was supposed to do so they wouldn't have to fight about me."

"Let me guess. It didn't work."

"Of course not. I was a kid, and I didn't know their problems weren't because of me. Another little gem from therapy." She sighed. "Even now, they've been divorced for years, but they still make snotty comments about each other when I talk to them. I can't be stuck in the middle, so I limit communication for my own sanity."

"Have you ever told them to stop?" It seemed silly to say it. He never thought twice about telling anyone in his family when they pissed him off.

"Not really. I tried once, but it just got ugly. More finger-pointing. I couldn't stomach it, so I dropped it."

Things about her started to click into place. The fact that she hadn't confronted him when she'd thought he'd cheated on her, the look on her face when he caught her in the hallway at the engagement party—she avoided conflict. Come to think of it, he couldn't remember a time when she even disagreed with him.

"So therapy fixed you all up, huh?"

"I'm working on it."

That's what she'd been referring to when they were at the block party. He was glad he waited to push to get these answers.

"We never went to therapy," he admitted. "After my mom was killed, I mean. Or anytime."

Kathy looked at him, clearly relieved he switched subjects.

"We were all so young, it probably didn't occur to my dad. Not that he would've taken us because"—he lowered his voice to imitate his dad—"*who needs that malarkey anyway?*"

She smiled. "Kind of scary how well you do that."

"I should be good at it. I've been listening to that man yell at me my whole life."

"Do you wish you had gone to therapy?"

He shifted his shoulders. "I don't know. Part of me thinks we wouldn't be so screwed up."

"How do you mean?"

"Jimmy is such a control freak. Part of the reason he didn't want to fall for Moira was because he knew he couldn't control her. He needs to keep everyone he cares about safe." He swallowed the rapidly forming lump in his throat. "Like he couldn't do for our mom."

Kathy's fingers caressed his pecs and stroked across his shoulders. "What about you? While I know you like to be in control in the bedroom, I don't see the same intensity in you as I do in Jimmy."

He licked his lips. He knew his greatest fear was being left. He'd noticed it first in his younger siblings, the fear of abandonment, long before he recognized it in himself. That fear was why he'd been so angry when Kathy disappeared from his life. But he wasn't ready to confess that. So he cracked a grin. "I'm the most normal of the bunch. Haven't you realized that yet?"

He should've known better than to think that would fly. Kathy pushed up off his chest, and he missed the warmth of her body. Scooping her hair behind her, she glared at him. "I offered you complete honesty, and you can't give me the same?" She shut her mouth, opened it as if to say more, but then just turned and got off the bed.

Kevin scrambled to the edge of the mattress and caught her arm. "Hey, I make jokes. That's who I am." He paused. "I'm not even sure of all the ways I'm fucked up."

She turned to face him and said, "But when I asked, something came into your head that you decided not to share."

"True." He swallowed hard again. If he wanted a relationship, a real one, he knew he needed to do the hard stuff. "The thought of being left scares me. First it pisses me off, but I know it's because I'll feel empty." He shook his head. "Now I feel like a total wuss."

He stood, still holding her hand. She stepped close to him, and her perky tits caught his attention. She kissed his cheek.

"I don't think you're a wuss. You did the manly thing and told the truth. Thank you."

He wasn't feeling too manly at the moment, but he'd take whatever he could from her.

She stroked his cheek. "I promise not to disappear on you again."

Grateful that he didn't have to explain that connection, he watched her walk from the room with her clothes in hand.

Kathy took her time in the bathroom, hoping Kevin wouldn't follow her. The sex had been amazing, but she'd expected that. Hell, she'd missed that. Everything that came after, though . . . not only had she not expected it, it rattled her. She didn't talk to anyone about her parents. Moira was about it. With anyone else, she always glossed over it. Past boyfriends just chalked it up to her not being close to her parents and most were relieved they didn't have to do the meet-the-parents thing.

Somehow Kevin managed to look beyond any easy answers and pushed for more. She wanted to give him more. She just hadn't counted on it feeling like this. She wasn't even sure what *this* was. A strange combination of anxiety and relief.

In that brief conversation they'd learned more about each other—the real, deep-down stuff—than they'd learned the entire time they'd been together before. Her plan to take it slow with him backfired in unimaginable ways. She couldn't figure out if it was a good thing. Her body was thrilled with the outcome of the afternoon. Her heart was still wary.

She cleaned up and dressed and found her bedroom empty. Kevin's clothes were gone and she worried that he'd taken off without saying good-bye. Then she shook her head. He wouldn't do that, especially now that he'd confessed how important a simple good-bye was to him.

She found him in the kitchen, unwrapping the sandwiches she'd bought for lunch. "I thought you had to leave."

"I have a little more time before anyone starts wondering where I am." He grinned. "We did have a lunch date after all."

She sat at her small table across from him at a loss for where to go from here.

He swallowed a bite of sandwich and then asked, "Are we okay?"

Nodding, she said, "Yeah. I'm just—" She waved her hand, still not finding the words.

"Yeah," he said quietly. "Surprised me too."

Looking into his eyes, she saw that he understood. Whatever they shared in bed was intense, even with the joking and games. "Do you regret it?" she asked.

"Hell no. However, if you ever repeat my confession to anyone, we might have issues, but telling you? I'm all good." He picked up the quickly shrinking sandwich. "Lying naked in bed after amazing sex, you could probably get me to confess anything."

"I'll keep that in mind. File it away for future use."

She'd only taken a few bites of her lunch when he crumpled his empty wrapper. He threw away his trash and came to her. "I hate to eat and run, but I have to get back to the office. I have a boss to impress, you know."

"Taking a long lunch to have sex with your girlfriend probably isn't the best way to make that impression."

"No job is worth giving up this kind of lunch. Maybe we should make it a regular thing."

Laughter bubbled up, but he was serious. "Really?"

"Why not? Our schedules are a little nuts. If we can sneak away for lunch and other festivities, we should."

The thought made her feel a little naughty, but in a totally good way. "It's doable. I'm the boss, after all."

"Excellent. I don't know when I'll be off tonight, but I'll give you a call. Maybe we can hang out."

"Sounds good." She rose to walk him to the door.

Before leaving, he kissed her breathless and murmured against her lips, "I won't be able to think about anything but you this afternoon."

She grinned, knowing her day would feel much the same. He left and she returned to her lunch, feeling out of sorts because she rarely took a leisurely lunch. But like she'd told Kevin, she was the boss. This was something she should've been doing all along.

Kevin strode into the office and his phone immediately bleeped with a text. The mayor wanted to see him. Crap. He eyed the work still waiting on his desk, work that he'd ignored to run around and do whatever Mayor Park wanted in an effort to outshine anyone else being considered for the position Kevin wanted. He sighed.

Time to go see what Park wanted now.

In the elevator, Kevin adjusted his tie and finger-combed his hair, hoping no one would be able to tell he'd just gotten laid. When he arrived at the mayor's office, he was ushered in immediately, as if he'd somehow kept Park waiting.

"Kevin," Park announced, his voice booming a little too much for Kevin's comfort. No one else was in the office, so he had no one to impress.

"Yes, sir. You wanted to see me?"

"Stop calling me sir. You sound just like your brother when you do that."

Kevin swallowed a groan. He could go his whole life without sounding like Jimmy and that would do him just fine.

Park pointed to the chair in front of his desk. "Have a seat." Then, instead of taking his usual seat behind the desk, he sat across from Kevin.

"I wanted to talk about the work you've put in on the tourism initiative. I really appreciate everything you've done."

This sounded like he was sending Kevin on his way, so Kevin did what he could to keep calm. He straightened his shoulders. "I've done my job, Mayor."

"No. You've gone above and beyond. Way above and beyond. I don't want you to think that goes unnoticed."

"Thank you." It wasn't a job offer, but at least the man recognized that Kevin had been working his ass off.

"I want to offer you the position of official tourism liaison to the mayor's office."

Kevin froze. He couldn't have heard that right. Park offered him the job?

"I hope you're interested because you already know everything we've done, everything I've been looking for."

"I am. Definitely." He inched forward on his chair.

"I can't offer you a pay increase. At least not until we get the new budget approved. But I can give you your own office."

"Okay."

"You don't need time to think about it?"

"With all due respect, sir, we all have to start some-where, and if my pay doesn't decrease with this move, what else do I have to lose?"

"I like the way you think." He stood and extended his hand. "Welcome aboard."

They shook hands and then the mayor handed him a bottle of champagne. "This is for you to celebrate with your girlfriend. Sheila will show you to your new office so you can get settled. Then take the rest of the day with Kathy."

Impressed that Park remembered Kathy's name, Kevin glanced at the bottle. "Thank you again."

"Don't get too used to short days, though."

Kevin chuckled. "I think I already know that."

"Let that girlfriend of yours know that there will be plenty more social engagements to attend in the near future." Park went back behind his desk. Before sitting, he added, "Tomorrow, nine o'clock. Be here ready to figure out how to coordinate with our new partners to take the bulk of this mess away from my office. After tomorrow, you should be the only person I have to deal with when it comes to tourism."

"Yes, sir."

Park glared at him. "Call me Bill when we're alone. Mayor Park in front of other people. Fair enough?"

"Absolutely. Bill." He lifted the bottle in his hand. "Thank you again. What about my current job and the work there?"

"Pass the work on. We'll see if we need to hire someone else or if the workload can be scattered."

Kevin nodded and left the office. He wanted to do nothing but run straight back to Kathy and tell her the good news, but he knew she'd be at work. Plus, he needed to get settled in his new office. He stopped at Sheila's desk. "The mayor said you'd be able to show me to my new office?"

"Congratulations. It's this way."

She stood and led him down the hall. The door she opened had apparently been a storage closet at one point. Sheila's mouth lifted in a smile as she handed him the key. "All yours."

"Is there furniture? A desk? Something?"

"The IT department is scheduled to be here first thing in the morning. Is there something particular you'd like in a desk? I can order one. Or you can look around online and send me a link to what you want."

He hated shopping. Although it wasn't her job to shop for him, Sheila had offered. "As long as it's a flat surface and has drawers, it'll work. And if the chair is halfway decent with wheels, I'll be happy." It wouldn't take much to beat the furniture he'd used downstairs.

"Okay. I'll get that ordered. It'll take a few days to get it. In the meantime, you can use the conference room." She pointed across the hall. "And two doors down, there's a break room with a fridge."

He took a deep breath. "Thank you. I appreciate the help."

"No problem."

For five full minutes, he stood staring into the empty closet. No windows and plenty of dust, but it was his. He'd done it. He'd begun to make his mark on the city. This was only the first step. He had no clue what the next step might be, but he was moving forward and that was all that mattered.

With his bottle of champagne tucked under his arm, he returned to his old desk to figure out who could handle the work he'd left sitting. While he was acquainted with his coworkers, he considered none of them friends. They had a pretty high turnover rate, so it hadn't been worth his time getting too chummy with most.

Trevor sat at the desk nearest him, so he started there.

"Hey, I've got a new position, so I'm moving upstairs. Mayor Park told me to pass on my current workload."

Trevor shot back in his chair. "What? That's bullshit. We all have our own work to do."

That was another reason not to make friends here. No congratulations, no "way to go."

Megan stood from her side of the cubicle wall. "Did I hear that right, Kevin? You got the promotion?"

He nodded and she eyed the bottle under his arm.

"Are you sharing?"

"Not with you guys. This is for my girlfriend."

She pouted. "Since when is there a girlfriend? Sheesh. You go running around with the mayor and everything changes." She walked around to his desk. "Can I have your chair? Mine has a squeaky wheel."

"Take whatever you want as long as you take some work with it."

"Deal." She tossed a file folder on the chair without even looking at the contents and wheeled it all back to the other side. Still standing, she asked, "So how'd you do it?"

"What?" he asked while looking around at who else he could drop work onto.

"Get the promotion. I kind of thought we were all anonymous down here."

"Choose not to be anonymous. Talk to everyone. Know their names and what they do. Look for opportunities."

For the next few hours he looked for opportunities to leave. He'd tried to get out of work early like Park had suggested. But as he packed up the few things that he kept at his desk, he talked to his coworkers and dumped current projects on them. No matter what he did, someone else had a question or needed something.

The only thing he had going for him was that he was sure Kathy was still at work. They'd taken a long lunch and he knew she'd stay until closing. He glanced at the clock. It was just about time for her to turn the lock, so he texted her.

Have excellent news and want to celebrate. Can I pick you up in fifteen?

Her response came quickly. Celebrate what?

Tell you when I get there.

I need to change. I'm not dressed to go out.

We can order pizza and eat in. Unless you want to go out. Your call.

Pizza!

Her text was followed by a series of emojis that he didn't even try to decipher. As he walked to his car, he thought about calling his family, but they would want to celebrate with him too. Tonight he wanted Kathy all to himself. He'd wait until the weekend to tell them.

Kathy raced back to her apartment. Kevin must've gotten the promotion he'd been working so hard for. It was the only thing that came to mind when he mentioned celebrating. She was so happy for him. That he wanted to celebrate with her made it extra special. This was the kind of thing that the old Kevin would've wanted to go to a bar to celebrate with every person he knew.

That he chose a quiet night alone with her said a lot.

At home, she cleared her coffee table in the living room so they could be comfortable while they ate and then she checked her fridge. Kevin was a beer drinker, but she didn't normally keep much on hand. She checked the clock. There wouldn't be time to run to the store to grab some for him. Maybe she could run out while they waited for the pizza after he got here.

Then she looked at herself. She wore the same clothes she had on earlier and she'd worked all afternoon in them. Although the shop was air-conditioned, she'd done a lot of running around, including handling a couple of deliveries because they'd been behind. She really wanted to wash up. As soon as she thought about how quickly she could shower, her doorbell rang.

She opened the door to Kevin standing in the hallway holding a bottle of champagne.

"Wow. You weren't kidding about celebrating." She swung the door wide for him to enter.

He stopped just over the threshold and leaned in to kiss her. "This is a gift from the mayor to welcome me to my new position as tourism board liaison."

"I knew it." Kathy jumped and wrapped her arms around him. "Congratulations."

His arms came around her. "Thanks."

She stepped back. "I was going to run out and grab you some beer while we waited for pizza. I don't have any."

"Nuh-uh." He tugged her close again. "I came here to be with you. I don't need beer."

"You don't like champagne."

"You do. I'll drink water. Or pop. I don't care."

"This is your celebration. You should get what you want, what you like."

"I like and want you."

She sighed. "You're being impossible. This is huge. You should've insisted we go out to celebrate."

"We can do that later after I tell my family. Tonight I

want us." His arm snaked around her waist and he nuzzled her neck.

Even as her brain fogged over at his touch, his words sank in. He hadn't even told his family yet. He'd only told her.

She had no idea how to feel about that. Special, definitely. Wary, a little. It wasn't like him to exclude his family from anything important in his life. "Don't you think you should call your family and tell them?"

"I'll tell them this weekend," he said against the sensitive skin on her neck.

She melted into his touch for a moment and then pulled away. "Let's order dinner. I've been working all day, and I need a shower. Then I want to hear all about the new job."

"Shower sounds good." The look he gave her let her know he was mentally undressing her.

She rolled her eyes. "Out of all the words that just came out of my mouth, the only one you heard was 'shower'?"

"That's the only one that leads to you being naked." His grin was purely sinful, and she had no way of resisting.

"Fine. Order dinner and meet me in the bathroom."

He was dialing before she even made it to the bathroom. She stripped and stood under the water, washing quickly. She might not have beer on hand to make Kevin's night, but a blow job in the shower would certainly make up for it. Moments later, as she was rinsing the shampoo from her hair, he stepped into the tub.

"I thought you were waiting for me."

"I said meet me here. I said nothing about waiting," she said with a pointed look.

He edged nearer to get under the spray. This tub was definitely not made for two. One day, when she had her own house, she was going to invest in the most awesome bathroom. He threaded his fingers into her tangled curls and brought her close for a kiss.

If the water hadn't already been hot, the kiss would've created enough steam to fill the room. His erection prodded her stomach and she stroked him. He groaned into her mouth.

"It's almost as if you didn't get off with me just this afternoon. Too much stress with your new job, huh? Need a release?" She pumped faster with her fist and his hips thrust into her palm. "Here. Turn this way." She angled him and then lowered herself.

She took him into her mouth and his palm slapped against the wet tile. "Fuck," he groaned.

"Better than a six-pack of beer?" she asked from her position on her knees in front of him.

"Fuck yeah."

Water cascaded down his shoulders in rivulets over his torso, but he blocked most of the spray from hitting her. She should've been cold, but when he looked at her like that, with nothing but heat and lust in his eyes, she was warmed from the inside out. She licked the head of his cock and down the shaft, enjoying toying with him a little to make up for what he'd done this afternoon.

She took him fully in her mouth again and sucked on him. He braced one arm on the tile and the other tangled in her hair again, this time guiding her at the pace he wanted, and she let him. Like she'd said earlier, Kevin liked to be in charge in the bedroom, and for the most part, she got off on it, so she let him. Even if it hadn't been her thing, tonight she would've given him this.

But with each time she was with Kevin she was finding that his way seemed to be her thing more and more.

She sucked and licked and stroked him until he came on a string of curses. He sank back until he was leaning against the wall. Kathy stood, kissing her way up his body, loving the feel of his muscles quiver under her touch.

"That was fucking amazing."

"The water's getting cold. Towels are in the cabinet. Pizza should be here soon."

He grabbed her wrist. "It's your turn."

"I don't need a turn. Tonight is your celebration. See you in the living room."

She closed the shower door behind her and dried off quickly.

"I'm gonna smell like a chick after this shower. You need to get some manly soap if I'm going to be spending more time here."

Kathy bit down on her smile. She loved the idea of him spending more time in her apartment. "What's wrong with smelling like a chick? I thought you liked the way I smell."

The water turned off and the door slid open. "I like the smell on you. Doesn't mean I want to smell like you."

"Boo hoo." She wrapped her hair in a towel, and he swatted her ass as she scooted out the door. In her bedroom, she tugged on a tank top and a pair of shorts. The doorbell rang as she let her hair fall from the towel.

"I'll get it," Kevin called.

She eyed him standing in the middle of her living room with a towel wrapped on his waist. "Yeah, I don't think so. Sometimes I have a delivery girl." She pointed at him. "And it's just unfair to show that to some girl who can't have it."

His chuckle was low and self-satisfied. Kathy grabbed her wallet and went to the door. It was a teenage boy standing in the hall who seemed very interested in Kathy's braless chest, so she opened the door a little wider. Kevin stood behind her. "Can you take the box, hon?"

"Sure," he answered, shooting the delivery guy a dirty look.

Kathy paid him and closed the door.

Kevin set the pizza on the table. "And you were worried about me showing something off? That kid's going to be spanking himself to images of your tits for the next month."

"I'm fully clothed."

"Wearing no bra." He cupped her breast and pinched her already hard nipple.

"I don't sleep in a bra. I saw no point in putting one on now."

"I'm not complaining. I love this. Just don't answer the door like that if you don't want me to answer in a towel."

"Fair enough." She plopped down on the couch and flipped up the lid on the box. "Now tell me all about your new job."

Chapter Twelve

Kevin sat in his underwear on Kathy's couch, and they shared pizza while he told her about his new job. He didn't have too much to tell, but he was excited to have someone to share it with. All in all, it was a damn good date.

"Mayor Park told me to let you know that there will be many social engagements in our future, so be prepared."

"Oh really? So now I'm supposed to take orders from you in the bedroom and orders from him in my free time?"

Kevin's eyes darkened. "Sweetheart, as much as I love the idea of you taking orders from me, I'll never ask you to do anything you don't already want to do. As for Park, I think that was his friendly way of saying that if I want to have any time to spend with you, it's probably going to be at work-related functions."

"That kind of sucks."

"Yeah, but I'll take whatever I can get. And if you get to network and grow your business out of it, it's a win-win, right?"

"I suppose, but don't count on me for everything. I'm excited and happy for you, but I can't commit to being at your beck and call for every social engagement you're expected to attend." Her face filled with worry.

"What's wrong?"

"I'm just picturing Moira's social calendar and that would make me sick. I'm more of a homebody, you know?"

"Okay." He watched her face carefully, unsure of where she was going with this.

As soon as he said okay, her entire body relaxed. Did she think this would be a fight?

"You'll come to some parties, though, right?"

"Of course. I'm not saying I won't ever join you, just that . . ."

"Don't automatically assume you're available."

Her face softened with the knowledge that he understood. And he did. He would never assume she would be available to be with him all the time. But they were a couple now and in every relationship, there was some give-and-take.

She settled back on the couch with a glass of champagne and continued to pepper him with questions. They talked and laughed and after a while they turned on the TV.

He took the remote from her hand. Clicking through the shows on her DVR, he groaned. "Really? Sappy movies and bad reality TV?"

"I have FBI shows too. Keep scrolling."

"I grew up with a cop and now my brother is one. I avoid all cop shows."

"You're no fun. What do you like to watch?"

"Sci-fi. Sometimes the History channel."

"Huh." She stared at him.

"What?"

"Weird choices for you."

"What did you expect?"

"Comedy all the way."

"Of course I watch comedies. Who doesn't?"

"Most comedies on TV aren't all that funny."

"Maybe you're watching the wrong ones." He clicked over to Netflix, found some of his favorite shows, and added them to her watch list. "Trust me."

"Famous last words," she said, but then she cuddled next to him and turned to watch TV.

They didn't even get through the first episode, and Kathy was sound asleep against him, her still-damp curls cool against his skin. Kevin knew he should wake her, send her to bed, and go home, but he enjoyed having her in his arms. And he was in no hurry to leave.

He pulled a yellow quilted blanket from the back of the couch, laid it over her, and turned to the news. What he hadn't said to Kathy when they were discussing TV viewing habits was that as of late, he'd had little time to watch anything for pleasure. He'd been watching every bit of city-related news he could find, afraid he might miss something crucial that would impact his new position.

His new position.

He liked the sound of that. Even though the job was now officially his, he knew he couldn't be any less vigilant. Tomorrow would be his first day as the official liaison and he needed to meet Park and come up with an agenda. Then he needed to meet with City Connections, the business with which they'd decided to partner.

While the news droned on in the background, Kevin opened his phone and made a list of what he had to get done tomorrow. It would've been easier with his laptop, but he hadn't brought it. At work he'd always used the crappy desktop and left his laptop at home. He might have to start traveling with it, especially if he was going to be spending more time at Kathy's apartment like this.

He glanced down at her. He definitely wanted to spend a lot more time like this. He stroked a hand over her curls and she turned into his touch.

"Damn," she mumbled. "I'm sorry. I didn't realize I was that tired."

"Don't worry about it. I didn't mean to wake you."

"You should have. Not much of a celebratory date." She pushed away from him to sit up. Her hair was rumpled and she was sleepy soft.

Kevin could imagine waking up to that every morning. The thought struck him hard, and for the first time in his life he didn't feel a second of panic. Everything with Kathy felt right, just the way it had five years ago, but this time he was ready for it.

"This was a perfect way to spend my celebration." He tucked a wild curl behind her ear. "Can I spend the night?"

She brushed her hand over her hair self-consciously. "If you want. I have to get up early though."

"That's fine. I'll have to get up to go home for clean clothes."

He realized that asking to spend the night might be pushing things between them. He'd agreed to take it slow, and it seemed like overnight everything had jumped to warp speed.

"If you'd prefer for me not to stay, that's okay too. I know we said we were going to go slow."

She smiled sweetly. "That kind of went out the window at lunch."

"Yeah, well, I didn't know if that meant you were ready to throw your whole plan out."

"I don't have a plan. But this feels right." She paused and looked into his eyes questioningly. "Doesn't it?"

"Hell, yeah it does." He was just glad that she felt the same as he did. "Let's go to bed."

He stood and while she folded the blanket for the back of the couch, he cleaned up their dinner.

In the bathroom, she handed him a fresh toothbrush. "You can just keep this here, for whenever."

They got ready and as they climbed into bed, he asked, "What's the likelihood of me convincing you to sleep naked?"

"Hmmm . . . I guess it all depends on how convincing you are."

And before they fell asleep he completely convinced her of all the benefits of sleeping naked.

At seven o'clock a few nights later, Kevin's phone rang. He considered ignoring it because he wanted to see Kathy, but the ringtone told him it was Jimmy. He knew better than to ignore Jimmy.

"Hello."

"Hey, shithead. You got a promotion and didn't tell us?"

"How the hell did you find out?"

"Did you forget I married a woman who does nothing but stick her nose into everyone's business all over the city?"

He should've known better. Moira had enough connections that she would've heard, probably before any other reporter did. "I planned on telling you all this weekend."

"Yeah, well, we don't like to wait. Get your ass down to O'Leary's Pub now. We're celebrating."

Kevin almost groaned, but he sucked it back. His siblings were happy for him and wanted to celebrate. "Let me call Kathy and see if she's up for it."

"Already done. Moira's picking her up so you have a designated driver to get home."

As usual, Jimmy controlled everyone's lives. "Okay. I'll be there soon."

He closed up his newly refinished office and headed out. At least with Kathy being his designated driver for the night, his brothers couldn't accuse him of being a pussy for ducking out early. Kathy always had to be at the shop at the ass crack of dawn, so she wouldn't be up for partying late.

When he arrived at O'Leary's, the bar was already busy. It was probably normal for a Friday night. He looked around and didn't see his family, so he fought through the mob while texting Jimmy. Where are you?

In the back.

He walked around people and dodged waitresses to get to the back room. He shouldn't have needed directions. If he'd waited two minutes, he would've heard the sound of the O'Malleys. One thing he could always say about his family was that they were never quiet.

"Hey, asshole, it's about time you showed up," Sean called from the table.

The family had a few tables shoved together and they took up a good portion of the back room. Jimmy stood and gave him a hug.

"Congrats, man. You should've told us."

They separated and Kevin looked at his sister-in-law. "I was going to tell all of you this weekend. I didn't plan on Mouthy Moira getting in the mix."

"You should've known better," she yelled. "I'm in every mix. Now sit down and have a beer."

He neared the table, his eyes scanning for the one person he really wanted to see, but she wasn't there. He sat down and opened his mouth to ask about Kathy, but Moira continued to talk.

"She ran to the bathroom. She'll be back in a minute.

Her seat is next to you." The whole time she talked, she poured beer from the pitcher in front of her.

From the other side of the table, Norah passed a plate of appetizers. "Celebratory food. Congrats. Tell us about the job."

"Not much to tell. I've moved from being a peon in one department to a peon in another."

"Shit. I can't believe it," Moira said. "Kevin O'Malley is being modest. He might still be a peon, but he's a peon with the mayor's ear."

He nodded because that much was true.

From the corner of his eye, he saw Kathy approaching. He stood and slid her chair from its spot for her. She edged to the side, as if avoiding any contact with him. What the hell?

She sat quickly.

"Is something wrong?"

She smiled. "No, why?" Her face gave away nothing.

"Because you're acting like you barely know me."

Her gaze shifted around the table. Everyone there—his whole family was coupled up. Kevin slid an arm around the back of her chair and leaned closer. "My family obviously knows we're dating."

"I know."

"Then what?"

"They're kind of overwhelming," she said quietly.

He pressed closer still until his lips touched the shell of her ear. "They're overwhelming, so that means you can't kiss me hello? I'm not understanding that." His lips closed on her lobe and her breath hitched.

"Man, you really are an asshole," Sean yelled again.

Kevin looked around the mass of Kathy's curls with lifted eyebrows. She stiffened next to him.

"We invite you out to hear about your fancy new job

and all you want to do is make out with your girlfriend. And you guys say I'm rude."

With that, Sean's girlfriend, Emma, shoved his shoulder. "Maybe if you didn't scream across the table and call people names, we wouldn't say that."

Kevin shifted so his arm sat comfortably on Kathy's shoulders. "I apologize, brother. I haven't seen my girlfriend in a few days. You have my attention now. What do you want to know?"

Kathy battled back the nerves that tightened every muscle in her body. She knew these people. She'd met them all before. But something felt different this time, and she didn't know if it was her or them or Kevin or what. When she and Kevin dated before, she'd met them, but they hadn't really interacted. They said hi or whatever, but that was it.

Tonight, they were all in her space, starting conversations and asking her questions. It was disconcerting.

Moira gave her a questioning smile from the other side of the table. Kathy forced her mouth to curve while Kevin offered the scant details he had on his new position.

"More money?" Tommy asked.

"Not yet. Maybe in the new budget, but I'm not holding my breath for that either."

Sean laughed boisterously. "So you're working longer hours, you don't get to see your girlfriend, and you're not making more money. You're getting screwed. That's Chicago politics at its finest."

Kevin shook his head at his brother, who was still laughing. "It's just another stepping-stone. I make this program work, I'll be able to do anything I want. I can move into the private sector or higher up in the government."

Norah spoke up then. "I always wondered if you planned to go into politics. I can totally see it."

"See what?"

"You'd make a perfect politician."

His eyes narrowed at his sister. "That doesn't sound like a compliment."

Kathy thought about the whole conversation. She'd never survive being in the spotlight with him as a politician. All the mudslinging and horrible things that people dredged up and spewed out. She felt sick just thinking about it.

She shook those thoughts loose. She and Kevin just started dating again. Who knew how far into the future such plans might be. She needed to not worry about things she couldn't control and focus on what she could. Having a good time and celebrating with Kevin and his family was something she could do.

"I agree with Norah. You have that smarmy smile that people won't quite know how to read," Kathy said.

Everyone at the table laughed, even Norah's hulking boyfriend, Kai. Norah pointed at Kevin. "'Smarmy' is the perfect word."

He looked at Kathy. "Smarmy? Aren't you supposed to be nice to me? This is a celebration."

Kathy patted his thigh. "You're also charming. You'd have the single female voting population swooning for you." She batted her eyelashes for extra effect.

Kevin removed his arm from her shoulder and slid his hand between her legs and squeezed her inner thigh. He lowered his voice and said, "You'll pay for that later."

She felt the heat rise in her cheeks and she squirmed in her chair, but he didn't move his hand. He simply returned his attention to his family and talked about his job prospects.

Thankfully, none of which revolved around running for office.

Hours passed quickly and Kathy found herself having fun. At least once she got used to the fact that the O'Malleys were really loud and their form of communication tended to include sarcasm and insults.

Chapter Thirteen

For the next two weeks, life was a blur. Kevin met with Brent, who was his City Connections counterpart. They had met with Mayor Park once, who made it clear to Kevin he wanted to be as hands-off as possible. Other than talking on the phone daily and one all-too-brief lunch date, he hadn't seen Kathy at all and it was taking its toll on him.

She wasn't pressuring him. In fact, she seemed about as cool as one could be, which was almost as irritating as Park's constant demands. He was beginning to feel like their relationship didn't matter as much to her as it did to him.

Every time he called to apologize and say he was working late, she said she understood. She couldn't wait up for him or meet for a late dinner or drinks because she had to get up so early. He stared at the empty wall of his office, wishing for a window to stare out. He needed to figure out how to make time to spend with Kathy and still make everything happen here.

Realistically, he knew the beginning of this new partnership was going to be the worst. Once they established everything, it would run a little smoother and it wouldn't be so time-consuming. He certainly wouldn't be expected to work sixty- or seventy-hour weeks forever.

A knock on his door drew his attention. No one came to his office. Most of his work was done by e-mail. If he had a meeting, he used the conference room. Although he loved the privacy of his office, he was a little embarrassed by the room itself.

"Come in."

Sheila pushed the door open. "You have a visitor."

He looked at her for more information, especially since he wasn't expecting anyone, but then Kathy pushed through the opening with a thanks to Sheila on the way. Kathy carried two plants and a plastic bag that smelled like dinner.

He stood from his chair. "What are you doing here?"

She set everything on the chair in front of his desk. "You've been working a lot and we haven't been able to spend any time together." She came over and kissed him. "I missed you."

Every concern he had about her lack of involvement disappeared in that instant. He reached past her and swung the door shut. Then returned his complete attention to kissing her thoroughly. He tasted her like she was the most expensive bottle of whiskey known to man. He savored her because he knew he wouldn't be spending the night with her no matter how much he wanted to. He'd be working late tonight like he did every night.

When he pulled away, he said, "Christ, I've missed that."

"Me too."

He stepped farther back because if he didn't, he would start undressing her and that wasn't a smart move in his new office. She smiled as if reading his thoughts, and looked around.

"You weren't kidding. It's bare-bones in here."

"It's nothing special, but it's mine."

"Hey, that makes it special. It's your office. In city hall. That's pretty cool."

He pointed at the stuff she'd carried in. "What's all this?"

"Plants, of course. No office is complete without them." At his grimace, she swatted a hand. "These are easy to care for and they'll totally brighten the space. And they're not too girly."

"In case you haven't noticed, I have zero sunlight. They'll be dead in a week."

"This is a ZZ plant and this is a peace lily. Both are excellent for little to no natural light. I chose them knowing that you were currently living in a closet." She chuckled as she said it and arranged the pots on his bookshelves. "There's a handy little card next to each of them with instructions about watering. I kept it simple."

She turned to face him and his heart tumbled. He had no idea how he'd managed to go so long without seeing her beautiful face.

She smiled. "What?"

"I can't get over how much I missed you."

She nodded.

He took her hand. "No. Like really missed you. We talk and I feel it every time we hang up, but seeing you now, it's like a kick to the gut. Not seeing you fucking sucks."

Her fingers stroked his jaw. "You just got a huge promotion and the project is demanding. I get it. When I opened the flower shop, I didn't do anything but sleep and work. And sometimes, I didn't even sleep. That's why I suggested that maybe this wasn't a good time to start a relationship."

Oh, hell no. She was not going to break up with him when they'd come this far.

"But we decided to make this work, so here I am."

Kevin was turning into an idiot. Never in his life had he spent so much time worrying about what a woman thought or how she felt or whether she was about to break up with him. With his thoughts racing, he kissed her again. Other couples managed this without a nervous breakdown. They could too.

When he pulled away, he asked, "You're doing okay with this?"

"Not really. I need to spend time with my boyfriend. It's hard to have a relationship with someone if you're never together. I need to be with you physically. I need to date."

His stomach sank. He'd figure this out.

"That's why I'm here. I know you don't have a ton of time, but everyone has to eat. Dinner is served. I figured you'd be tired of pizza, so I got Chinese." She began to set the food on his desk.

"Wait." He glanced around, and then grabbed the bag from her. "Let's do a picnic."

He plopped on the floor. Patting the spot next to him he said, "Carpet's clean. Brand-new."

She sat beside him and they opened the cartons of food.

"This way, we can share." He held a forkful of fried rice to her mouth.

She looked at his thigh brushing hers. "I'm sure that was your first thought."

"You naked is always my first thought. Touching you my second. If I get to my third thought, I'll be really uncomfortable, so tell me about your day instead."

She burst out laughing, and Kevin knew they had to find a way to spend more time together. He wanted to be able to come home to her and tell her about his day and hold her throughout the night.

Why the hell couldn't he?

"What do you think about spending the night at my apartment?"

"When?"

"Tonight."

She looked up from her carton of food. "I can't stay here that late."

"I'll give you my key. Go home, pack a bag and go to my place. You can crawl into my bed and wait for me."

"How are you going to get in if I fall asleep?"

"I have a spare." He thought of the magnetic box Jimmy had made him put under his car long ago.

"You sure that won't be weird for you?"

"What?"

"Having me in your house when you're not there."

"I don't have anything to hide." He leaned over the food and kissed her lips. "I really want to spend the night with you." Another kiss. "And wake up with you."

"Okay," she whispered, a little breathless.

Yeah, they'd figure this out. There was no way he was going to lose her again.

Kathy was glad she'd surprised Kevin at work. The impromptu picnic on his office floor was a much-needed break for both of them. Now she stood in her apartment trying to figure what to pack. It shouldn't be so difficult. It was one night. And she'd probably sleep naked. So all she really needed were clothes for work tomorrow.

But then she started to think about taking a shower. Should she bring some shampoo and conditioner? Kevin probably didn't even know what conditioner was. What about a toothbrush? Just because she had an extra for him didn't mean he'd have one for her. It wasn't like this sleepover had been planned.

Why did everything stress her out so much?

After shoving some clothes into a bag, she went to the kitchen and opened the fridge. She grabbed a tube of chocolate chip cookie dough and cut it open. Cookie dough had been her go-to stress reliever for years. She'd been eating it since she was old enough to sneak the package and open it by herself.

She remembered the first time her mother had come to her apartment and found the open package in the fridge. Her mom had questioned why Kathy hadn't finished baking them. For a few minutes, Kathy had felt like a nine-year-old all over again, trying to figure out the right words to say to keep the peace. Then she admitted the truth: she had no intention of baking them. She liked the dough raw.

Her mother of course threw a fit because raw dough could make her sick. Kathy had let her ramble with the litany of horrible illnesses that might befall her. She'd been tempted to take a bite right then in front of her mom, but she didn't have the guts to do that. Moira would have. Kathy wished she had the courage—or at least the don't-give-a-damn—Moira had.

She sighed and plopped down on her couch. This was ridiculous. She was a grown woman in an adult relationship. Her boyfriend had given her a key to his apartment so she could wait for him. It shouldn't conjure memories of her mother and being stressed out with her family.

It was no big deal. In fact, it was a good sign that he wanted to keep their relationship moving forward.

It wasn't like he'd cleaned out half his closet and invited her in.

Damn. Why did her brain go there? Was that what she wanted? With a groan, she wrapped up the remaining dough and tossed it on the table. She wanted to be with Kevin.

She was falling for him and it was freaking her out.

She'd been through enough therapy to be able to recognize that. She squared her shoulders. Yeah, falling for someone was scary.

Falling for a guy she didn't totally trust even scarier.

Maybe she needed to trust her gut. Freaking out was a warning sign. She'd wanted to take it slow and as she'd pointed out to Kevin, slow went out the window when she pulled him into her bed. His key weighed heavily in her pocket. He was expecting her. What would he do if she wasn't there?

He'd be pissed. Her stomach tumbled. She shouldn't just blow him off, but if she called or texted, he'd talk her into going to his apartment. He had all the smooth words to convince her.

She needed to wrap her head around what she was doing and where they were going. Standing up, she grabbed her cookie dough to put in the fridge. She turned her phone off and went to take a shower.

When she crawled into bed a while later, she didn't feel any better. She lay awake for a long time, staring at the clock wondering where Kevin was and whether he was angry with her.

Chapter Fourteen

Kevin was dog-ass tired as he dragged himself into his apartment. No lights were on and as soon as he stepped through the door, he knew Kathy wasn't there. He felt the lack of her presence.

Well, damn. He pulled out his phone and sent her a text. Everything okay? I thought you were coming to my house.

He loosened his tie as he walked through the apartment with his phone in his hand, waiting for a response. He tried calling, but the phone went straight to voice mail, so she had it turned off. Why would she do that?

He stripped and went to the bathroom to take a shower. Thinking back over their evening together, he couldn't come up with any reason why she would've changed her mind. When he dried off, he still hadn't heard from her and his anger was mounting.

He had half a mind to go to her apartment and demand to know why she hadn't come over and was ignoring him now. But he also knew that if she wasn't already asleep, she would be by the time he got there. Making a scene by waking all her neighbors wouldn't win him any points.

So he crawled into bed alone and set his alarm. Kathy might be avoiding him now, but he'd get to the bottom of it first thing in the morning.

When his alarm rang, Kevin slapped at it and didn't want to move. He made a mental deal with himself that if Kathy had sent him a text to explain last night, he could sleep in. Maybe it had been a simple misunderstanding.

He swiped his phone on, the bright blue light nearly blinding him. No texts. No calls. She'd been awake for at least a half hour, so she would've seen his text and missed call from last night.

Unless she hadn't turned her phone back on yet.

He rolled over with his phone in his hand, willing it to buzz with some acknowledgment.

He dozed off and when he rolled over twenty minutes later, there was still nothing. He got out of bed, determined to get some answers. The thought of calling or texting crossed his mind, but that was too easy to ignore. She couldn't pretend he didn't exist if he was standing in her shop.

The drive to Love in Bloom was fast, considering most of the world was still asleep. He peered through the front door, but saw no sign of her, so he walked around to the alley. He rang the bell meant for delivery drivers.

When the metal door clanged open, Kathy stared at him with a startled look on her face. Her eyes were impossibly wide. "Hi. What are you doing here?"

"You were supposed to come to my apartment last night."

"I know. I was really tired, and I fell asleep." Her eyes shifted away and he knew she wasn't telling the whole truth.

"Can I come in?"

She nodded and stepped back, still holding the heavy door open. She made no move to give him a kiss. What the hell happened between dinner and bed last night?

The door thunked shut with a loud clatter. Kathy brushed past him and went to her office. He followed. Memories of the orgasm he'd given her there assaulted him. He cleared his throat to focus.

"Why didn't you come over?"

She moved behind her desk and sat down. "I told you—"

He stayed standing, hating the distance the desk created between them. "Cut the crap. You could've gone to my place and fallen asleep. You decided not to come over, and then you turned your phone off to avoid me."

His words were sharper than he'd intended and she gripped her hands together in her lap. She looked like a kid getting reprimanded by her parents. That's not what this was supposed to be. He just wanted to understand what was going on in her head. He moved around the desk and squatted in front of her.

He put his hand over her clasped ones. "What's wrong?"

"I freaked out."

"About what?"

"This. Us. Going to your apartment, spending time there without you, spending the night with you. All of it."

His thumb stroked her hand. "Why didn't you just tell me?"

"I knew if I called you, you would convince me to come over."

He smiled because she was right. He'd wanted to spend the night with her so of course he would've tried to talk her into it. But he would've tried to fix this first. "Why were you freaking out?"

"I'm not sure. It felt really fast all of a sudden."

"You're the one who initiated sex. You said you were ready."

Her shoulders sagged. "I know that. And it's not sex. It's everything." She took a deep breath and flexed her hands, stretching her fingers out, forcing him to release her. "I think mostly it was the key."

"The key?"

"I had the key to your apartment in my pocket, and you weren't going to be home. That's a lot of trust."

"I do trust you."

She licked her lips and stared into his eyes. "But I don't fully trust you."

It felt like someone had just forced a rock down his throat and into his empty stomach. He'd known this. She had plenty of reason not to trust him, but he'd been doing everything possible to change that.

She wrapped her fingers around his. "I know you're trying and I recognize that you're not the same guy you were five years ago. But I don't know how to get rid of this gut-level reaction of not trusting you. It's not fair to you."

"Yeah, it is. I've slept with a lot of people and I can't even guarantee that I didn't sleep around when we were together. I've led a life of very casual relationships. I always thought everyone was on the same page with me. You weren't and there's no changing that. But I'm willing to do anything you need to prove that you can trust me now. I won't cheat on you. I won't lie to you."

She bit her lip. Every time she got quiet like this he felt like she was going to kick him to the curb.

"Swapping keys is too fast. I need to see you and spend time with you."

"I know."

"I know you *know*, but I don't think you can make it happen. We've been trying for weeks now."

"We can make this happen. In fact, I have some work functions to go to and I'm hoping you'll be my date. Even if you don't stay for the whole thing. I know it's not quite the date you're looking for, but my appearance is mostly for show. I have to chat some people up, but that's all."

She sighed and he half expected her to shoot him down. "Give me the details. I'll be there. Maybe even go home with you after."

He stood and pulled her up with him, his heart so much lighter than it had been moments ago. He loved the press of her body against his. "So you'll spend the night with me as long as I don't send you to my place alone."

She nodded slowly. "I really like having sex with you."

He laughed. "I really like having sex with you too." He lowered his mouth to hers for a deep kiss. "I'd like to have lots more sex with you."

She threw her head back and laughed with him. He took advantage of the moment and kissed her neck. Her breath hitched when his tongue made contact, and her hand pushed his shoulder.

"As much as I'd love a repeat performance here, I have a delivery due any minute."

He smiled. "I can wait until the delivery is done."

With a chuckle she said, "Anna will be in soon after. We have a crazy busy weekend."

"Fine," he said dramatically.

"Text me the details for your fancy parties, and I'll do my best to be there."

"No blowing me off. If you can't make it or don't want to, say so."

"And if I say I don't want to go, you won't try to talk me into it?"

"Of course I'll try to talk you into it. It's not my fault you can't help but fall for my charm." He stroked her cheek. "In all seriousness, if you're freaked out, you need to tell me, so we can deal with it. No running away and avoiding me."

"Okay," she whispered.

He pressed a kiss to her lips. "I'll call you later."

When Moira strode through the door of the flower shop, Kathy couldn't help but smile. Her best friend always came with good advice and great food. What more could she ask for in a friend?

Today she needed a healthy dose of both. Kathy waved to Anna and said, "I'm headed to lunch. Call if you need anything."

Anna nodded. "Have fun. Hey, Moira. How's it going?"

"Good. How about with you?"

"Same. How's married life?"

"No different. Jimmy and I have been living together for long enough that the only thing that's changed is using 'Mrs. O'Malley.' Makes me sound old. And of course, my mother is pressuring me to give her grandchildren now."

Anna laughed. "Moms do that. Enjoy your lunch. Bring her back in a better mood," she said with a chin tilt toward Kathy.

Moira looped her arm through Kathy's as they headed out the door. "So what was that all about?"

"Rough night. And morning."

"What did Kevin do now?"

"Nothing bad. This is all on me."

They walked in the late summer sun to a burger place around the corner. Kathy loved that they didn't need to discuss where they would go.

"Well?" Moira prompted.

Kathy huffed. "I'm an idiot. Kevin and I haven't been able to see much of each other lately. He's been working a ton of hours and I get that. I'm not mad, but you know, I want to see my boyfriend."

Moira made a face.

"What?"

"Just weird hearing you refer to Kevin O'Malley as your boyfriend."

Kathy nudged her friend's shoulder. "Would you prefer lover?" She added breathless emphasis on *lover*.

"Hell no. But go on with your story."

"So I went to his office to surprise him with dinner and an office plant last night."

"Oh no." Moira stopped in her tracks. "Please tell me he wasn't screwing his secretary on his desk."

"What? No!" Kathy shook her head. "You really do think the worst of him."

"How can I not?"

Kathy began to think that maybe Moira wasn't the best person to talk to about this, but then she didn't really have anyone else she was close enough to. They continued down the street.

"For the record, he doesn't have a secretary."

Moira snorted.

"We had a picnic on his office floor. He asked me to spend the night at his place."

"Okay." Moira drew the word out as if waiting for a bomb to drop.

"He gave me the key to his apartment so I could go there and wait for him."

Moira pulled open the door to the restaurant. "Still not seeing a problem."

"I know. That's why I'm an idiot." They went to the counter, placed their orders, and sat at a table to wait for their food.

Once they were settled, Kathy finished her story, telling Moira about freaking out, blowing Kevin off, and him coming to the shop this morning.

"I give him credit for waiting until morning. Kind of surprising when I think about it. Those O'Malley boys aren't known for their restraint. I'd have expected him to pound on your door when you didn't show up."

"Me too, I guess. But he said when my phone went to voice mail, he knew it was off and I was probably asleep. So at least he wasn't worried."

"Be glad for that. Jimmy would've had the SWAT team knocking down my door."

Kathy laughed because that sounded like exactly what Jimmy would do. Their number was called and Moira grabbed their food. When she returned to the table, they spread everything out and dug in.

"So what's really the problem?" Moira asked.

"Ultimately, I don't trust him."

"Understandable."

"Yeah. And he totally owns that, which makes it worse. He's trying. He really is. I just don't know what to do. He gave me his freaking key to go to his apartment without him. That's total trust. He had nothing to hide."

"That's good. That's what you need from him, right? Complete transparency?"

"In a way, yeah. But I don't want to be the kind of woman who's always checking up on him and verifying things just to make sure he can be trusted. I can't live like that. I need to be able to trust."

"It's not like you're asking too much. What does he say?"

"That he'll do whatever I need to gain my trust."

Moira put her burger down. "What does that mean?"

Kathy rested her head on her hand. "I don't even know."

"Maybe you're saying you're giving him another chance, but you're not."

"Huh?"

"What did he say about the last time you guys were together? Why did he cheat?"

Kathy's stomach tumbled again. This wasn't a good conversation to have with Moira. Moira was there after Kathy had caught him last time. Or thought she'd caught him. "We're not even sure he did cheat," Kathy said quietly.

"We're not? Since when?"

"Since Kevin and I talked about it."

"Oh, this'll be good. That man can talk his way out of anything. No wonder you're so twisted up about whether you can trust him." Moira leaned closer, her ample chest pushing forward. "Maybe you just can't."

Kathy leaned back in her seat. "See? That's a problem." She pointed at Moira. "You can't be objective when it comes to Kevin."

"I don't need to be objective. I need to be in your corner. Which I am. Always."

"When I saw him with that woman five years ago . . . I

didn't confront him. I turned tail and left. I came to you and being the best friend that you are, you bashed and berated him."

"One of my favorite pastimes," Moira said with a smile.

"But an objective friend might've questioned what I saw and if I'd asked him about it. If I had, I would've found out that he hadn't slept with her."

"What?" Moira's voice was loud enough that other people turned.

Kathy hung her head.

Moira clamped her mouth shut for a minute, sucked in a breath through her nose, and then asked, "Do you believe him?"

Kathy nodded. "I know you think he's lying to get me to trust him, but it's what he said after that made me believe him."

She explained the rest of the conversation, including Kevin's admission that there might've been other drunken hookups. "He thought we were casual. I didn't. Both of us felt that it wasn't casual, though. He just wasn't ready."

"Stupid O'Malley."

Kathy looked at her friend for further explanation.

"The whole lot of them are emotionally stunted. God forbid they just admit how they feel."

Kathy laughed and it was more at herself than at what Moira had said. Kathy herself was every bit as emotionally stunted.

Moira reached out and covered Kathy's hand with hers. "You need to decide what matters. What might've happened five years ago or what you might have today. If you can't really give him a chance, let him go."

Kathy nodded. She knew Moira was right. She wanted to give Kevin—to give them—a chance. She thought she was ready. The real question was whether she believed he was ready this time.

"I mean, you could make him suffer some first. I'd be on board for that."

"Remind me never to get on your bad side."

Moira winked.

Chapter Fifteen

Kathy felt good about where her life was. Better than she'd felt in a long time. Kevin had been true to his word. He called when he said he would, and if she said she didn't have time to talk or couldn't meet him, he left her alone. Mostly. He whined a little. Maybe tried to get her to change her mind, but no real pressure.

They'd gone to some big society function two nights ago, and as much as she'd wanted to go home with him, she'd been exhausted and needed to leave early to get some rest. Now she was getting ready for a charity benefit on the beach. She could think of worse ways to spend an evening.

And Anna was opening the shop in the morning, so she could spend the night at Kevin's apartment without having to rush out or crash early. She smoothed a hand over the sundress she wore and debated whether to put her hair up.

Kevin loved her hair down, but the late August heat made her curls go wild. She decided on a compromise and gathered the sides and clipped them at the top of her head. She just finished swiping on mascara when her bell rang.

When she opened the door, Kevin was pacing in the

hall, talking on his phone. She had no idea what he was talking about or to whom, but he was irritated. It showed in every line of his body, but his voice remained calm and deceptively seductive. The man was like a chameleon.

As he turned and saw her, she saw another shade to him. His body still carried the stress, his voice the calm, but now his eyes reflected desire. She briefly wondered what a stranger would see looking at him. He blinked and shook his head, returning his focus to the phone.

"No. That's not acceptable. I don't care that you can't make it. Someone from your company should be there, especially to deal with the issues that arise. That's part of your job." He ran a hand through his hair, making a mess of what had been neatly combed.

Kathy locked up and nodded toward the door to let him know they could leave. He continued to firmly let the person on the other end of the line know how displeased he was. It was weird listening to him talk like that.

Outside, she glanced up and down the block for his SUV, but it was nowhere in sight. He tugged her elbow and led her to a car, where a driver got out and opened the door for them. She turned and glanced at Kevin with a raised eyebrow before sliding in. He simply smiled in return.

He disconnected his call, took a seat beside her, and closed the door. Before she had a chance to ask about the call, he gripped his phone tightly in his fist as if he planned to throw it, and he let out a guttural yell. Then he hit the side of his fist against the door.

Kathy's heart skipped. She sat silently and waited.

Kevin closed his eyes and laid his head on the back of the seat. After a few deep breaths, he opened one eye and said, "Sorry about that. I had to let the frustration out somehow."

She still sat staring at him, her hands clasped in her lap.

Kevin jolted forward and leaned toward her. She jumped back. He grabbed her hand. "Did I scare you? I didn't mean to. That . . . That had nothing to do with you."

"I know."

She felt ridiculous for being startled.

"I would never, *ever*, hurt you."

"I know that too." She might not be able to control that visceral reaction to any kind of conflict around her, but she believed him.

His hand gently caressed hers. "What's wrong?"

"Nothing." She forced a smile. "What happened?" She pointed at his phone that was currently lying on the seat between them.

"I'll get to that. What's wrong?" he asked again.

"It's nothing." She tried to wave it off, but he wouldn't have it. She took a deep breath. "It's not a big deal. I told you I don't deal well with conflict. I'm not afraid of you. I know you were upset about something else. I can't control that immediate reaction though. I'm okay." This time the smile she gave him was genuine.

He leaned close and kissed her. His warm lips pressed against hers and when his tongue entered her mouth, it was instant comfort. Judging by the ease in his shoulders, the kiss had the same effect on him. When they separated, she touched his cheek, the stubble growing there rasping her palm.

"I needed that. Should've done it back in your apartment."

"You were a little busy yelling at someone."

"I didn't yell."

She smiled. "You yelled without raising your voice. It was quite effective."

"He had it coming."

"Who?"

"Brent. The City Connections guy who is supposed to be working with me. He's fucking this up. I have no idea how he even got this job, but he has no clue. We've been working together. All the time I wanted to spend with you had been spent with him."

"And?"

"And tonight the asshole isn't showing up. He's supposed to be working with businesses to make the city a tourist destination. If events flop, we look bad."

"But this is an established event. Moira told me all about it. She comes every year."

"Great. So Mouthy Moira will be there to watch it flop for the first time because Brent doesn't know how to do his job."

Kathy reached over and ran a hand down Kevin's thigh. "You'll be fine. The event will happen, people will have fun, and no one will remember the little glitches."

He caught her hand. "Let's hope they're just little glitches." He lifted her hand and kissed the center of her palm. "I'm glad you're with me."

"We all need someone to talk us off the ledge now and again."

"Usually that's Jimmy, but he wouldn't get this." He toyed with her fingers as he spoke. "Who's your person?"

She didn't even need to think. "Moira."

He reached over and brushed her hair off her shoulder, allowing his fingers to linger on her skin where her shoulder met her neck. "I'd like to take on that role."

"I'm not sure you're the talking down type."

"Of course I am."

"You're more like the knock down the walls type."

"For you, I could be both."

She didn't believe that for a moment, but she warmed at the idea that he was willing to try to be anything she needed.

The car slowed and the driver looked at them in the rearview mirror. "Would you like me to park, or let you out here?"

"Here is fine," Kevin answered.

As they stepped from the car, she asked, "You never told me what the deal was with the fancy car and driver. Why didn't you drive?"

"I don't get many perks with my new job. This is city business, so the mayor springs for a driver."

"Check you out. Wait till your brothers hear about this."

He took her hand and led her to the beachfront building. "They won't find out anything."

"Hmm . . . sounds like blackmail information."

"I'm sure we can work something out to keep this a secret." He flashed her a smile while opening the door. His dark hair was still mussed from running his fingers through it, giving him a rakish look as he grinned.

Unfortunately, it was the last genuine smile she saw from him all night.

Chapter Sixteen

Kevin had never seriously considered homicide. Tonight changed that. Brent had fucked him over good. The valet service that he supposedly booked flaked, so there was no valet parking. The caterer served excellent food, but complained that she hadn't gotten accurate numbers, and she was worried about running out of food. Brent was supposed to guide the event and he wasn't even there.

It wasn't Kevin's job to fix this or to make sure it ran smoothly. He was expected to attend as the mayor's representative as they tried to convince other businesses and organizations that Chicago was the place to host conferences and conventions. The next move was to bring more TV and movies here to film. But if they couldn't even pull off an established charity function, who the hell would trust them with anything else?

So to save face, he spent the night running interference and relying on Kathy for ridiculous things like making sure the waitstaff didn't take a smoke break outside the door where guests would see them. Another time he'd asked her to check with the organization to see if their event organizer needed anything. He simply couldn't be everywhere at once.

When he wasn't smiling his way through networking with many of Chicago's connected and elite, he was plotting his revenge against Brent. The night was wrapping up, and he had no idea where Kathy was. He hadn't seen her and part of him feared she'd left.

He stood near the door, saying good-bye to guests as they left. He felt foolish for thinking this would've been a nice date for him and Kathy. He'd envisioned a walk on the beach, being able to watch the sun set. As he shook hands with another guest, one who appeared adequately impressed with both Kevin's bogus city hall title and the way the event had been run, Kevin had another business card slipped into his palm. He apologized yet again for Brent's absence, but promised to get their contact information into the right hands.

Which wouldn't be Brent's if he had anything to say about it.

A snort and a laugh drew his attention and when Kevin scanned the room, his gaze landed on Kathy and the snorting came from Moira, who stood beside her. Kathy's face lit with her laughter and she was beautiful. When her eyes locked on his, he realized without a doubt that he loved her.

The notion was both frightening and amazing. He smiled and abandoned his post at the door. When he reached her, he took her hand and kissed her cheek.

"How's the new job going?" Moira asked.

"I'm surviving."

"That doesn't sound too promising."

"I can't control who I work with."

She narrowed her eyes as she looked up at him. "Was that a dig at me?"

"Huh? No. I don't work with you. Although, since you're

here, I hope I can call on our familial bond to get a good review."

"I don't review people like you. I talk about the organizations and charities and the events they produce."

A sudden idea struck him. Although he'd been making a joke about using his relationship with her, he realized it might be worth it. "You could though."

"I could what?"

"You could write an article about the mayor's new initiative and how we're working with City Connections to improve tourism for the city."

The look on Moira's face changed and he recognized it. Her interest was piqued. Jimmy had told him that she'd been working on a number of different projects that went deeper than her usual charity pieces. "Let's set up a time to talk," he continued. "I can give you all the information and access you need."

What reporter didn't love an exclusive?

Kathy yawned and guilt kicked him again. He held her hand. Moira looked at their joined hands and back at him. There was a warning in her eyes that he didn't want to think about.

"The two of you always talking business. I'm glad I have a job that ends when I turn the lock on the door," Kathy said.

"That's not true. You think about flowers and arrangements and vendors and stuff when you're not at the shop," Moira argued.

"But I don't live my job like you guys do."

Kevin took a deep breath. She was right. He had been living his job, much like he'd seen his father do his whole life. "I'm done living it. At least for tonight. Are you ready to get out of here?"

"Whenever you are."

"I'll call you later," he said to Moira.

"Be good," she responded.

"Where's the fun in that?"

"You got me there. I almost couldn't even say it without laughing. I was channeling Jimmy."

Kevin smiled and waved and led Kathy toward the door. "I'm so sorry about tonight."

"Why?"

"I promised you a date and then I didn't do anything but impose on you. I bet you didn't even get to enjoy yourself."

"Well, you'd be wrong. I had a great time. I met a lot of people and hung out with my best friend. So it wasn't quite a date, but at least the night's still young."

"How early do you have to be up tomorrow?" He feared the answer because he really wanted to spend the night with her, making love to her, showing her how much he cared about her.

"I don't. Anna is opening, so I can go in whenever I want."

"That's the best news I've heard all night. How about a walk on the beach?"

"Sure."

Holding her hand, he led them out the rear of the building, which opened to the lakefront. He paused just outside the door to allow her to kick off her shoes. A breeze picked up, swirling her skirt around her thighs. She slapped a hand on it with a laugh.

"I'll carry your shoes so you can keep yourself decent." He slipped the shoes from her hand and interlocked his fingers with hers again.

The cool night air blew across them from the lake. Dark waves rolled on the horizon as they walked through the sand. Kevin looked over the water and had the urge to scream to the world that he loved Kathy.

"This is nice," Kathy whispered.

Her words crashed against his thoughts like the waves against rocks. "Nice. Not quite what I'd been hoping for in an evening spent with you."

She pulled him to a stop. "I'm fine, Kevin. Things are hard right now, but we're handling it. Our midday rendezvous tide me over more than I thought they would. When I said this is nice, I meant it. I'm taking a romantic stroll on the beach with my sexy boyfriend."

"I want more of this."

"We'll get there."

In a sudden flash, he had a great idea. "Let's go away for a weekend together. We'll leave everyone and everything behind. Can Anna cover for a weekend by herself?"

Kathy's brows furrowed. "Probably. I've never taken a whole weekend off, but I don't see why not."

"You haven't had a weekend off since you opened the shop?" What the hell kind of life had she been living?

"Nope."

"Then we're definitely going away. Give me a couple of weeks and I'll plan it all." His mind raced with ideas about where they could go.

"Bossy."

He shook his head. "Nope. Just being your person. You might not need to be talked down from a ledge, but you need a vacation. I'll handle it."

She smiled softly up at him and then yawned. Covering her mouth, she said, "I'm sorry. I don't know what has gotten into me."

"Let's head to the car."

When they got back to the front of the building, he waved to the car that sat waiting for them. "Your place or mine?"

"Yours is fine."

His night just did a one-eighty. He wanted Kathy in his

home. He wanted her there all the time, but after the key incident, he knew he couldn't pressure her into more. He opened the door to the car and waited for her to slide in.

He sat beside her and fought the urge to make out with her like a teenager because he knew he wouldn't stop at making out.

"So did the night turn out to be a success?" she asked.

He studied her face and although he knew she asked about his work, he answered thinking only about her. "I think so."

Falling in love wasn't something he'd spent much time thinking about until all of his siblings had taken the plunge. Then he was surrounded. Even then, it was more of an abstract idea of something he wanted to have one day.

Knowing that day was today should've scared him. Instead, he felt at peace.

Well, peaceful except for the intense desire to fuck Kathy's brains out. But that was all his hormones and cock. His heart, his heart was at peace in a way he'd never experienced.

"What are you thinking about? It's making me a little nervous. You're never this quiet."

"Us." He took her hand. "I'm glad we reconnected and that you're giving me another chance."

"Me too." Her answering smile was soft, but the lust in her eyes matched the feeling in his gut. Thankfully, there was little traffic and they were almost at his apartment.

When the driver parked, Kevin handed him a couple of bills and slid from the car, still holding Kathy's hand and her gaze. As soon as they were standing on the sidewalk, he pulled her to him and kissed her. He wanted her to feel what he felt underneath the lust and desire.

But he couldn't say it. Not yet.

He pulled her face away from his, but kept the rest of her body in place. "Let's take this upstairs," she whispered.

Walking backward, he led her toward the steps of the two flat. She laughed against his lips. "We're gonna fall. Let's be adults and walk. I promise that once we're inside your apartment, I won't say a word. I'll just strip immediately."

Her words had him hard and he spun and yanked her to the steps. He shoved the old heavy door open, holding it for Kathy because he knew if she wasn't prepared for it, it would slam against her. Then he patted her ass to get her to go up the stairs in front of him.

"Pushy." She jogged up the stairs. With a flick of her eyes over her shoulder she added, "I think I like it."

That had him racing behind her with keys in hand. The door was unlocked in record time. True to her word, she kept her lips together and slipped her sandals off. Then she reached behind her and released the zipper of her dress. The material began to gape in the front, but Kevin moved to her and held the straps.

"I'll take care of this." He moved the straps from her shoulders and kissed the soft skin. He made his way across her collarbone to her neck.

He let the dress slip a few inches to reveal the top swell of her breasts, and he paid close attention on his path south. Peeling back the cups of her bra, he sucked on each nipple in turn until Kathy sucked in a breath.

The dress slid from his grasp as he moved back to her mouth. Her tongue made him forget what he'd been thinking. Her fingers moved quickly to remove his tie and unbutton his shirt before he regained his ability to think.

He stilled her hands. "We're going at my pace tonight."

"We're always doing things your way. Maybe it's my turn."

"Trust me. This is all about you."

He let the dress pool at her feet and then tugged her to follow him through his apartment. He might not be able to tell her how he felt, but before the night was through, he would show her.

Kathy followed Kevin to his bedroom. He never failed to completely turn her on with his bedroom games of control and bossiness. But tonight felt different. It wasn't the frustration she'd felt earlier at his complete neglect of her and their date. That she understood. She didn't like it, but she understood.

It wasn't even how that slight irritation had disappeared when he'd looked at her on the beach and in the car back to his place.

Something shifted and it was uncomfortable, different, but not necessarily bad. She just couldn't put her finger on it.

So she allowed him to lead her through his apartment and make demands of her body because she knew she would come out the other side feeling sated and wonderful.

The rest could wait.

She reached around to unclasp her bra.

"Did I tell you to do that?"

She simply cocked an eyebrow at him. Bossiness was one thing, but she had lines for the control she'd give him.

After turning the bedside lamp on low, leaving a warm glow through the room, he neared her and tugged the satin from her body. "Just for tonight. Let me do this. Let me do it all."

Her heart rate kicked up. Something in his eyes shot through her. This was important, but she still wasn't seeing the why of it. Yet she wanted to trust him, so she nodded. He stripped down, leaving his suit in a pile on the floor. As much as she wanted to reach for him, to stroke his hard cock, to give him some relief, she stood still and waited.

He pulled her toward the bed. When she was lying on her back, he stretched out beside her and began a slow, torturous assault on her body. He stroked and caressed and kissed, swallowing her moans as he brought her to the brink of orgasm repeatedly.

Using his hands and then his mouth and tongue, he lit a fire under her skin everywhere he touched. Every nerve burned, her blood raced white hot.

"Why are you doing this to me? Do you want me to beg?"

"No, sweetheart. I want to be deep inside you so we can go there together." He rose above her and plunged into her in one long, smooth stroke. His rhythmic thrusts continued to keep her on edge, even as she tried to shift and angle her hips or lock her ankles around his waist to pull him deeper.

Oh, but Lord, the man knew what he was doing. Her body was moving to a different plane. When he finally let them both go, *explosive* couldn't even begin to describe the orgasm that rocked them.

Kevin continued his slow slide in and out of her body as the tremors and aftershocks continued to ebb and flow. He gave her a smirk that told her he planned to make her come again, which at this point sounded impossible, but her body had a mind of its own. And at the moment, Kevin controlled it.

He peppered her face with kisses. A fresh orgasm built

and he seated himself deep inside her body. With his lips on her ear, he whispered, "I love you."

She froze.

He rocked, and her body belonged to him. She broke in ways she'd never felt before. He must've known because he simply held her afterward. He hadn't completely collapsed on her, but his body continued to cover hers.

Her brain was filled with white noise. Nothing filtered through. No thoughts. No sound. But her heart was erratic, and it wasn't just the wild ride of multiple orgasms. She kept her eyes closed as her body floated on that alternate plane. Slowly, her brain started to function.

Kevin had said he loved her.

He was a smooth talker, but he wasn't the kind of guy to use those words lightly. She knew that about him. But would he use them in the heat of the moment? She didn't want to think so, but that would mean that he believed he was in love with her.

What was she supposed to do with that?

He began to stir on top of her. His breathing regulated. He pushed away and pulled out of her. As he took care of the condom, she kept her eyes closed because she was still trying to process his words.

The mattress dipped when he returned to her side. His fingers skimmed her ribs and goose bumps rose. She lifted her heavy eyelids to look at him. His eyes were bright.

"Hey," he said, his voice rough and scratchy and downright sexy.

"Hey, yourself," she whispered, hoping she sounded playful and not scared.

"I'm usually more in control of my mouth than that. Somehow you manage to make me lose my mind every time I'm inside you."

Yeah, she knew that feeling.

His palm settled flat against her hip, anchoring her to him. "But what I said was true. I didn't mean to say it right now because I know you weren't ready to hear it, but now it's out there."

She sighed and threw an arm across her face. This was worse than him just being careless.

He pulled her arm away and levered himself over her body once again so they were nose to nose. "I'm not expecting you to say it in return." He kissed her gently. "But in the craziness tonight, when it seemed like everything was going wrong, I looked over and saw you and it hit me. You make me incredibly happy. I'm a better person with you in my life. I do love you. And I'll wait as long as it takes for you to realize you love me too."

Kathy stopped breathing. It was the only explanation for the sharp pain in her chest. Either that or she was having a heart attack. Her eyes filled, and she felt stupid. She closed her eyes against the tears. She had no reason to cry, so it must be the lack of oxygen.

She wanted to tell him she loved him too. Part of her did, she was sure. But the part of her that still feared trusting him poked at her and made her hold back. She had no doubt that Kevin cared about her. But love? She wasn't sure he truly understood what that meant. Even if he did, was he really ready for the commitment he said he wanted?

"You okay?" he whispered as he nuzzled her neck. "No freak-outs in my bed. Only good things happen here."

Her laugh took her by surprise. It bubbled up and pushed past whatever was blocking her chest and throat. "Someone's full of himself as usual," she said.

"Ah, but there's no denying it."

Just like that, he put her at ease with his simple flirtation. "Are you as good in other rooms?" she asked.

"I'm good everywhere."

"Prove it."

"Give me a few minutes and I will."

She slapped his ass. "You don't need a few minutes for what I want. I'm hungry. Go find me some food."

He groaned, but pushed off the bed. "As you wish."

Kevin left Kathy lying across his bed as he stepped into his underwear. He walked to the kitchen wanting to kick his own ass. How the fuck did those words slip out of his mouth? He'd never spoken those words to a woman. Ever.

Yet buried inside Kathy, he couldn't hold them back. Even though he knew it was a mistake and she would freak out.

And freak the fuck out she did.

He opened the refrigerator to look at his options. He should've thought about food earlier and maybe stopped at the store, but everything with Brent had just gotten progressively worse this afternoon and nothing else entered his head. He had a loaf of bread and eggs, so he could make breakfast. It was better than cold cereal.

As he moved around the kitchen prepping the food, he heard Kathy moving and the water running in the bathroom. He gave her space to wrap her head around what he'd said. He meant every word of it. Although he'd thought saying it would be scary, he felt pretty damn good right now.

He scrambled the eggs and made toast. He set butter on the counter next to the orange juice. For the first time, he wished he had a kitchen table. He didn't have anywhere to eat. On the rare occasions he ate at home, he stood at the kitchen counter or sat on the couch in front of the TV.

He never thought about sharing a meal with someone else as something he might be missing out on.

Now he was thinking just that.

Kathy came into the kitchen wearing one of his T-shirts with her hair piled high on her head. A few springy curls escaped and danced around her face. She took the glass from his hand and sipped his juice. She eyed the pan on the stove. "Hmm . . . better than I expected."

"What did you expect?"

"A bag of chips and a bottle of beer."

"You don't like beer."

"I know," she said with a smile, and kissed him.

"You think that little of me?" He scooped the eggs onto two plates.

"Nah. I'm just joking. I actually thought you might have leftover pizza in your fridge. Or a frozen one. Pizza seems to be your go-to meal."

"Not mine. It's your go-to meal."

She took the plate he handed her and studied him. "So we're always eating pizza because I like it?"

"I don't have anything against pizza. But you really like it."

"You're a pretty good boyfriend."

He sighed and shook his head. "We need to work on your vocabulary. 'Pretty good' is an insufficient modifier. I think for Christmas I'm getting you a thesaurus."

She took a bite of eggs. "Maybe you just need to inspire me to come up with a better way to describe you."

"You're plenty inspired when you're screaming my name in bed."

She laughed. "That I am."

They stood in the kitchen, leaning against the counter, eating breakfast at night. Kathy seemed to regain her composure, and Kevin wasn't sure where to go from here.

Just pretend he hadn't admitted he was madly in love with her?

"So what are you going to do about what's-his-name? Brent, was it?"

Looked like they were ignoring his feelings. "I don't know. It's not like I'm his boss. We're basically equals in different departments."

"But he does have a boss."

"I'm sure he does."

"So go over his head."

"Seems like a douchey thing to do."

"More douchey than ditching you at an event he was supposed to be in charge of? And ruining our date on top of it?" She scooped up the last of her eggs and set her plate in the sink.

"You make a damn good point." But he'd never been the kind of guy to tattle on someone. He preferred to handle things himself.

Kathy stood close and laid a palm on his chest. "Do me a favor and don't punch him out."

Her fingers were distracting him, so he held her hand still. "What makes you think I'd do that?"

"If I know anything about you O'Malley boys it's that you lead with your fists. Even when you're just messing around it's shove and push and slap. I can only imagine what happens if you're truly pissed off. And tonight, you were pissed."

"Was it that obvious?"

"Not to everyone, I don't think. I saw it in your body language, but your voice was very smooth politician. Mayor Park would've been proud."

"You don't say it like it's a good thing."

"It's unnerving to watch you like that. You become

someone different. Constantly changing. It's as if I'm not sure which version is the real you."

He slid his arms around her, pulling her close. Her comment hit home. There were times he wasn't sure who he was. "When I'm with you, I promise I'm real. The rest of the time, I'm whoever I need to be."

Her lips skimmed his jaw. "I don't think I could do that. Be something I'm not."

"One of the many things I love about you."

She jolted at his use of the word *love*, but then continued to kiss and nibble her way to his ear and his neck.

"Are you ready to go back to bed?" he asked.

"I'm ready to spend the night in your bed. I'm not ready to sleep though. We could talk and stuff."

He began walking her backward out of the kitchen. "I'm all about the stuff when we're together. We can talk on the phone when we're at work. Or before bed when we can't be together."

"How much energy do you have?"

"Enough to satisfy you."

"I have no doubt."

As they settled in his bed once again, Kevin could think of nothing else he enjoyed more than having Kathy in his arms. He wanted to make this a more permanent situation, but he knew he couldn't suggest it now.

He just needed to figure out how to move things along a little faster. Once he proved to her that she could trust him, that he wouldn't do anything to hurt her again, they could move forward.

Kevin sat on a stool at McGinty's bar waiting for the Savage Tools hockey team to come through the door. Both of his younger brothers played on the team, and they routinely came to the bar to drink after practice and games. They'd played hard tonight to win, and Kevin knew they'd want to celebrate.

Moments later the first few guys came flying through the door. He ordered beers for his brothers while he waited. When they came in, he waved them over to the bar. Sean slapped him on the back.

"Good to see you out at a game again. You should play with us."

Tommy laughed. "Nah. He's ready for the old-timers' league."

Kevin snatched the bottle of beer from his baby brother's hand. "I'm not that old." With a smile, he returned the bottle to Tommy. "Even if I wanted to play again, I don't have the time right now. This job is kicking my ass."

Sean said, "That sucks."

Kevin looked around. "Where are your ladies?"

Tommy took a drink. "They both have to work early, so they don't watch our late games."

Kevin was a little relieved Emma and Deirdre weren't there. He needed time with his brothers because he needed their advice. It was irksome enough having to ask his little brothers for help without being teased by their girlfriends.

"So what's up?" Sean asked as he sat on the stool beside Kevin. Tommy took the stool on the other side of him, and they both stared.

"I wanted to ask you guys something and figured this would be a good time."

"Shoot," Sean said.

Kevin drank from his bottle and tried to figure out how to frame the question so he wouldn't sound like an asshole.

"God, how bad is it?" Tommy asked.

"It's not bad. It's about me and Kathy."

"You fucked it up already, huh?" Sean reached around him and pushed Tommy. "You owe me twenty."

"What the fuck? You guys bet on whether I'll fuck up my relationship with Kathy?"

"Not whether. When." Tommy shrugged. "It's kind of a given." He fished in his pocket, but Kevin stopped him.

"First, I didn't fuck it up. We're still very much together. Second, you're both assholes for betting against me. I can't believe I wanted your advice."

"Come on, man. What is it?" Sean asked.

Kevin thought about his other option, Jimmy, which didn't sound any better. "I fucked things up with her before, and she doesn't trust me. I get it. I deserve it. But I need to figure out how to get her to trust me."

"Dude, I got this. I might not know much, but this I do know. You can tell her all you want, but you need to show her you can be trusted." Sean leaned his elbows back on the bar and looked like he'd just answered all of life's questions.

"How do I do that?"

"Show her she has nothing to worry about."

Tommy leaned forward. "Right after Deirdre and I got married, an old friend called and Deirdre answered my phone."

"Ouch," Sean said with a smile. "I think Emma would've removed a body part if that had been me. Probably a part I really like."

"Deirdre's not like that. But she was hurt. It was all over her face, man. I would've done anything to make sure I never saw that again."

"What'd you do?" Kevin asked.

"I called Chrissy back in front of Deirdre. Offered to put it on speaker so she could hear the conversation. Then I let Chrissy know I'm off the market."

Kevin laughed. "I already tried that. I made general announcements to everyone that I was off the market because Kathy was my girlfriend. She told me I was being over the top."

"But she still doesn't trust you," Tommy said.

Kevin shook his head.

Tommy added, "I deleted all other contacts from my phone. The only women left are clients, friends, and family. I did it without Deirdre asking. It just felt right. Like I said, I never want to see that look on her face again."

Kevin shook his head. "I don't have the numbers of random hookups in my phone. I use my phone for work too much. I only have family in there. I'm always at work. When could I possibly cheat on her? I'm lucky to steal time for her. I can't find time for another woman."

Sean smacked his shoulder. "But she doesn't know that. She just knows that you say you're at work."

Kevin drained his bottle. What was he supposed to do? Set up nanny cams in his office so Kathy could see him working?

"Emma doubted my ability to be responsible. I finished the coursework for motorcycle repair, and I've been at the same job to show her I can. If you need to call Kathy from work to let her know where you are and what you're doing, do it. It's a fucking phone call. I know you. You don't do that."

"How the fuck do you know what I do?" He set his empty bottle on the bar and waved the bartender over to order another round.

"Because ever since you moved out, you've focused on your life. You're only in our lives when you're with us. When you're at work, you're there a thousand percent. No one else crosses your mind." Sean scooped up the fresh bottle and gulped.

"I'm supposed to be paying attention when I'm at work."

Tommy took his bottle. "But you don't forget other people exist. How many dates have you broken?"

Kevin opened his mouth to argue and realized that he couldn't. While he didn't think Kathy held the broken dates against him because she understood why he'd broken them, he still broke them.

"Like Jimmy always says, man. Priorities. Get 'em." Tommy took his bottle and slid off his stool. "I'm gonna go talk to the guys before we head out. Good luck. Thanks for the beer."

"Anytime."

He spun on his stool and braced his arms on the bar. "Did I really neglect you guys after I moved out?"

Sean shrugged. "We were grown, so I wouldn't say neglect, but you had no idea what was going on, and then you got all pissy that you were in the dark."

Sean was right. He had felt out of the loop a lot recently. Looked like he had a lot to remedy in his life. He slid his untouched bottle of beer in front of Sean. "Enjoy your night. Thanks for the advice. I have a lot to think about."

"Anytime. Especially if you're buying."

Kevin smiled. He'd missed having his brothers around all the time. He just hadn't realized how much. Time for him to figure out how to find balance in his life. First for Kathy, then for his family.

Chapter Seventeen

Kathy needed a quiet night at home. After everything that had happened with Kevin the other night, her head had been spinning. She'd wanted to just blurt out that she loved him too, but she wasn't ready to be that vulnerable. She couldn't quite figure out why she was still holding back, though. Kevin was a changed man. He'd done nothing to make her think he'd cheat.

She sat on her couch with a glass of wine and a Lifetime TV movie where she was guaranteed a happy ending. Unfortunately, while she'd hoped for a light, fluffy movie, she'd gotten stalker-of-the-week thriller. Just as the bad guy lurked outside the heroine's window, Kathy's doorbell rang.

She jumped and yelped. Laughing at herself, she went to the door. Kevin stood on her doorstep.

"Hey, what are you doing here?"

"I know we didn't have any plans, but I need to talk."

"Come on in."

He followed her through the door and locked up as she returned to her spot on the couch. He eyed the TV, so she muted it. "What's up?"

"I have something for you."

"Ooo . . . I like presents." She smiled and held out her hand.

"I hope you stay that excited." He set a key ring and a piece of paper on the table.

"What's that?"

"It's not what you think." He rubbed the back of his neck in the way he always did when he was nervous. "Well, it is, but for a different reason."

She sat back and waited for the reason because this was beginning to feel like pushy O'Malley syndrome.

"Those are keys to my apartment. I'm not trying to make you nervous. I want to prove I have nothing to hide. You can come over day or night, with or without warning, whether or not I'm there. I'll never be upset. You would be a welcome surprise at any time. I have nothing to hide. Snoop through my underwear drawer, dig through my closet, look under my bed. Whatever you need."

"Aren't you worried I might find your porn stash?"

He laughed. "Anyone with half a brain knows you watch porn online." He reached for the paper on the table. "Speaking of which," he said, as he handed the slip to her. "This is the password to my laptop and my phone. If you want access to my social media accounts, too, say the word. I couldn't remember the passwords off the top of my head."

Kathy sat in stunned silence.

"Say something."

"I . . . I don't know what to say." Suddenly she was overwhelmed with emotion and tears filled her eyes.

"Ah, fuck. How'd I mess this up again?"

"No, no, you didn't." She blinked back the tears.

"I don't know what else to do to show you that you can trust me. I'm in this, Kathy, whatever it takes, however long it takes."

"Oh, God. Shut up and kiss me already."

He took her face in his hands and brought her close. His lips were soft against hers but his tongue was insistent. His taste was heady. Kathy got lost in the moment and the emotion behind the kiss and Kevin's gesture.

He loved her.

She pushed him back on the couch and rose over him until she could straddle his thighs. She rocked her hips and felt him harden beneath her.

He tugged the band out of her hair to set it free. Her curls created a curtain around them as they kissed.

Kevin flexed his fingers on her hips, holding her tightly to him. He pulled his mouth from hers and rained kisses down her neck. "You feel so good."

"You too," she managed, rubbing against him, making herself wet.

He growled and bit down on her neck. "Fuck. I need to be inside you now."

Kevin flipped them over so he was on top of her and her legs wrapped around his waist. He pushed her T-shirt up and mumbled praise for her lack of bra. He continued the thrust and grind against her as his mouth latched on to her nipple.

She arched against him, nails scraping and yanking at his shirt. She reached between them and unsnapped his jeans. "Thought you need to be inside me."

"I do." He grabbed her sleep pants and yanked them off in one quick move, tossing them over his shoulder. Before stripping off his jeans, he fished a condom from his wallet and set it on the couch beside her leg.

While he pulled his shirt over his head, Kathy rolled the condom on him. The muscles of his thighs and abdomen flexed and he hissed at her touch. Once he was sheathed, she stroked him again.

"Nuh-uh." He pushed her back into position. He stroked her with his fingers a couple of times, spreading her moisture, making sure she was ready. Then he sank in. He drove into her hard and fast, not allowing her to control anything.

And she didn't care.

He'd been doing what he could to regain her trust, give her what she needed. She could give back.

Her orgasm built, and he picked up the pace, rising above her instinctively. One hand restrained her arms over her head, his other hand played her clit like a fine-tuned instrument until she was panting and then screaming his name. When he released her arms, he settled close to her again and pumped into her slowly, she knew because he enjoyed the pulsations of her body pulling at him, drawing him in.

He nuzzled her neck and she stroked his hair. His muscles tensed as his own release was imminent.

She whispered, "I'm in too. Whatever it takes."

She hoped those words would be enough for now.

Kevin's job was finally looking up. While he'd planned to talk to City Connections about Brent, as it turned out, he didn't have to. They figured it out on their own and fired him. They'd promoted from within so training Brent's replacement would go quickly.

Kevin's days and nights had been busy as he covered for the hole Brent left. He hadn't spent much time with Kathy at all, but they had plans to go away for the weekend together. He loved the idea of having her to himself for an entire weekend. They booked a bed and breakfast in Lake Geneva. If he needed to work around the clock to make sure everything ran smoothly so he could have the weekend, he would.

Brent's replacement was Marnie, and Kevin had spoken to her multiple times over the last few days. She was supposed to spend the afternoon with him at city hall to get the lay of the land here and learn the calendar system and meet his contacts.

He managed to get most of his desk cleared of pressing matters just after lunch. Then he took time to text Kathy to see how her day was going.

> Aren't you supposed to be working?
>
> I'll be meeting with Brent's replacement all afternoon and probably into the evening, so I wanted to text now.

She texted him a picture of a chocolate shake. Too bad you didn't meet me for lunch.

> If we met for lunch, that's the last thing I'd be thinking about.
>
> You have a dirty mind.
>
> I'll show you exactly how dirty this weekend.
>
> I wish we didn't have to wait till the weekend.
>
> Me too. You could always send me pictures.
>
> I don't think so. Use your imagination.
>
> I'd rather wait for the real thing.
>
> Me too.

Sheila knocked on his door. "Marnie Wilcox is here. I put her in the conference room."

"Thanks, Sheila."

> I gotta go. Time for meetings.
>
> Talk to you later.

Kevin grabbed his notepad filled with ideas and notes for Marnie and headed to the conference room, hoping he wouldn't look like a love-struck teenager who'd just been texting his girlfriend.

"Hi, Marnie. Kevin O'Malley." He entered the conference room and extended his hand.

The woman stood and walked to meet him and shake his hand. She was small, barely five feet, with short blond hair and wide blue eyes. She looked a little like a fairy, which was nothing like he'd pictured her based on her voice.

"Kevin, nice to finally put a face to the voice."

Yeah, the deep whiskey voice definitely didn't match the rest of the package.

"Let's have a seat and get to work. We have a lot of notes to go over and then I'll take you around to meet some people."

"Sounds good," Marnie answered. "We've been working really hard to fix the miscommunication and mess on our end. Brent really did a number on us. We're embarrassed about that. And when I say 'we,' I do include myself. I was part of the committee that put Brent in place. He talked a hell of a good game."

They sat at the table. Kevin set his papers down, glad he wasn't the only one fooled by Brent and his empty promises. "Yeah, he did, and I'm glad he's gone."

"I can guarantee those mistakes won't happen again. I'm not perfect and I have a lot to learn, but I'm going to work my butt off to make up for it."

"I'm just glad the problems were all caught early enough. Really, less than a month in. That can all be attributed to normal growing pains. Anyone looking in from the outside wouldn't think any different."

"City Connections definitely appreciates your discretion."

"We're all in this together."

Kevin knew better than to burn bridges in a city like Chicago. You never knew when you might want to call in a favor. And City Connections had literal connections all over the country.

Kevin and Marnie worked for hours, ordered dinner in to work through, and made a ton of headway in streamlining the processes they had in place. Then they moved on to planning the media and communications for the winter.

Marnie was easy to talk to and bounce ideas off, definitely easier to work with than Brent. She came prepared to work. As he took her through city hall, she took notes on every single person he introduced her to. After working with Brent, it wasn't hard to impress Kevin, but from everything he saw, Marnie was hitting it out of the park.

Her ideas for bringing more tourism to the city this winter sounded great. She planned to spend the rest of the week working with her social media people to create slogans and graphics. Kevin would be completely free for the weekend. He wouldn't have to worry about anything but enjoying himself with Kathy.

After closing up the shop, Kathy went home and took a shower. She wanted to go through her closet to plan what to pack for her weekend. Although she was getting ahead of herself, she had to work extra hours until the weekend to make up for asking Anna to do it all while she was gone. With her suitcase on the bed, she had begun to sift through her underwear drawer when her phone rang.

She answered without checking, assuming it was Kevin. He was the only person who called her this late.

"Hello."

"Kathy." Her mom's cold, clipped voice zipped across the line.

Crap. She should've checked. She always needed to brace herself to talk to her mom. She dropped the nightie she was holding and sank to the edge of the bed. "Hi, Mom. What's up?"

"I wanted to remind you that your cousin Christy's engagement party is Saturday and I need you to pick me up at three. And I told her mother you would bring ten table centerpieces."

Kathy clenched her jaw. Nothing like being volunteered to work. For free. "I can arrange the centerpieces, but I can't go."

"What? I told you about the party weeks ago."

Kathy took a slow, deep breath. "You told me about it without giving me any other information, like the exact time and date. I'm sorry, but I never committed to going. I have a business to run and I have plans."

"You can't just decide not to go. I accepted the invitation."

Kathy's stomach churned. She'd never, ever told her mother no, but she wasn't about to give up her first weekend away with Kevin for a cousin she didn't even like. "I'm an adult, Mom. If they wanted to invite me, they should've sent me an invitation, and then I could've either accepted or declined."

"Fine then." Her mother hung up.

Kathy's heart raced. Her mother hung up on her. That was not a good sign. She stared at the phone and considered calling her back to apologize. Instinct told her to, but if she did, it would be the equivalent of accepting the invitation. And she couldn't do that.

She hadn't felt like this since she was a small child, and she watched her parents argue over whether she should be able to take ballet classes. She'd asked if she could and while her mother agreed, her dad thought it was a waste of money. They'd yelled and bickered and then stopped talking to each other for days.

After that, Kathy made sure she never did anything to cause another fight. That horrible memory was enough to last a lifetime. She'd been sure their marriage was over, that they would divorce. Looking back now, she knew she wasn't at fault and that her parents didn't belong together, but that feeling never left.

Now it was back.

She dropped her phone to prevent herself from calling her mother, picked up her keys, and drove into downtown. Kevin said he was working late. He said he wanted to be her person. If someone could talk her down and remind her why this weekend was important, it was him. That was what they were supposed to do for each other.

Her hands were still shaking as she pulled into the after-hours parking lot and grabbed a ticket. She didn't even bother to look at the prices. Never in her life had she felt the need to see another human being as much as she did right now. She felt like she was going to fall apart even though she knew it was impossible.

The security guard checked her in as she passed through the metal detector and she went upstairs. When the doors swished open, she walked to Kevin's office, but it was empty. Her chest felt hollow as it tightened again. She should've called first. She must've missed him. And she hadn't even brought her phone to call him.

She struggled to breathe. A sound behind her caught her attention. She walked a few steps down the hall and then she heard his voice. Kevin. She almost bolted toward him, but he wasn't alone. Through the glass of the conference room, she saw them together.

He was sitting with a blond woman, sharing a drink,

laughing. The woman leaned forward and laid a hand on his arm.

Kathy flashed to a memory of five years ago. Her surprising Kevin when he said he had to work late. Him coming home with a blonde on his arm. Seemed as though Kevin had a type.

And it wasn't her.

Kathy forced air into her lungs, past the tennis ball–sized lump lodged in her throat. She swallowed, despite the lack of spit in her mouth. Neither of them noticed her, so she did what she did best: she turned and left.

Chapter Eighteen

By the time Kathy hit the highway, she was crying so hard she could barely see. She pulled over onto the shoulder until the worst of it subsided. Since she didn't have her phone, she decided to just drive to Moira's house and prayed that her best friend would be home. And that Jimmy wouldn't be. The last thing she needed was to see another O'Malley.

Rejoining traffic, Kathy focused on breathing steadily and not crashing. She cleared her mind of everything but flowers. She pictured images of daisies and orchids and lilies. Anything but people.

When she got to Moira's street, she was relieved to see Moira's car parked in front of the house. She parked behind Moira's car and went to the front door. Moira answered, took one look at her, and asked, "What the hell happened?"

Kathy fell apart again because she didn't know where to start. Moira pulled her into the house.

In between halting breaths, Kathy asked if Jimmy was there, and Moira told her he was with his dad.

Moira pulled her over to the couch, sat her down, and then disappeared to the kitchen. She reappeared a few minutes later with a glass of water and a bottle of whiskey. Kathy took the water with shaky hands. After a few sips, she explained about the phone call with her mom.

"Good for you," Moira said. "It's about time you stood up for yourself. It's not okay for her to assume you'll re-arrange your life to suit her wants. Is this why you're so upset? She'll come around, sweetie. Damn, I've said worse to my mother without trying."

Kathy shook her head. "No. I mean, yeah." She took a deep breath, or at least tried to. "I wanted to call her back and apologize."

"Oh no."

"But I didn't. I put my phone down and left. I wanted to see Kevin. He's supposed to make me feel better, right?"

Moira nodded, but her face filled with worry.

Kathy swallowed and continued to explain what happened when she got downtown.

"You think he's cheating?"

Kathy lifted a shoulder. "It was the same as five years ago. He told me he was working late. He wasn't expecting me. I showed up and he was with a blonde, laughing and drinking."

"Wait a minute. Didn't you tell me that he didn't cheat with that blonde five years ago?"

"So he said. But he didn't say he didn't cheat. Just not with her." Kathy finished her water and opened the whiskey. She splashed some into her water glass.

"Were they doing anything inappropriate?"

"Like what?" She took a sip of whiskey. The liquid burned her already raw throat and splashed in her empty stomach. She immediately knew she'd regret the move.

"Touching, kissing, sitting too close?"

Kathy sat back and closed her eyes, picturing what she'd seen. "He was being Kevin. No closer than with anyone. The woman touched his arm while she laughed."

"Babe. You were upset about your mom, and I think your emotions ran away. Sounds like you jumped to conclusions. Did they jump apart when they saw you? Anything suspicious?"

"They never saw me. I left."

"Crap. Kathy, you can't keep doing this."

"Doing what?"

"Sabotaging everything. I'm not Kevin's biggest fan. We all know this. But the man is trying. You completely cut him off at the knees."

Kathy gulped the rest of her liquor. "I can't help the way I reacted. It was a gut feeling. And you're probably right. Maybe he wasn't cheating or even thinking about it. But what does that say about us? It's a pretty messed up relationship." She poured another glass. "I think I'm spending the night. Is that okay?"

"Anytime."

She didn't want to think about what Moira had said out of fear that her friend was right. It was easier to believe that Kevin would screw up again, that he couldn't be trusted. Another tear rolled down her cheek as she slugged back more whiskey. It didn't matter that her heart knew the truth.

Early the next morning, Kathy was up and out the door of Moira's house, leaving a brief thank-you note behind. Sleep had been mostly nonexistent last night and she felt no better about anything in her life. She had no deliveries this morning, but instead of indulging in a leisurely coffee and reading Facebook posts, Kathy decided a run was in order.

Since starting to date Kevin, she hadn't been running nearly as regularly, mostly because if she was in bed with him, she had no desire to leave. The thought stuck in her tight throat. She needed to run to make sense of her feelings.

She left her music and earbuds in her apartment. Today she wanted to hear her thoughts with the city as her backdrop. After some quick stretches, she jogged slowly down the block. Her body was sluggish and her muscles tight, but she pushed forward.

For as long as she could remember, running offered her peace. Traffic swooshed by along Lawrence Avenue and she jogged around pedestrians shopping in the various stores. A bus rumbled, filling the air with black exhaust, so she turned the corner. Kids were already out, playing in front yards, enjoying the last few summer days before having to go back to school.

Kathy thought back to yesterday, and allowed all of the horrible emotions wash over her. She still hadn't heard from her mother, which worried her. It wasn't like she had spare family to run to. She picked up the pace.

Everything she'd said to her mom was right. Her weekend was more important than some party that she'd known nothing about. And thinking about her weekend made her think about Kevin. Her heart lurched.

Now that she was done crying, she processed what Moira had said. She pictured Kevin and the blonde in the conference room. She didn't like the friendly way the woman had touched Kevin, but it hadn't been sexual.

But Kathy despised her reaction more. She hated that the first thought she had was that Kevin would cheat.

Her head was all kinds of fucked up. How the hell had she thought she was ready for any real relationship, much less one with a man she didn't trust? She'd thought she could do this, but she was failing miserably.

She punished her body by running harder and faster than she had since high school. She wanted to break everything down so she couldn't feel anymore. She wasn't done fixing herself, so she knew what had to be done.

It would mean more pain for both her and Kevin. But continuing on like this wasn't any good for either of them.

Chapter Nineteen

Kevin sat hunched over his desk typing another memo. As different as this new job was, some things didn't change at all. He couldn't begin to count how many hours a day he spent at his computer typing and revising and e-mailing. But the rush to get his desk clear today would be worth it because this weekend, he would be free.

Just him and Kathy. A whole weekend where they had nothing to do but sleep, talk, fuck, and eat.

Well, maybe she might want to do some sightseeing or shopping or some other girly shit, and for her, he'd suck it up. As long as she remained naked in bed with him the rest of the time. Maybe they needed to write up a contract for how this weekend should go. He stared at the blinking cursor on the screen. He needed to focus on his job.

A soft knock had him looking up and when he saw Kathy standing in the doorway, he blinked, sure he was hallucinating. When she didn't disappear, he stood. "Hey, what are you doing here?"

"I need to talk to you and it couldn't wait." She came into the room and closed the door behind her.

The serious look on her face scared him. In his gut, he knew he was losing his weekend with her. "What is it?"

She moved forward slowly and set his keys on his desk. "This isn't working. Let me know what I owe you for the bed and breakfast. You probably won't be able to get your deposit back."

He stared at the keys for a full minute and processed what she said. Then it finally sank in. "You're breaking up with me?"

She nodded and backed away.

"What the hell happened?" His voice was a little louder than he'd intended, but what the fuck had she expected?

Her eyes widened as she looked at him. "Look, I don't want a scene. I promised you I wouldn't just disappear like I did last time. So I'm saying good-bye."

She reached for the door.

"That's all I get? You swing by my office to be sure there won't be a scene. You don't offer me any explanation. Just drop my fucking key and say good-bye? What the hell is that?" He rounded his desk to stop her.

She spun before opening the door. "You said things were different and as much as we want them to be, they're not."

"What are you talking about?"

He watched as she took a deep, halting, shaky breath, sure she'd give him something, some information that he could refute. Instead she licked her lips and then pressed them together before speaking. "I wish you could understand how hard just doing this much was for me. Yes, it was a total cop-out to come while you were at work because I knew you wouldn't cause a scene here, but I can't do this. Please just let me go."

Her eyes were so sad and scared, he couldn't push her, no matter how much he wanted to. "I'll call you later. This isn't over."

She opened the door. "Yes it is. It has to be."

And she walked out.

Kevin stared after her for a long time and tried to figure out what he could've done to screw up. They'd texted yesterday before his meeting with Marnie. They hadn't had any contact since then. He searched his brain and came up empty.

Then he went back to work. He accepted that maybe he'd lose part of his weekend away with Kathy, but this was a hiccup, a bump in the road. He'd figure out what had upset her and they'd fix it. She was overreacting to something simple. It had to be.

They weren't over. No way.

It took all afternoon to write the few e-mails he had. His focus was all over the place. He couldn't get Kathy's eyes out of his head. He'd never seen them so completely despondent. As much as he wanted to dismiss what she'd said, he knew he couldn't. When he left the office, he went straight to her apartment. No lights were on, but he rang anyway. Then he tried her phone. Voice mail.

"Kathy, we need to talk. I gave you the afternoon to calm down. Now I deserve an explanation. I'm at your place. Where are you?"

He went back and sat in his car and waited. He drove by the flower shop, saw that it was closed, lights off, and went back to her apartment. He called again. As the phone rang in his ear, he expected her voice mail again because she was clearly avoiding him and any confrontation.

"Stop calling me."

"Wait."

"What?"

He swallowed and his brain scrambled to figure out what to say. He hadn't considered that she'd answer. "Please talk to me. We can fix this."

"No, we can't. It's over."

"You can't just say that and not give me a reason or anything."

"I did give you a reason. You weren't listening. Good-bye, Kevin." Then she disconnected.

As he drove to the store to grab some beer and a bottle of whiskey, he replayed the conversation in his office. As far as reasons went, what she'd offered was weak as fuck. What she'd said made no sense and now he was getting pissed off. He paid for his purchase and texted Jimmy to say he was on his way over to get drunk.

He'd followed his younger brothers' advice to get the girl and it had seemed like it worked, but something had fallen apart. Maybe Jimmy had some words of wisdom. After parking near Jimmy's house, he grabbed his liquor and went up the stairs. Jimmy met him at the front door.

"What happened?"

"I don't even fucking know," Kevin answered.

They went into the living room and sat on the couch. Kevin handed Jimmy a beer, and they both twisted the caps off the bottles. "Moira home?"

"Nope."

Kevin downed half the bottle and prayed for clarity. "Things have been good, man. More than good. We were supposed to go away this weekend. We've been dealing with all of the shit from the past and handling it." He gulped more. At least he'd *thought* they'd been handling it. "My hours at work have been rough, but even that, we've been dealing with."

"So what happened?" As usual, Jimmy nursed his beer as he listened.

"She showed up at my office today, slapped my apartment keys on my desk, and said, 'It's over.'" He twisted the cap off the whiskey and drank straight from the bottle.

"Wait. What keys?" Jimmy scooted forward and braced his elbows on his knees. "You didn't say it was so serious that you were swapping keys."

Kevin finished his beer and opened another. "We didn't swap. I gave her my keys to help her trust me. I wanted to prove to her that I have nothing to hide. I'm not bringing other chicks home to bang when I'm not with her, you know? She wasn't ready to share keys because she didn't trust me."

He sank back on the couch cradling the whiskey in one arm. "I really thought I was earning that trust."

"She was here last night. Moira said she was really upset."

"Kathy was here?" He took another shot of whiskey.

"Yeah. Before I came home. By the time I got here, she was asleep on the couch. Moira didn't give me the details, but she said Kathy was a mess and it was about you. I just figured you guys had a fight."

"Nope. We don't fight." He took a swig.

"Everyone fights."

Kevin shook his head. "Well, Kathy doesn't fight. Ever. She gets upset and then she fucking runs away."

The front door clicked and Moira came in. She took one look at Kevin and Jimmy and said, "Shit."

"'Bout sums it up, babe," Kevin said. "Can you give me the insight I'm missing? Kathy broke up with me and won't tell me why."

He popped the top on another beer. His third? He lost count. Didn't matter. The alcohol was hitting his empty stomach hard.

Moira sighed and sat next to him on the couch. Weird. She never got within touching distance. Then she did the unthinkable: she placed a hand on his thigh. If he were sober, he'd crack a joke. Of course, Jimmy would beat his ass for that.

When Kevin looked at her, Moira's face was filled with pity. Damn. This wasn't going to be good.

"She saw you yesterday."

"Saw me where?"

She took a deep breath. "She talked to her mom last night and was upset, and she came to see you at your office."

"No, she didn't."

Moira stiffened and she arched an eyebrow. "Yes. She did."

Kevin shook his head and it felt like his eyeballs were rolling around in his skull.

Moira nudged his leg. "She saw you with some blonde sharing a drink and laughing."

"Huh?" He blinked slowly and deliberately. "Marnie? That's the only blonde I was with yesterday. Kathy knew I was meeting with Marnie. I *told* her. I didn't lie. It wasn't secret."

Moira held up her hands. "Look, as impossible as it seems, I defended you. Her emotions were raw. She was messed up from talking with her mom. You've never seen what that does to her, have you?"

He shook his head. "She told me about her parents. About her childhood, but she doesn't say much."

"They turn her inside out. And this was worse. She was coming to you for comfort, and she saw you with this Marnie person."

"She's a colleague!" Kevin stood and nearly dropped his bottle of whiskey. "For fuck's sake."

"What are you doing?"

"I didn't fucking cheat on her. I wouldn't do that!"

"You don't need to yell at me. I told you, I defended you. I didn't think you cheated on her. I just don't think she was ready to hear it. She jumped to conclusions because she was upset."

He set the alcohol on the table. He was done drinking. He needed to think. He needed a plan. "What the fuck do I do?"

"Sleep it off," Jimmy said. "You can't do a damn thing like this."

"Always with the words of wisdom. Good thing you have Moira to do the talking for you." Kevin sat back on the couch, which he needed because the room had begun to spin. Maybe Jimmy had a point. He looked at Moira.

"I don't know, Kevin. I don't know if there's anything you can do."

"Don't say that. There's gotta be something." His throat closed and his eyes burned. No fucking way was he going out like this. Crying like a baby and giving up. He snatched the bottle of whiskey off the table and drank until the lump in his throat eased.

Jimmy stood and cleared the table. Moira took the bottle from Kevin's hand. "This won't fix it," she said. "I'll try talking to her again tomorrow. Get some sleep."

He rested his head on the back of the couch. Moira got up and returned with a pillow and blanket.

He opened one eye and looked at her. "I'm sorry I was such an asshole to you when we were growing up. You know it was just because I liked you. You know that, right? Jimmy's lucky to have you."

"He sure the hell is," Moira said.

Kevin sat for a while and thought about Kathy and everything they'd been fighting for. He'd sworn he wouldn't hurt her again, and yet he knew that she was sitting at home hurting right now. He had to talk to her. He stood and the room was still spinning. Using the app on his phone, he called for a car.

Then he did what he learned to do as a teenager—he snuck out of the O'Malley house.

Chapter Twenty

Kathy sat in the dark in her apartment with nothing but the glow of her TV to keep her company. It wasn't all that late, but she could hear the comings and goings of her neighbors as they enjoyed their weekend. She normally missed out on such things because she was usually in bed. Tonight, she knew she wouldn't sleep.

She'd spent the entire day thinking about everything she'd seen, heard, and said. She'd let Moira's words sink in and after a lot of debate, she realized that it didn't matter if Kevin had cheated. The problem was with her. She automatically went there.

She might never trust Kevin.

Who wanted to be in a relationship like that?

A thump sounded at her door, startling her.

"Hey, Kathy, it's me. Open up."

It was Kevin, but it didn't sound quite like him. She went to the door and peeked through the peephole. He leaned with his arms braced against the door frame.

"Open up. I know you're in there." He lifted his head and looked at the closed door.

She realized then that he sounded funny because he was drunk.

He thunked his head against the door. "Please open the door. I need to see you. I need to explain."

"There's nothing to explain," she said through the closed door.

"I won't come in. I won't even ask to. Please just let me talk to you. See your face."

As much as she didn't want to open the door, part of her wanted nothing more than to be in his arms, so looking at his face seemed to be a fair compromise. She unlocked the door and cracked it open. "How did you get in the building?"

"Mrs. Thomas let me in. I think she likes me." He gave her a smile that broke her heart even more because Kathy liked him too.

"Moira told me you came to the office yesterday."

She closed her eyes because there was so much about yesterday she wished she could forget.

"You should've come all the way into the office. I would've introduced you to Marnie." He stepped closer and raised his hand as if to touch her. "There's nothing going on with me and Marnie. I don't want her. I only want you."

God, she wanted to believe that. She wanted to wrap herself up in those words and live in them forever.

"I told you that this is what I want." He waved a hand between them. "It's not a game for me. I'm not fucking around." As he spoke, his voice got louder, but she was pretty sure he was unaware.

"I know."

His shoulders sagged. "If you know I'm not fucking around, then why the hell am I standing in the hall instead of lying in your bed? We can still have our weekend." He moved closer still like he wanted to come in.

Kathy pulled the door close and held up a hand. "We're not getting back together."

"What?"

"This can't work, Kevin. It's not just about you."

"Don't fucking give me the it's-not-you-it's-me speech. Fuck that."

"This isn't a clichéd speech. Don't you get it? I saw you with another woman, and I immediately assumed you were cheating on me. That was my first thought. No matter how much we think we can make this work, it's not. What I said earlier stands. Good-bye." She slipped behind the door and closed it.

She squeezed her eyes shut as she flipped the lock.

"You said you were in this. Whatever it takes. That's what you said."

She pressed her forehead and her palm against the cool wood. A tear trekked down her cheek. "I was wrong," she whispered. "I'm not strong enough."

Another thump against the door startled her. "I'm not leaving, Kathy. I'm not giving up."

She heard him slide down the door. He couldn't stay there, and she knew he would. Stepping away from the door, she turned off her TV, grabbed her phone, and closed herself into the dark of her bedroom. Then she dialed Moira.

"Hello?" Moira asked groggily.

"I'm sorry to wake you, but I didn't know who else to call."

"Kathy?"

"Yeah. Kevin is here and he's drunk. He's sitting in the hallway of my apartment building refusing to leave. I'm afraid one of my neighbors will call the police."

"He's what? Hold on. Jimmy. Get up. Kevin left."

Kathy heard movement on the other end and waited patiently. Mumbling was quickly followed by a loud stream of curses by Jimmy. Then Moira returned. "Are you okay?"

"I'm fine. He's been in the hall the whole time."

"I'm sorry. We thought he went to sleep."

"He was there?"

"Of course. He came here to get drunk after your broke up with him. He's heartbroken, Kath."

He wasn't the only one.

"Jimmy's getting dressed now. He'll come get him."

"Thanks."

"Are you sure you're okay?"

"I will be. I hope."

"I think you should step back and reconsider. He really loves you."

There was that word again. Love. Love wasn't enough, no matter what people said or what everyone was taught as a child. "I know. I'll talk to you later."

Kathy disconnected, powered off her phone, and pulled the blanket over her head. She didn't want to hear Jimmy's arrival or the fight that would surely follow.

Kevin pulled his knees to his chest and rested his forehead on them. At some point Kathy would come to her senses and open the door to let him in. Even if it was just because she felt sorry for him or because she was embarrassed that he was sitting in her hallway drunk, she'd let him in. Then he could really talk to her and make her understand.

They were supposed to be together. They loved each other. He knew it. Why didn't she? You don't fucking walk away from something like that because it got hard.

He heard the exterior door open and close with people

coming and going to enjoy their weekend. He should be enjoying his, not sitting drunk on a stinky carpet.

Suddenly a shadow loomed over him. "What the hell is it about the O'Malley boys needing to be drunk and stupid over a broken heart?"

Fucking Jimmy.

Kevin looked up at his big brother. The man who always had his life together, who always knew what he wanted and got it. The guy who never fucked up. Jimmy crossed his arms over his broad chest.

"How did you get here?"

"Don't worry. Didn't drive. Called a car."

"Good to know there's still a little brain function in there." He held out a hand. "Let's go."

Kevin shook his head. "Not leaving."

"You can't stay. She doesn't want you here."

"She'll come around."

"Even if she does, it won't happen tonight. Not like this."

Kevin put his head back on his knees and curled his hands on the back of his head. He didn't want to hear this.

Jimmy sat on the floor beside him. "What did she say?" he asked.

"She knows I didn't cheat on her. But that's not enough. She's so afraid I will that she's quitting."

"Damn."

"As soon as things get hard she runs away. She won't stay and fight."

"Maybe that's a sign, man."

"I can't give up."

"You can't make her want this either."

His stomach roiled with the alcohol and stress. "She

does want it. She just doesn't know how to do it. She's scared."

"Everyone's scared. Sitting in front of her door won't change that. It'll only make things worse. How did you think this would fix anything?"

"Moira said Kathy saw me with Marnie. I had to tell her I didn't cheat. I wouldn't do that to her. I promised her I wouldn't hurt her again. I had to tell her."

"And you told her."

"But it wasn't enough."

"Come on." Jimmy stood and grabbed Kevin's arm to haul him off the floor. "You need to sleep it off and come up with a better plan. This just makes you look pathetic."

"I am pathetic. I love her." He stumbled as he followed Jimmy down the hall.

"I know." He held Kevin's shoulders to keep him steady. "Does she know?"

"I keep telling her. Don't know if she believes me."

Jimmy pushed the door open and a blast of night air hit them. Kevin's stomach was still churning, and he paused next to the car.

"If you're gonna be sick, do it before you get in."

"I'm not gonna be sick. I'm fine." He turned to tell his brother to stop being an asshole, but the sudden movement was just enough to disturb his stomach the wrong way, and all the alcohol made a trip up his throat. The whiskey was definitely worse coming up than it was going down.

"Fuck," Jimmy said. Although he'd jumped out of the way, puke had splashed on his shoes.

Kevin held on to the front of the car until the vomiting passed and his stomach stopped clenching. Jimmy returned and handed him a bottle of water. "Here."

Always prepared. Always perfect.

"You're a fucking asshole. You know that?"

"Me? I just handed you a bottle of water so you don't dehydrate. How does that make me an asshole?"

Kevin swished water through his mouth and spit. Then he took a drink. "You never fuck up. You do everything right. You're always there to catch us when we screw up."

"I'm your brother. It's my job to be here. Drink the water."

Kevin did as he was told.

"Better?"

"Fine."

Jimmy opened the door for him and then got behind the wheel. "For the record, I've done my share of screwing up. I'm not perfect. I look at you guys—you, Sean, Tommy, and Norah—and I think I messed up pretty bad. You guys don't know how to have normal relationships and that's probably my fault. I wish I knew how to help you fix this, but I don't."

"Take another look at them. They all figured it out. They're happy. It might've been rough, but they found someone to love who loves them. What more could you want?"

"Nothing." Jimmy started the car. "Does she love you?"

"She hasn't said it, but she does. I know she does." He leaned his forehead against the cool glass of the window and let his big brother drive him home.

Chapter Twenty-One

It had taken all of Kathy's willpower not to sit by her door to listen to Jimmy and Kevin talk. She'd known the minute Jimmy had gotten there because she'd had to buzz him in. Their deep voices murmured through the door for a while, but she couldn't make out the words. She tried to convince herself that whatever they said didn't matter. Kevin didn't matter because they were over.

But she had never been very good at lying to herself.

Instead, she left through her back door to go to the flower shop and work on the centerpieces she'd promised her mother for the engagement party. Even though her mother had hung up on her, Kathy knew she would still expect to be able to pick up the flowers. Darcy Hendricks was not the kind of woman who made a promise and then didn't deliver. It would make her look bad to the rest of the family.

Kathy worked by the glow of a couple of low lights. She laughed at her thoughts. She'd never cared much about what her family had thought about her. She'd only gone to family events because her mother expected her to. At this moment, she began to question all of the expectations.

Kathy always did what was expected of her. Even now, making these centerpieces for a cousin she didn't like.

She stared at the sprig of baby's breath in her hand. Why was she doing this? Her mother had hung up on her and hadn't attempted to contact her since.

With the finishing touches on the centerpieces, she stood back and admired her work. They were simple, but pretty. Then she decided it was time for a dose of reality. She came here to avoid Kevin. Her therapist would say that she worked on the centerpieces to avoid thinking about how hurt she was. She was devastated.

Fighting with her mother scared her. Seeing Kevin with another woman freaked her out and triggered irrational thoughts. And now she was paying the price for all of it. She sank into the chair in her office and cried. She allowed herself to feel everything she'd been avoiding, the deep hurt and anger and confusion. All of it hit her and she was miserable.

At some point she'd fallen asleep with her head on her desk. She heard movement in the store and she checked her phone. Anna was right on time to open. Kathy scrubbed her hands over her face, knowing there was no disguising the fact she'd been crying or that she'd slept in the office.

"Hey, Anna," she called from the office door so she wouldn't scare her.

"What are you doing here? I thought you were heading for your weekend away."

As if she needed the reminder of where she was supposed to be. "I came in last night to work on those centerpieces for my mom in case she decides to come in to get them. I don't even know for sure if she will."

"Are you okay?"

"I'll be fine. Give me a call if you have any problems."

"I won't be calling. Enjoy your weekend."

Kathy just nodded and left. When she got home, she crawled into bed and cried some more. She cried thinking about Kevin. She wanted to call him and apologize, but she wasn't even sure what she should apologize for. A litany of reasons entered her head: jumping to conclusions about him, not trusting him when he'd worked so hard to gain her trust, not talking to him when he'd asked, breaking his heart, not telling him she loved him. That last one was probably the worst of it. If she had told him, how would that have changed things?

It wouldn't have, not really. Another round of tears flooded her face. She loved him but she didn't know how to trust him. She didn't trust anyone easily. Hell, maybe she didn't really know how to love him either. What did she have for a role model?

Thinking of her parents made her feel even worse because she couldn't pick up the phone to ask her mom what she'd thought. Although they weren't close friends, Kathy would normally talk to her mom about the man in her life. Kathy sometimes asked her mom's opinion or advice on things. Rarely did she follow the advice, but she at least talked to her. Now she had no one.

She must've dozed off again because the ringing of her phone startled her. When she saw her mom's name on the screen, her heart raced. "Hi, Mom."

"It's one o'clock. Will you be here at three with the centerpieces?"

Oh my God. I can't believe her. Kathy's heart cracked again. "No, Mom. I'm not. I'm not going to Christy's stupid party. First of all, I've never liked Christy. She treats me like crap. Second, I wasn't invited, you were. Third, I told you I had plans this weekend. They were plans with my boyfriend. We were supposed to go away for the weekend. But now we're not because I broke up with him. I'm lying in bed right now crying my eyes out because I broke up with a man I loved. I don't give a fuck that Christy's getting married."

Silence met her and Kathy was sure that her mother had hung up again, but then she heard her breathing. So Kathy kept going. "You never asked, Mom. You never asked why I didn't want to go. I'm upset right now, but you wouldn't have asked why. It's like my feelings don't matter. I made the centerpieces. You can pick them up at the shop. Anna will give them to you."

Then she hung up on her mother. And it felt freeing. It didn't matter if her mother called back, Kathy would survive. She took a deep, albeit shaky, breath. She could picture her mother staring at the phone in disbelief.

The thought made Kathy smile. She texted Moira to tell her she'd just hung up on her mother. If anyone would cheer for her over that, it would be Moira.

Sure enough, seconds later, she had a string of emojis filling her screen.

She dragged herself out of bed and took her tube of cookie dough out of the refrigerator. Sitting on the couch, she ate the raw dough with a spoon, seeking some comfort. All of her insides felt twisted and tangled. All she'd ever wanted in life was a simple, easy relationship, someone to love and come home to every day. A man to share her life with.

She didn't know why it had to be hard. Love wasn't supposed to be hard, was it? Moira and Jimmy didn't make it look hard. Neither did any of the O'Learys now that she thought about it. They might not have perfect relationships, but she couldn't remember Moira ever talking about any of them feeling like she did right now.

Kathy chewed on some dough. There were a couple of weeks where Jimmy avoided Moira because she wasn't quite the woman he thought he wanted, but he came around pretty quickly. Maybe for someone looking in from the outside it never looked that hard, but when you're the one in the middle of it, it sucks.

Her doorbell rang, pulling her from her thoughts. She glanced down at her messy clothes and shrugged. If someone wanted to show up uninvited and without warning, she wasn't about to dress up. She opened the door and was surprised to see her mother standing there.

"Mom."

"Are you going to let me in?"

"Sure." She opened the door and set her cookie dough on the table. Her mom came in. She was obviously dressed for the party, wearing a simple black skirt and blue blouse. Kathy stared at her, still in shock and half expecting to be yelled at.

"You can stop staring like an open-mouthed fish now. I'm the same woman you've known your whole life." She pointed to the cookie dough. "Still too lazy to bake them I see."

"It's better raw."

"No. You used it as comfort when you were too young to use the oven." Her mom gripped her hands together and looked her in the eye.

The statement was true, but Kathy had no idea that her mother had known.

"We need to talk."

"I don't need a lecture, Mom."

"This isn't a lecture, although you do deserve one. Sit down."

Kathy sighed, but did as she was told. She curled her

feet up and sat in the corner of the couch. Her mother sat beside her, close enough to touch. Weird.

"I'm not sure where to start," Mom said.

"The beginning is usually the best."

She shot Kathy a look. "Why didn't you tell me you were seeing someone?"

Kathy shrugged.

"Don't give me that."

"Because I really liked him. It was special."

"And?"

"And I didn't want you to ruin it." Kathy slapped a hand over her mouth.

"Truth gets easier after a time, doesn't it? We messed up with you. We knew it, but we didn't know how to fix it. And you made it easy because you never stirred the waters. On the phone today, you said Christy treats you poorly, but you've never said anything. Why?"

"Why would I? It would just start a fight."

"So what? Sometimes you need to fight to get to the other side. To air the problems instead of stepping around them and pretending they aren't there."

Kathy sat in silence. She'd often spoke to her therapist about healthy fighting. The thing was, she wasn't sure she could distinguish healthy versus unhealthy arguing. All of it made her feel horrible.

Her mom's stare weighed heavily on her and Kathy began to fidget while she waited for her mom to speak again. "You spoke rudely to me today. It made me very angry, just as it did the other day when we talked."

"I know."

"I got mad and I hung up on you."

Kathy nodded. She didn't need the play-by-play.

"What did you think was going to happen?"

Kathy shrugged. "After today? I was pretty sure I was never going to hear from you again."

"What?"

Kathy stared at her.

"You seriously thought that the bit you said to me would do more damage than the crap I endured from your father over the years? That I would stop talking to you, my daughter, over it?" She laughed. "People fight, Kathy. Sometimes the fights are ugly and people need a break."

"I was really surprised to see you today."

"You said you were heartbroken. There is no place I belong but here."

Even though she thought she was done crying, Kathy managed to find more tears that slid down her face.

After a good cry, the first thing her mother did was try to convince her that the cookie dough really was better if it was baked. Fresh, warm chocolate chip cookies topped cold dough any day of the week, or so she said. So while Kathy took a shower and put on fresh clothes, Darcy baked cookies. By the time she came back to the kitchen, cookies sat on a plate waiting for her. Chocolate melted on her tongue. Maybe her mom was onto something.

"Now tell me about this man who broke your heart."

"He didn't. I broke his."

"Then why are you the one sitting around crying?"

Kathy sat at the table and played with a cookie. She explained her past with Kevin and what happened over the last few days.

"Do you believe nothing was going on with the blonde in the office?"

Kathy nodded.

"Then what's the problem?"

"Now you sound like Kevin. The problem is me. I saw

him with another woman and my immediate thought was that he was cheating on me just like five years ago. I don't trust him, even though I thought I could. I want to, but I don't."

"That is a problem with you. It's a choice you make. The problem is not in the thought you had, but what you did about it."

"What do you mean?"

"Did you go to him and ask him who the woman was? Did you spill a drink on him? Slap her and tell her to keep her hands off your man?"

Kathy snorted at the image of her mother doing any of those things. "No. I left."

"That was your mistake. If you want him, you have to be willing to fight for him."

"So every time I see him with another woman I should slap her?"

"That's not what I'm saying and you know it. You're smarter than that. You shouldn't be running away with your tail between your legs, that's for sure."

Kathy opened her mouth to argue and realized that her mom was right. She always ran away so she didn't have to deal with any conflict. "I can't. Just the thought of starting a fight ties me up in knots."

"Get over it. You can't live life without fighting." She paused and looked at Kathy. "Well, I suppose you could, but it wouldn't be much of a life worth living. Who wants a life where you're not willing to fight for anything?"

"But you and Dad fought all the time. It was horrible. I can't live like that."

Her mother grunted. "You should know by now not to use us as an example of anything other than how not to do marriage." She shook her head slightly. "We were a mess, but we kept trying to hold on. We weren't fighting *for* anything, just against each other. All the time."

"But where's the line? How do I know when I've stepped too far in fighting for something I want that will ruin what we have? At some point the two of you did that and didn't realize it."

"I don't have an answer. You have to pay attention. We didn't."

"That doesn't help. I can't spend my life wondering if this fight will be the one that sends him packing. That's why I don't fight."

Her mother offered a mirthless smile. "If one fight can do that, he was never yours. That's not love. If it's love, he'll be fighting to hold on. You'll know he's trying to hold on to you."

Kathy wanted to believe her mother. She'd come back after all, even after Kathy had been mean and hurtful. But she was Kathy's mother. It was probably in the mom handbook that she had to give Kathy countless chances. How many chances would Kevin give her?

Kevin worked through the weekend with a hangover and moved right into the week. He filled his days with meetings and memos and his nights with alcohol so that he wouldn't think about Kathy. If he didn't give his brain the ability to rest, she had no chance to invade his senses to remind him how lonely his days were or how cold his bed was. Jimmy and Moira had taken to nagging him via text incessantly every day.

When he stopped answering them, Jimmy sent their other siblings in his stead. He was half tempted to block all their numbers, but he couldn't do that. He knew they were worried about him. Right now, though, he wished they understood that he needed to be left alone.

A sharp knock sounded on his closed office door. "Yes."

The door swung open and Deb stuck her head in. "Hey. Long time, no see. I like the new digs," she said with a smirk.

"It's an office. And I don't have to share."

She let herself in and closed the door behind her before taking the seat across from his desk. "You haven't responded to the invitation for the cocktail reception for tonight."

"Why do you need me to respond? You know I'm expected to be there, so I'll be there." He dropped his pen. "Why does Park want me there for this thing anyway? I've been swamped with getting the new tourism board stuff off the ground. Why pull me into this meet and greet? He doesn't need me for that."

Deb leaned an arm on his desk. "Park likes you. Most of the city council is going to be there tonight. Your tourism board thing is working. I think Park wants to show you off. You're the face of it after all."

Kevin rolled his eyes. He didn't need to be the face of anything.

"Speaking of . . ." She pointed in a circle at him. "You might want to do something about yours. You're looking a little ragged these days."

Kevin scrubbed a hand over his chin. Damn. He'd forgotten to shave again.

"The scruff isn't half bad, but the dark circles that say you haven't slept won't win you any awards."

"Good thing I'm not looking for any." He grew more suspicious by the minute with this conversation. "Why are you really here, Deb?" It wasn't like her to stop by to chat.

"Some of us are a little worried about you."

"Us?" Who the hell even paid attention to him?

"Look, I've tried the nice approach, but that's not working. And let's face it, I suck at beating around the bush. Sheila noticed first, you know, since you walk past her desk every morning. You've scared no fewer than three interns with your growling this week. You look like hell, O'Malley. What's going on with you?"

He really didn't want to bring his personal life into the office. He never did, and it had served him well over the years. "Nothing. Haven't been sleeping well."

Her snort would've rivaled any Moira would've given him. "Yeah, I believe that. Guess that means it's woman trouble. Do I want to know what you did to screw it up?"

"First, I'm not discussing my personal life with you. Second, even if I were, what's to say I was the one who screwed up?"

"Because most of the time, it's the guy who does the screwing up. I'm sorry your love life is a mess, and I hate to be the bearer of inconvenient news, but your girl is providing the flowers and centerpieces for tonight. Hope that won't be a problem."

"No problem with me." Except when Deb referred to Kathy as his girl it was like a knife to his heart. Yeah, he still thought of her as his, and it was painful to remind himself that she didn't want him to have those thoughts.

Deb stood and smoothed her already perfect skirt. "See you tonight then. You might want to go home and take a nap or something. Stay away from the hair of the dog though. You won't make a good impression on the council members if you smell of whiskey."

Then she spun on her heel and left. Deb was a sharp woman, both in speech and intellect. She was downright frightening. Kevin processed everything she'd said. He needed to make a good impression with the city council. Chicago was still very much a you-scratch-my-back-I'll-scratch-yours kind of city.

But more importantly, Kathy might be there, especially if he showed up early enough. He could totally arrive during setup under the pretense of work and be able to see her. He hadn't seen her since he'd shown up drunk at her apartment last weekend and even then he'd only seen a glimpse of her through a partially open door.

He closed his computer and cleared his desk. Tonight he'd make his move. Seeing Kathy would be a test. If she looked as miserable as he felt, he'd confront her. But if she looked like she'd moved on, unaffected by their breakup, he would accept that Jimmy was right. He can't make her want him or fight for them. And maybe he was wrong all along and she didn't love him.

Chapter Twenty-Two

Kevin had talked with Marnie on his way home to make sure she planned on being at the meet and greet. They both needed to promote the partnership to the city council together. She assured him that not only would she be there, but that she'd also worked with Deb closely to fix another ball Brent had dropped. She'd personally contacted venues and caterers and event coordinators and then Kevin tuned her out because he didn't give a damn who would be in attendance.

He showered and considered shaving, but decided not to. He'd grown accustomed to the scruff. He trimmed it a little and thought about maybe growing a beard. He wore a suit even though he would've preferred jeans and a T-shirt. The lack of sleep, the overconsumption of alcohol, and constant tug of sadness couldn't be disguised by a suit, no matter how classy.

He drove to the venue and entered through the back entrance, as if he needed to make sure things were on track. He scoped the area looking for Deb, Kathy, or Anna, but only found the catering staff. He went into the dining area and saw Deb barking orders stiffly at the head caterer. She could be such a hard-ass sometimes. But the caterer took it in stride. Deb turned and saw him. She didn't say anything, but gave him a look with an arched brow.

He held his arms out for her to inspect his appearance. She offered a sharp nod and went back to her business. He returned to his quiet search for Kathy. The front door opened, and Kathy came in carrying two small centerpieces. She didn't look up or notice him at all. She was completely focused on her task. She placed the centerpieces on tables and then walked the room making small adjustments.

She didn't look out of sorts, but she wasn't herself either. He'd seen her work, watched her get lost in her love of designing the perfect arrangement. That's not what he was witnessing here. She stepped away from a table, tilted her head, spun the piece, and then turned it back. Kathy was doubting the work in front of her.

He couldn't see her face, but her body was stiff. She moved to another table and yanked a flower from the arrangement and tucked it into her pocket. Then she shook her head, still unhappy with the appearance.

"It's fine, Kathy," Deb called from the other side of the room.

Kevin got the impression that they'd been at this awhile. Kathy disappeared out the front door again and returned with an armful of flowers. This time, when she came through the door, she did see him. Her feet froze, but her arms loosened, and she dropped the flowers.

"Crap," she mumbled.

Kevin raced across the room to help pick up the mess.

"What are you doing here?" she asked in a sharp whisper as she grabbed a bundle.

"I have to be at the event," he answered.

"The event doesn't start for two hours. You never come

during setup. I would've been long gone before you got here."

"I know." He gently placed a pile of flowers in her arms and stared directly into her eyes. There he saw what he needed. She was as lost and upset as he was. "Can we talk?"

"No. Not now. I'm not ready for this. I have to prep. I—"

"Take a breath."

She slowly inhaled and stood with her flowers. She set them on the table and turned to face him. "I've been doing a lot of thinking."

"Yeah?"

"I'd like to talk to you if you're willing to talk to me."

He stepped closer and touched the curls that were springing around her face. "Of course I'll talk to you."

She swallowed hard. "Maybe later tonight. When you're done here? I'll come back, and we can have a drink and talk?"

"We should be done by eight. I'll wait for you."

"Okay." She smiled and ducked her head before turning away to finish her work.

For the first time in nearly a week, Kevin felt a glimmer of hope. He found a quiet corner to sit and wait for the event to start. He worked on his phone sending e-mails and making notes on ideas he had now that his brain started to clear. He did his best not to stare at Kathy while she worked, but she distracted him as she buzzed around making minor adjustments that he didn't think anyone would notice. But she would. She noticed the small things.

A little while later, Deb came and sat across from him. "For a guy who didn't want to cop to having woman trouble, this is pretty telling."

"What? I came to the event early to see if you need any help."

She glared at his blatant lie. "Things straightened out?" she asked as she hitched a thumb over her shoulder to where Kathy worked.

"Not yet, but we're meeting later to talk."

"Good because a mopey florist cannot be good for business. Don't get me wrong, she still does good work, but she's just . . . flat."

It hurt to hear someone like Deb, who barely knew Kathy, describe her that way. But he knew that he'd done nothing wrong. He just needed Kathy to realize that he loved her enough that they could make this work. They could be happy.

She had to want to get back together. That was the only reason why she would want to talk, right? Otherwise, she would've just told him to get out of her way and let her work. He held tight to that thought, the idea that she wanted to fix this. They just needed a plan.

Kathy finished setting up for the reception for the mayor and went home. Anna was closing up for the night, so Kathy was free. She'd spent every day thinking about calling Kevin and what she would say and how to say it. She'd been trying to work up the nerve to do it. She hadn't considered that he would show up early tonight to confront her.

But she should have. She should've known that was exactly the kind of thing he'd do. Except she'd dismissed all thoughts of him trying because she'd pushed him away so hard. She was convinced he'd really given up. It had been nearly a week, and he hadn't attempted to contact her at all.

Seeing him tonight had stolen her breath. He'd looked

every bit as sexy as he usually did in his suit, but he hadn't shaved in at least a few days. He had the beginning of a beard going on, and she'd wanted to reach out and stroke it. Then their eyes met and the incredible sadness in his struck her. It matched what she'd been feeling since he left.

God, how she'd missed him.

She wasn't sure if she could convince him that they could fix this. That she was fixable. But she wanted to try. So after she showered and changed and practiced what she wanted to say to Kevin, she watched the clock tick by. She didn't want to get there too early because she'd interrupt his work. This was a big night for him. She didn't know exactly what the reception was about, but she'd heard Deb talk about it enough to know that Mayor Park was showing Kevin off to a lot of people. Part of her had wanted to be by his side to celebrate his success with him, but she no longer had that right.

She took a cab back to the reception partly because she didn't want to deal with traffic and parking and partly because if this conversation with Kevin went as planned, she didn't want them to have two cars. He'd come home with her. When the driver pulled up in front of the building, Kathy sat for a moment.

"This is it."

"I know. Sorry. Nerves." She paid the driver and pulled the door handle. She walked through the front door again and saw the reception as a guest would. The room took on a different glow than it had when she'd been setting up. She held her clutch tightly in her palm and looked around the room. Most of the guests were already gone. Mayor Park was shaking hands with someone off to the side. The party was definitely winding down.

She decided to wait at the bar for Kevin to find her. If

he didn't show in a little while, she'd text him to let him know she was here. She sat on a stool and ordered a glass of wine. Then she mentally rehearsed what she needed to say. Again. The rehearsal filled her mind so much that she didn't notice Kevin beside her until he touched her back.

"You look beautiful."

Her heart squeezed at his words, and her blood raced at his touch. She wished she could just turn and kiss him and allow that to be enough. To turn back time and pretend the last week didn't exist.

"Thank you. How was the reception?"

"Same as always. Lots of talking."

"You're good at that." She shifted on her stool. "Do you want to order a drink?"

He shook his head. "I've had enough."

"Can we get something more private? A table maybe?"

"Absolutely." He held a hand out and waited for her to stand. When she walked past him he placed his hand on the small of her back as he always did. It felt natural, right.

As they passed the mayor, Kevin said good-bye, and they sat at a quiet corner table. She set her wineglass down and toyed with the stem as her well-practiced words fled her mind. "Thank you for agreeing to talk with me."

He placed a hand over hers and waited until she raised her gaze to meet his. "I was a little surprised you asked," he said. "I came here early tonight as a test. I needed to see for myself if we were really done."

She swallowed hard. "I thought I wanted to be." She shook her head. "No, that's not right. I thought I needed to be. But I couldn't. I've been miserable."

"Me too." He picked up her hand and stroked his thumb over the back.

"I wish I could just pretend none of that happened."

"We can't." He spoke sharply and she knew he was angry, even though he hadn't yet shown any sign of it.

"I know."

"What changed?"

"Huh?"

"What changed since last week? Why do you want to talk to me now when you wouldn't then?"

"I couldn't talk to you then. I knew what would happen. You'd use your charm and your kisses to convince me to ignore how I felt. And I'd let you."

He slipped his hand away from hers. "So you pushed me away instead. What the hell sense does that make?"

"None, really. I wasn't being fair to either of us. I was upset after a fight with my mother. I saw you with Marnie and my initial thought was that you were cheating on me."

His eyes flashed with anger and he opened his mouth, but she stopped him with a raised hand. "I know nothing was happening there. Even after I stepped back and realized that, there was something fundamentally wrong. Don't you see? I want to trust you and believe you won't cheat, but the first time I saw you alone with a woman, that was my instinct. That wasn't fair to you. What does that say about our relationship?"

His shoulders slumped a little, and he rubbed a hand over his face. "What are you getting at?"

She took a sip of wine and then twirled the base of the glass as she tried to formulate her words. "My mom came to see me. Actually, she called and I yelled at her and I was mean and nasty. At least more than I have been at any point in my life. I thought she'd disown me. Instead, she came to my apartment."

Picking up the glass, she finished her wine and looked directly at Kevin. "It was the first time in my life that I not only talked back to my mother, but also that I felt that she wasn't going to just walk away. I know it probably sounds stupid to someone like you, but I grew up feeling like I might lose them."

"What do you mean, someone like me?"

She waved a hand in the air. "You O'Malleys. You're all assholes to each other. Fighting and yelling and yet, no matter what, you have each other's backs in an instant." Her throat got tight and her eyes burned. "I've never felt that. I know logically that my mother loves me. I know that I'd have to do something really, really horrendous for her to completely drop out of my life, and yet, I still feel the need to not rock the boat."

"Until last weekend."

Kathy nodded. "She expected me to go to some stupid engagement party, but we were supposed to go away together. That's what started it. It snowballed from there, but the short of it is that my mother pointed out that it's my choice whether or not I trust you. I can't control those immediate feelings of jealousy and fear and insecurity."

"Kathy, I won't cheat on you. There's no one else I want."

"I get that. You've done everything possible to show me that I can trust you. It's going to take time. But my mom's point was that instead of confronting you, I did the same thing I did five years ago. I ran. I didn't fight."

"Your mom told you to fight with me?"

Kathy laughed. "Actually she offered a number of suggestions ranging from throwing a drink in your face to slapping the other woman."

Kevin burst into laughter.

"What is so funny?"

He reached for her hand again. "Sweetheart, you are not the drink-throwing, face-slapping type."

She tugged her hand back. "Maybe it's time I become one."

A sly smile crossed his face. "Are you saying you want to fight?"

"It's about time I learned to fight for something."

"It'll get tiresome. My job puts me in the company of a lot of women. Are you planning on slapping them all? The bail fees might get exorbitant."

"This isn't a joke."

"Who's laughing?" He stood and moved so he sat beside her. He put an arm on the back of her chair. "I love you, Kathy. But neither of us wants to be in a relationship where we're doing nothing but fighting. Your mom is right in that you have to make the choice to trust me. Part of that just has to be faith."

"Are you saying that you don't think we can work?" Her eyes filled again. She'd held out all her hope on this one conversation to fix everything.

"Of course I'm not saying that." He cradled her cheek. "You don't need to beat back other women to be with me. You just have to be willing to fight me. Tell me when you're feeling insecure or scared or pissed off. Be brave enough to tell me that. Be strong enough to take it when I fight back. Be sure enough to know that I'm not going anywhere."

"How?"

"That's where faith comes in. You have to be willing to take that leap. Regardless of how scary it is."

Could she do that? Suddenly, all of the thinking and prep work she'd done for days for this conversation didn't matter because Kevin didn't think she was up for this. She saw it in his eyes.

He stroked her cheek again, and she leaned into his touch.

"We both deserve something better than a relationship where there is no trust. That trust has to go both ways. I have to trust that you'll come to me, no matter how bad things seem. Right now, all you want to do is run away. I get it. That's your defense mechanism. But if I'm willing to open every part of me to give you whatever you need, you have to be willing to do the same." He slipped away from the table and stood. "As much as I want to take you home right now and spend the night with you, you were right about that too. It would be easy. And I don't think you're ready to give me what I need."

Then he turned and left her staring at him. Just when she didn't think her heart could break any more, it did.

Chapter Twenty-Three

Walking away from Kathy at that moment was the hardest thing Kevin had ever done in his life. But he couldn't continue on with the constant push and pull that they'd been doing. If he was going to be all in with this relationship, she needed to be too. And not just to say it, but to really believe it and live it. He shoved through the doors and walked to his car. By the time he stuck the key in the ignition, his hands were shaking.

Fuck, he wanted a drink.

He'd stayed sober all night because he wanted a clear head to talk to Kathy. Now he was regretting that decision. He no longer wanted to think straight or feel anything. Oblivion was starting to sound pretty damn good. Because he just walked away from the best thing he had. He'd needed to. It was the right decision and nothing told him that more than her reaction to what he'd said.

She let him go.

Not even a word of protest. She wasn't ready to fight for them. Or fight with him. No matter what she'd said. The words sounded great, but like she said, when you're a person who's good with words, they don't carry much weight.

He started the engine and drove to his apartment. He and Kathy needed more space. She needed to figure out what she really wanted, what she was willing to put out there. He'd hoped that the past week apart had been enough. It was killing him to not be with her.

By the time he got into his apartment, his thirst for alcohol had waned, but he popped the cap off a bottle of beer anyway. What he wanted to do was call Kathy and go to her, but this time, it was her move. She needed to decide if she was really in this relationship, if she was ready to put the work in.

Just as he raised the bottle to his lips, there was a knock at his door. He went to answer, confused as to who would show up at his apartment. He hadn't expected to see Kathy standing there looking pissed off.

"That was a shitty thing to do," she said as she pushed past him and entered his apartment without invitation.

She must've taken his stunned silence as permission to continue. She turned on him, pointed, opened her mouth, and then stopped. She took a deep breath and crossed her arms.

Damn. She was shutting down again. That was too bad because she looked damn good with some fire in her.

"You came all the way over here to yell at me and now you're not going to do it?" he said.

"I didn't come to yell."

He answered with a raised brow. He knew a pissed-off woman when he saw one.

"Yes, I'm angry. Talking to you tonight was hard for me, and you acted like it was nothing. I know I screwed up and I want to fix it. I tried to tell you and I feel like you dismissed that." Tears welled up in her eyes.

He didn't care anymore about pushing her or waiting to see if she was ready. She was here, and so he pulled her into his arms and held her. "I wasn't dismissing you. I want you to want this as much as I do. I need you to be pissed off at me and fight with me when you are instead of shutting down and holding it in. 'Cause, let's face it. I'm gonna do a whole lotta shit to piss you off. It's in my nature. If you can't let me have it now and then, we'll never survive."

Her shoulders shook with her laughter. "I'm trying. I am. I don't know how to do that."

"What?"

She eased back and looked up at him. "Fight."

"Come on. Everyone knows how to fight."

She shook her head. "Nope. I've always been too afraid. Every time I've ever had a boyfriend, and things got rough, we broke up. That was it. The end."

"You sure you're best friends with Moira? Because I've seen the O'Learys fight. They're not as rowdy as the O'Malleys, but they get into it."

"I'm not stupid. I know people fight. I've seen it happen, and it makes me uncomfortable. I usually leave."

He thought about that. Every time he and his brothers had gotten into something, even if it was playful, Kathy had made herself scarce. "You can do your best or your worst and you won't scare me away."

She paused before offering a quick nod. "Okay."

He held her upper arms and pushed her gently back from his embrace. "So let me have it."

"What?"

"You came in here pissed off, saying it was a shitty thing to do." He held his hands out for her to continue, but he also saw she had no steam left.

But she straightened her shoulders and stiffened her

spine. "You're an asshole. I asked if we could talk, and you made it sound like we had a chance, you gave me hope. When I said I wanted to learn to fight for us, you laughed."

"I didn't—"

Her hand flicked up. "Don't interrupt me. You absolutely *did* laugh at me. You thought I was being cute when all I did was try to make a point. That hurt."

Fuck. Her point struck home. He had done that to her. And worse, he was doing it again. He stood there, thinking about how cute it was that she was going to fight, and her words actually carried weight and meaning.

He set his beer on the table beside them and reached for her. He held her head, threading his fingers through her curls, and kissed her. "I'm a fucking asshole."

"Yeah, you are, but why are you copping to it so easily?"

He rested his forehead against hers. "I pushed you like I needed you to prove something to me, as if I needed to teach you something, and in one quick sentence, you showed me. I asked you to fight with me, to tell me when you were feeling insecure or upset. And then I treated your concerns like they were cute. I'm sorry."

"I don't like this," she whispered. "Fighting."

"It's not like we do it all the time."

"My parents did."

"But they didn't belong together. You know that. Did they ever love each other?"

She lifted her shoulders. "I didn't bother asking my mom. I'm not sure I want the answer."

"I know the answer here. We belong together." His fingers skimmed down her arms. "Can you spend the night?"

She nodded. "I've missed you."

"Not nearly as much as I've missed you."

He knew things weren't perfect, but they'd figure it out. They were definitely on the right path.

* * *

Kathy had no idea how she'd been roped into going to a hockey game and then out for drinks with the O'Malley family on a Sunday afternoon, but that's where she found herself a week later. She and Kevin watched Tommy, Sean, and Kai on the ice and cheered with Norah, Deirdre, and Emma in the stands. Her life felt balanced and normal. She and Kevin were happy and working.

And she'd found herself surrounded by a whole new family who accepted her.

She and Kevin still didn't see each other as often as she'd like, which was part of why she was sitting at McGinty's drinking with a bunch of hockey players at four in the afternoon, but they were working on it. Kevin had brought up the idea of them moving in together a couple of times. She thought it was a little too early yet, but the thought no longer scared the crap out of her. The idea of settling down with Kevin was beginning to feel like it was where she belonged, and that made her happy.

She sipped on a margarita because the bartender looked at her like she was crazy for asking for a cosmo. Judging by the amount of tequila burning her throat, she shouldn't have asked for a margarita either. Kevin was on his second beer and he was in party mode. She hadn't seen him like this in a long time. He'd shaken off all vestiges of city-hall, suit-wearing Kevin, and he was just another loud-mouthed, cursing O'Malley.

He wasn't vulgar or disrespectful, just different. She'd forgotten this side of him. The side that needed to let loose. He moved from one group of people to the next. At tables, at the bar, it didn't matter. He spoke with everyone. When he was like this, she could see him being a politician. He was good at charming everyone.

Kathy sat by herself. She'd talked with players' wives and girlfriends, but she was talked out. She didn't know how Kevin did this. He never ran out of things to say. Kevin came by, kissed the side of her head, and asked, "Need another drink?"

"No, this one isn't all that good. I think I'm going to head out."

"Come on, let's stay for a while. We haven't been out like this in a long time. Not just for fun. No work, or networking, or responsibility."

He was right, but she wasn't having much fun. "You can stay." They'd come in separate cars, but had planned on going home together.

"No. Stay and we'll leave together. A half hour." He offered a broad smile and wiggled his eyebrows at her. His charm always worked on her and he knew it.

"Thirty minutes for real," she said.

"Yep."

Then he was gone again. Kathy turned her drink in circles and played with the condensation dripping on the glass. Kevin was having a good time, and she didn't want to ruin his fun, but that's what she felt like she was doing.

"Hi. Is it okay if I sit here?" one of the hockey players asked.

She looked up. His dark hair was artfully messy and he was built much like Kevin's brother Sean—long and lean.

"Sure," she said.

"I'm Craig," he said with an extended hand.

She shook his hand. "Kathy."

"I don't think I've seen you at a game before."

"This was my first one."

"Who do you know on the team?"

"Sean and Tommy O'Malley. Their older brother Kevin is my boyfriend." She checked the time on her phone.

"Have somewhere to be?"

"Not really, but I'm tired and ready to head out." She peered behind him at Kevin, who was still standing at the bar. "My boyfriend, however, still doesn't look ready to go."

"I'm leaving in a few minutes. I could give you a ride if you want."

"Thanks, but I have my car. I told Kevin I'd wait a half hour. Just feels like a long thirty minutes."

"Can I at least get you a drink since you're stuck here?"

She shook her head. "I already tried a margarita, and it about killed me."

Craig laughed. "Someone should've warned you that beer and whiskey are the only safe options here."

"I'll keep that in mind for next time." She laughed.

"Let me know if you change your mind."

She watched Kevin make his rounds and tamped down her jealousy when two young women stopped him near the bar and were standing much too close for a simple conversation. They were obviously flirting with him.

He smiled, said something, and they laughed. One stroked his arm. He didn't brush them away or step out of reach. It didn't look like he was pointing her out to them as his girlfriend either. Kathy took a deep breath. She couldn't control the actions of other people. Kevin was coming home with her.

He loved her. She had no doubt.

But when one of the women leaned over to whisper in Kevin's ear, Kathy lost whatever patience she had. She slid from her stool and walked to Kevin and the women. Taking a page from his book, she stepped next to him and simply said, "Hey, babe. Care to introduce me to your friends?"

Her words were sharp enough that even if the women were drunk or stupid, they'd understand her meaning.

Kevin leaned back and put an arm around her shoulder. "Hey, sweetheart." He pointed to the women and said, "This is Tiffany and Sam. This is my girlfriend, Kathy."

At least he had the decency to introduce her as his girlfriend. "Hi," she said.

The women looked her up and down with a smile. "See you later, Kevin," one of them said before flouncing off.

He turned to Kathy. "Please tell me you weren't jealous of some puck bunnies."

"Jealous? Hardly. I'm tired of being here. I'm not having a good time."

"You looked like you were having a good time with that hockey player." He took a swig of his beer.

"What?" She thought back and realized that he was talking about Craig. "Craig sat down and we talked. I immediately told him I was here with you. Can you say the same?" She didn't wait for a response because she wasn't sure she wanted to hear the answer. She was being bitchy and it was uncalled for. She closed her eyes, took a deep breath, and then said, "Look. You're having a good time. I don't want to ruin that. Have fun hanging out with your brothers and their teammates. Come over later. I'll be at home."

He looked from her face to the crowded bar. "You sure?"

"Yes."

"Okay. I'll be over in a while." He kissed her cheek.

When she pulled away, a pit settled in her stomach. He hadn't bothered to offer to walk her out. He hadn't even given her a real kiss. It shouldn't have bothered her, but something nagged. By the time she got home, she'd worked herself into a frenzy with thoughts about why Kevin wanted to stay at the bar and what the hell he'd meant by puck bunnies.

She parked in front of her apartment and tried to calm herself, but nothing seemed to work. She knew she was being irrational, so she changed into running gear, tied on her gym shoes, and went for a run.

The moment her shoes slapped the pavement, her head started to clear. She filled her lungs with the cool early fall breeze in the late afternoon sun. She told herself she was seeing the dark side to everything.

Kevin was a good-looking guy and women would flirt with him. Men flirted with her too. She dismissed it because it didn't mean anything. She loved Kevin.

The thought rang out as clear as light blue sky above her. She loved Kevin.

Which was why she got pissed when he flirted with other women. She turned the corner and crossed the street without waiting for the signal. Traffic was light, so she had no cars to dodge. Her momentum felt too good to slow.

She was irritated by his actions at the bar. Her irritation fueled her pace. It wasn't about whether or not he would cheat or even if she trusted him not to. She didn't like the way he'd treated her. They were supposed to be on a date. He'd said he wanted to spend time with her, but he hung out with everyone but her.

As she reached her block, she slowed to a walk to catch her breath. Nearing her building, she saw Kevin leaning against the gate leading into her courtyard. Hands tucked into his jeans pockets, he watched her walk.

Most guys would've waited in the car or at least played with their phone while waiting, but Kevin had been looking for her.

Of course, she liked that, but she had something to say to him before she would let that knowledge warm her.

* * *

Kevin had been watching up and down the block for the last ten minutes. When Kathy hadn't answered her phone or her door, he began to worry that things weren't okay between them. Over the past two weeks, their relationship had been working, but at McGinty's this afternoon, something was off.

"Hey," she said, the breeze blowing her ponytail forward.

"Well, I'm glad my guess was right and you went running and weren't ignoring me."

"I didn't expect to see you for hours." She reached down to her ankle and snagged her key. When she straightened, she looked him in the eye. "We need to talk."

Ah, fuck. Like every man he knew, he hated those words. He followed her into the building and into her apartment without saying a word. Once inside, he asked, "Is this a sit-on-the-couch kind of talk or yelling-in-the-living-room kind of talk?" He tried for levity he wasn't feeling.

She turned to face him. "Closer to the latter."

She toed off her shoes and kicked them aside. Then she crossed her arms and huffed out a breath.

Before she could launch into yelling at him, he raised his hands and said, "I'm sorry you weren't having a good time at the bar. I wanted to spend some time together. When I got there, I just wanted to let loose. I can't remember the last time I went out just to drink with my brothers."

"I don't care about that."

Now he was truly baffled.

"I'm pissed because of the way you treated me. You had me tag along to this dive bar and then you abandoned me so you could flirt with—what did you call them?— puck bunnies."

He stepped forward and reached for her hand. "I told you, you don't have anything to be jealous of."

"I'm not jealous!"

Her harsh yell startled Kevin into releasing her hand. Her light brown eyes, the color of cool whiskey, were now burning hot. He'd never seen such a fierce look on her face. He stood in stunned silence.

"I get that you are charming and you're a talker. You talk to everyone in that friendly let-me-get-to-know-you way. It's who you are. In fact, it's one of the things I like about you. But I didn't like you charming those women when I was in the room, waiting to hang out with you. You said yourself that you wanted to spend time with me."

As sick as it made him, seeing her pissed off and yelling at him was a turn-on. "I wasn't trying to charm them. Yeah, they were flirting, and I'm a guy, so I enjoy it. But they meant nothing. Harmless conversation. Why do we have to keep talking about this? You either trust that I'm going to be faithful or not."

"God, would you listen to yourself? I don't think you were making plans to fuck them. I'm trying to tell you that I don't like the way I felt when I was in the bar with you. At first, I recognized that my reaction was a little irrational. And if you'd called me on that, I'd understand. But I went for a run to clear my head and it did wonders. You asked me to come to that bar with you." She came close, pointing a finger. "You should've spent time with me. Even if it meant ignoring your fans."

He smiled, even though it might've caused her to physically hurt him.

She shoved his chest. "This isn't funny, asshole. I felt like you were testing me at the bar and that was a dick move."

"What?" She'd lost him again. Sometimes he wished

he'd spent more time with his sister because then he might have a shot at understanding the female mind.

"I think you wanted this." There went her arms flailing again.

"You think I intentionally pissed you off? Why the hell would I do that?"

"To make me fight with you. That's what you've been pushing for, isn't it? To make me prove that I love you? It's a crappy way to treat me."

He was so mesmerized by her body, her fluid movements as she yelled, that he almost missed the words. "What'd you say?"

She crossed her arms again and clenched her jaw. "I said it's a crappy way to treat me."

"Before that."

Her brow furrowed and instead of waiting for her to retrace her thoughts, he said, "You said I wanted you to prove that you love me."

She shook her head, waiting for more.

"Do you?"

"Of course, I love you. You know that."

"But you've never said it." He moved in again, pulling her body into his embrace. Her arms were trapped between their bodies. "I don't need you to prove a damn thing, Kathy. I love you."

She sighed and relaxed in his arms, wiggling her own free. "This wasn't exactly how I thought I'd say it to you the first time."

"I'm sorry I ignored you at the bar. You're right. I should've been with you."

"Or next time, you can go alone. I don't need to be with you all the time. I'm okay with you hanging out without me. That was way more your thing than mine."

His smile broadened.

"What are you smiling at?"

He walked her backward until she was against the door, and he was flush against her body. "First, you fought with me. Like really fought, no shutting down and running away. With a little practice, you'll be able to give the O'Malleys a run for their money. Second, you fucking love me."

She tilted her head up. "Why does the fight get top billing?"

"Because you know what happens after a fight?"

"What?"

"Makeup sex."

Her laugh filled the room, and it was the best sound in the world. She wrapped her arms around his neck and drew him down for a kiss.

"I love you, Kevin O'Malley. You taught me that I don't have to be afraid to fight with you or for you. Now I'm really looking forward to you teaching me all about makeup sex."

"I love the sound of that."

Epilogue

Two months later

Kathy stood in her new kitchen washing glasses and putting them in her cabinet. Correction—their cabinet. Kevin had spent every day wearing her down to convince her they should live together. While she argued and held out for a while, she couldn't ignore his excellent points.

She loved waking up next to him. She loved being in his arms and sharing news about their day before falling asleep.

Bottom line—she loved him.

It made no sense to wait. He'd done the obligatory dinner with the parents. Twice, since she couldn't have her parents in the same room. And she'd spent tons more time with the O'Malleys. They were a loud, lovable bunch.

With that thought, her second favorite O'Malley came bounding in the kitchen. Moira had her hair pulled high on her head.

"You know, having access to a group of able-bodied men certainly comes in handy when you have to move," Moira said as she grabbed a glass and dried it.

"Lucky me, I have access to two families' worth. I can't believe Liam, Carmen, Maggie, and Shane all came to help me move."

"Why not? If you have a big family, use them."

"They're not really my family."

"Sure they are. Plus, now you have the O'Malleys."

Kathy opened the fridge. "Speaking of, do you think this is enough beer? They should be here with the truck any minute."

She grabbed a bottle and handed it to Moira.

"That'll be plenty." She put the bottle back in the fridge.

"You're not drinking beer? I have wine if you want."

Moira's gaze shifted. "No. I'm good with a glass of water."

Kathy narrowed her eyes at her best friend. Moira's lips were pressed together and Kathy could see she was bursting to talk. Then it hit Kathy. "Oh, my God. You're pregnant."

Moira's eyes got wide, almost big enough to match her smile. She nodded, but said, "Shh. We're not supposed to be telling anyone yet. It's still early."

"I thought you guys were going to wait."

Moira shrugged. "I thought so too. Nature has its own plan."

Kathy hugged her tight. "I'm so happy for you. You're happy, right? And Jimmy?"

Moira laughed. "Jimmy's thrilled, but if you thought he was controlling before . . . whew. It's a fight every day."

Kathy pulled away, still smiling. "I think you can handle him."

"You know it." Noise from the other end of the condo caught their attention.

Tommy came into the kitchen carrying two boxes. "Hey, Kathy, where do you want these?"

Based on the black marker on the side in Kevin's scrawl, she said, "Put them over there on the table. Kevin wasn't too meticulous in how he packed, but that says 'kitchen' on it."

She and Kevin had made trips in their cars throughout the week to bring most of her stuff over. Kevin had still been packing last night.

Yelling in the living room had Kathy abandoning the dishes to see what the problem was. Sean and Kevin stood over Kevin's overturned coffee table and three boxes.

"You should've told me to slow down," Sean was yelling.

"Why the fuck were you moving so fast?" Kevin yelled back.

Sean's arms flew up. "So sorry, old man, I didn't know you wouldn't be able to keep up."

Kathy's heart picked up pace, but her stomach didn't churn. Definitely a good sign. O'Malley conflict wasn't bothering her the way it used to. Weird.

Jimmy burst into the room. "What the hell is going on? I heard your big mouths all the way downstairs."

Moira stood beside Kathy with her hands on her hips. "The boys are arguing over who the bigger idiot is." She bent over and righted a box that sounded like it contained a baby's rattle.

Kathy winced and then checked the side of the box. Kevin's writing stared back at her. She shouldn't have felt relief, but she did. It was another box marked KITCHEN, so it was probably his dishes.

Moira hefted the box, but Jimmy immediately snatched it from her. Moira rolled her eyes. "I'll check the damage."

Kathy looked at Sean and then Kevin. "It's not a big deal."

Kevin crossed his arms.

"I'm sure Sean wasn't trying to break anything any

more than you were. Accidents happen." She went to Kevin and kissed his cheek. "Your brothers are doing us a huge favor by helping."

"It's not a help if they break all my shit."

He sounded like a mopey kid.

Kathy stroked his back as her arms circled him. "And if you'd taken more time to pack things properly, they would've been better protected."

"Ooo, she owned you," Sean called. "Tell him, Kathy."

Then Sean left the room and they were alone for a moment.

"Yeah, tell me, Kathy."

"Tell you what? How I own you?" she teased.

"You know you do. I'm glad you finally came to your senses and realized what a good idea this is."

She held him tighter. "So am I."

They had approximately two minutes of quiet before Liam, Carmen, Maggie, and Shane came into the room carrying boxes.

Liam said, "If we all make one more trip, I think we can get it all done."

Kathy stepped back. "That's my cue to order the pizza then." She swatted Kevin. "Go get our stuff so we can settle in."

"Our stuff. I like the way that sounds."

She smiled at him and called for pizza.

Kevin sat on the floor of their living room surrounded by his family and friends. And yeah, he could look at Moira and actually think of her as a friend now. They'd all pitched in to get him and Kathy moved into their condo. The truck had been returned and now they all sat around eating pizza and drinking beer. Jimmy was already hooking up the TV and stereo, as if Kevin couldn't figure out how to do it correctly on his own.

But if his big brother wanted to step in, Kevin wasn't about to stop him. He looked across to Kathy, who was laughing with Maggie and Emma. She sipped on a glass of wine—obviously a glass she'd owned because he'd never thought to buy wineglasses. Even in jeans and a ratty T-shirt smeared with dust and dirt from the move, she was beautiful. He couldn't imagine being any happier.

Kathy called Carmen to sit closer and Liam's girlfriend flashed a diamond on her left hand. The women all oohed and ahhed over the jewelry. Carmen's face brightened with a smile as she looked at her fiancé.

Just then, Jimmy got the stereo turned on, filling the room with music. Moira stood and began a hip-wiggling dance. The other women soon followed suit, kicking empty boxes out of the way. The men sat back and watched, until Emma crooked her finger at Sean, who made a face but stood and went to her.

Without a word, Tommy followed suit, wrapping his arms around his wife. Kevin didn't wait for an invitation. He stepped behind Kathy and gripped her hips to pull her to his body. He kissed her exposed neck, loving the way her body pressed into his in reaction.

She turned and wrapped her arms around his neck. "Hi."

"Still okay with everything?" he whispered.

"Way more than okay. I'm so happy we're doing this."

"Yeah?"

"Yeah."

He held her close as they moved to the beat. With his lips on the shell of her ear, he said, "I love you."

"I love you too."

He'd never tire of hearing her say that, and in that moment, with her in his arms, declaring her love for him, surrounded by people who cared about them, the timing would never be more perfect. When the song ended and a new one began, he stepped away and said, "I'll be right back."

She smiled and waved as her hips swiveled to the rhythm. He ducked into their bedroom and dug through his briefcase. He'd been carrying the ring around with him for a couple of weeks. He hadn't planned on proposing so soon—hadn't even planned on getting a ring yet—but when he saw this one, he knew Kathy had to have it. He didn't second-guess it or even feel a pang of nervousness.

He tucked the jewelry box in his pocket and returned to the living room. Kathy continued to dance alone and he grabbed her arm and pulled her into his embrace. He kissed her lips and with his forehead touching hers he said, "You have any idea how happy you make me?"

She smirked. "I might have some idea. Goes both ways."

"There's only one thing that would make me happier."

She snorted. "That's not happening with a house full of people."

He laughed and shook his head. "Not even close."

Then he dropped to one knee with the ring in his hand. "Kathy Hendricks, will you marry me?"

Everyone around them had frozen as soon as he hit the floor. Kathy's hand flew to her mouth and her eyes grew wide.

He waited, but fear began to claw up his neck. His family stared at them for what felt like an eternity. He took her hand and stroked his thumb over her knuckles.

"How could you do this in front of everybody?" Kathy asked.

His hand wobbled the ring as he doubted the perfection of his timing. "I want everyone to know how much I love you."

She tugged her hand and ran from the room.

Kevin stood.

"Bro—" Sean started, sympathy in his eyes.

Kevin shook him off and went after Kathy. When he entered the bedroom, her back was to him. He closed the door quietly. He hadn't considered that they'd fight on the day he proposed, but if it was going to happen, he wanted it to be private. One humiliation per night was more than enough.

"You promised me no more running away." As soon as the door clicked, she spun and threw herself at him. What the hell?

She kissed his neck, his cheek, and worked her way to his mouth. Her tongue caressed his and they kissed until a moan rumbled up her throat. He pulled back.

"You're not going to yell at me?"

"Why would I do that?"

"I asked you to marry me and you ran away."

She laughed. "Got you good, didn't I?"

"Huh? You were playing me?"

"A little," she said with a flirty smirk. "You should know me well enough by now that I don't like to be the center of attention. And if I'm going to throw myself at the man I plan to marry, I sure as hell won't do it in front of everyone we know." Her fingers toyed with the hair at the back of his neck.

He held her hips and processed her words. "So that's a yes?"

"Of course it's a yes."

"Yes, you'll marry me?"

She laughed, a deep hearty laugh. "Yes, Kevin O'Malley, I will marry you."

From the other side of the door a chorus of cheers and yells sounded. Kathy's eyes popped wide again and she hid her face in the crook of his neck.

"Get used to it, babe. The O'Malleys will always be up in our business."

"I guess that's the price I pay for having people who love me, huh?"

"Yeah. That's what family's for." His hand tilted her chin up so he could look in her eyes again. "Ready to go celebrate?"

"Yeah."

He turned to open the door, but she held his elbow. "Wait."

He stifled a groan. "What now? You can't pull that card twice. I'm not falling for it."

"It's not official until I have a ring on my finger." She held out her left hand and wiggled her fingers at him.

He took the ring from its box and slid it onto her finger. It was a little loose, but she closed her fist to keep it in place.

"Now let's go show it off." He led her out of the bedroom and they were immediately engulfed in hugs and pats on the back and congratulations.

Moira hugged him and said, "Get it right."

"I will."

Kathy nudged her friend and said, "He already has."

Kevin kissed her again with a backdrop of cheers and yells from his family. It was about as perfect a night as he could ask for. It was definitely an excellent way to start their life together.

Keep reading for
more of the O'Malley Brothers
and more romance in

Through Your Eyes

by Shannyn Schroeder.

On sale now!

Deirdre Murphy stepped out of the international terminal at O'Hare Airport, into the blustery wind of Chicago. She disliked the crowds and held no love for the cold, but as soon as she stepped to the curb, she felt freedom. It had been months since she'd left this city to return home to Ireland, but something about this place put her at ease. Or maybe it was simply escaping her family and the responsibilities she'd left behind.

She scanned the curb for her cousin Maggie and, for the life of her, couldn't remember what Maggie's car looked like. Suddenly, loud honking preceded a pickup truck whipping into a spot in front of her. Deirdre looked up and saw Maggie's smiling face.

Deirdre grabbed her suitcases and her shoulder bag, but before she got to the curb, Maggie was flying at her and wrapping her arms around her. If her hands hadn't been full, Deirdre would've returned the embrace. Maybe.

"I'm so glad you're back! And just in time for St. Paddy's Day." Her cousin chuckled. "You thought you were coming to hang out, but I had ulterior motives in getting you here. You can work at the bar with us. It's a blast."

Deirdre clenched her jaw. Working at O'Leary's Pub was the last thing she wanted to do. Her entire life had been about her own family's pub, and that was the single most important reason she'd wanted to leave home.

Maggie pulled away, but nudged her shoulder. "Really. It's fun. And it's only one day. You'll make a crap ton of money in tips just for having the accent." She paused and lowered her voice. "I *know* you don't want to be there all the time."

In fact, Maggie did know. She was the only person Deirdre had confided in. Maggie grabbed a suitcase and shoved it on the backseat of the truck.

"Whose truck is this?"

"Shane's. My car is having issues, so I dropped him off at work so I could use his truck."

Deirdre watched Maggie as she spoke about her boyfriend. She was so happy that it was evident in her entire body. Deirdre wondered if she looked the same when she spoke about Rory. She doubted it. Something was off between them, now more than ever.

After they were buckled up, Maggie reached across the seat. "Well? Let me see."

"What?" Deirdre asked, her stomach plummeting because she knew exactly what Maggie wanted to see.

"Your Christmas present." She paused. "Shit. He didn't propose, did he?"

Deirdre shook her head. "On the upside, I'm here." She forced a smile. "He bought me the plane ticket."

A flash of Christmas night came to her. Rory had watched her open the present, and she'd swallowed her disappointment when she'd realized it wasn't an engagement ring.

He'd held her hand. *I've never seen you as happy as you were in Chicago. Your face lit up my computer screen. Go back and have a good time.*

"What is it?" Maggie's question pulled her from the past.

"I don't know. I'm thrilled to be here, but things between me and Rory . . . something's not right."

Maggie pulled out into traffic, then asked, "Is he cheating on you?"

Deirdre shrugged. She never would've considered it, but then Maggie put her thoughts into words.

"I mean, I don't really know him well, but what guy sends his girlfriend halfway around the world?"

Deirdre bit her lip. "Rory's not like that. We've been friends since we were tots. He wouldn't do anything to hurt me."

"Not to be a bitch, but one way to keep you in the dark is to send you thousands of miles away."

Deirdre laughed. "Saying you don't want to be a bitch doesn't make it so."

Maggie feigned offense.

"I can't imagine Rory would be able to have a girl on the side without my family or his knowing. And they certainly wouldn't keep it from me."

Maggie had gotten on the highway, and the rush of traffic and the crazy crisscrossing of the pavement mesmerized Deirdre. She loved so much about this city. "It doesn't really matter why he sent me here. I'm here and I'm going to enjoy myself."

"More than last time, I hope."

"What do you mean? I had fun last fall."

"Girl, you did little more than work and go to church with my mom." Her hand flew up. "Not that we all don't appreciate you taking on that task."

Deirdre laughed again. "I don't mind. It seems to make Aunt Eileen happy to have someone attend with her."

While not as devout as her family believed, Deirdre liked the familiarity and rhythm of mass. It gave her peace that she didn't find at home.

They exited the highway and began winding down residential streets. Deirdre was content to watch the scenery, but as usual, Maggie continued the conversation.

"Okay, since there was no engagement, give me the scoop. Are you still a virgin?"

"Why wouldn't I be?"

"Come on, if Rory had proposed, we both know your panties would've dropped as soon as the ring slipped on your finger."

Deirdre felt her cheeks heat. She didn't have a sister of her own, and she'd never talk so openly with her brothers. As uncomfortable as the conversation made her, she realized that she'd missed Maggie and her brazen nature.

Plus, she was right. Deirdre had only been saving herself for marriage because it seemed like something Rory wanted.

"What's that Beyoncé song? He should've put a ring on it?" She laughed with her cousin even though she didn't feel the levity her remark should've caused.

Before she knew it, they were in front of the O'Leary house and Deirdre was filled with longing once again. She loved that although the O'Learys ran their own pub, they had a real house. Deirdre's family lived above their pub, so there was no escaping it. Ever.

They hauled her luggage into the house, and Eileen came from the kitchen to greet them. "I have tea on. I thought you could use some after the trip."

Deirdre nodded. "Thank you. It sounds lovely."

"I'll take your bags upstairs. The room is the same. No one has used it since you left."

"Let me help." Deirdre hefted one of her bags. As they headed up the stairs, she asked, "So Aunt Eileen is really all right with you living with Shane?"

"Why wouldn't she be?"

"I just thought . . . I don't know. My mom is so excited at the simple thought of marriage."

"Come on. Your mom isn't that old-fashioned. I'm sure if you and Rory wanted to live together, she'd be okay with it." She tossed the suitcase on the bed and then plopped beside it.

Deirdre unzipped the case and flipped the lid. Maybe her mom wouldn't care. Rory always seemed to think it would be an issue. Just like he wanted to wait to have sex. Now he'd sent her back to Chicago.

That unsettled feeling returned.

"Leave this for later. Let's go have tea and catch up."

"Don't you have to get Shane?"

"Not till later. We have plenty of time."

Back in the kitchen, Aunt Eileen was filling the teapot. A plate of cookies sat beside it on a tray. The same way her mom served tea at home.

Without turning, Eileen said, "I'll have you know that I spoke with the McDonoughs. They'd love to have you back at the bakery."

Maggie snickered.

"What?"

"I just think it's ridiculous that the McDonoughs have owned that bakery for probably longer than I've been alive, but they leave the name Blackstone's."

"Blackstone's is an institution." Eileen's voice stiffened.

Deirdre wasn't sure if she was being serious.

"If I owned a bakery that was that good, you better

believe I'd have my name plastered all over it. I'd want people to know it was me."

Deirdre didn't understand that. She'd be happy in the background. It was enough to create something that people would enjoy, even if they had no idea who had done it.

Eileen lifted the tray. Deirdre rushed forward. "Let me."

They moved to the dining room table. She found comfort in the routine of having tea and cookies. As different as life was in Chicago, she liked knowing that family traditions were consistent.

Tommy's phone rang as he finished giving his client after-care instructions. He said good-bye to the client and answered the phone. "Hey, Jimmy, what's up?"

"I need you to get Norah's birthday cake from Blackstone's."

"Why me?"

"Because Sean isn't answering and Norah shouldn't have to get her own cake. It's all paid for. Just pick it up."

He hadn't gone to Blackstone's since Cupcake had gone back to Ireland. He'd never gotten the chance to ask her out, and going to the bakery would just be a reminder of his failure. "Get Kevin to pick it up."

"Not gonna happen. Stop being a dick and get the cake for our sister."

He was being a dick, but he didn't need Jimmy to point it out. He also needed to get over it. There were other girls. He'd barely had a conversation with Deirdre, even at the urging of Moira, who was Deirdre's cousin and Jimmy's fiancée. "Fine."

He disconnected and caught Kai staring at him. Tommy thought that his boss would've lightened up since getting together with Norah. Some things, unfortunately, didn't change. "Yeah, Kai, I took a personal call, but I was done with my client." Then a thought hit him. "You want to pick up Norah's birthday cake?"

"Why the hell would I want to do that?"

"She's your girlfriend."

"She's your sister. And it's your family that wants to do dinner. Besides, I have to go pick her up."

Tommy sighed. Back to getting over himself. He waited a little while, hoping for a walk-in client, but only one came in and Puck, the other tattoo artist, beat him to the counter.

"I'm out of here," Tommy called to Kai. "See you at the house."

Outside, a blast of cold wind slapped at him. He couldn't wait for spring. He wasn't as bad as his brother Sean, who couldn't wait for warm weather so he could ride his motorcycle. For Tommy, it was just being outside, hanging with people. During the winter, everyone tended to disappear and hibernate. Loneliness always hit him over the winter.

Which was why he missed having a girlfriend. A steady girl kept the loneliness at bay. And the regular sex didn't hurt, either. He drove to the bakery and found a parking spot in front. It was near closing and the business was empty.

He walked through the door and a sweet scent filled the air. The place hadn't changed much over the years. The fake cakes they had on display were different, changing with the times, showing popular themes, but the classics remained on a high shelf near the ceiling.

One of his earliest memories was coming here with his dad and Jimmy to pick out his birthday cake. His dad had hoisted him up on his shoulders and told him to pick any cake design he wanted. He couldn't have been more than four or five. It wasn't long after his mom had been killed, but the memory was such a happy one. He didn't remember feeling sad.

That realization made him feel crappy.

No one came from the back, so he called out, "Hello? I'm here to pick up a cake."

From the back room, with her head down, she came toward him.

"Cupcake," he whispered.

She moved to the counter opposite him and turned her back to dig through a stack of order slips. Her reddish-brown hair trailed down her back in a ponytail. Without any greeting, she asked, "Name?"

"O'Malley."

She spun with the pink slips in her hand. Her light blue eyes were wide, and the sprinkling of freckles across her nose reminded him how cute she was.

"You're back," he said.

"*Another* cake for O'Malley?"

He lifted a shoulder. "There are five of us."

"It's good to know you're not eating all this cake. I was beginning to think you had a wicked sweet tooth."

"Uh, your cousin Moira told me you went back to Ireland."

The papers in her hands crinkled, and a blush swept across her cheeks. "I did."

"Are you staying long?"

"I'm not sure." She focused on the slips, flipping through them, looking for his order.

When she found it, she pulled it from the stack and

looked up. She waved it at him with a smile. "I'll be right back."

She disappeared to the back room, and Tommy sucked in a deep breath. This was it. He had another chance. All he had to do was open his mouth.

Why hadn't Moira said anything? She knew he had a thing for her cousin. Maybe she was the one who'd put Jimmy up to making him get the cake. That definitely sounded like a Moira move. But to get Jimmy involved, that took skill. Moira was obviously better than he'd given her credit for.

Deirdre returned carrying a box. She slid it on the counter between them and lifted the lid. "Here you go."

He barely glanced at it. No one would care if something was misspelled. His gaze locked on hers as she lowered the lid.

"Would you like to go out sometime?"

She stared at him for so long, he began to wonder if he'd really spoken aloud.

"Uh . . . I have a boyfriend."

"Oh." The disappointment hit him hard. Again, he had to question why Moira wouldn't tell him. This was the kind of pertinent information you gave a guy before he made a fool of himself.

"Your order is all paid for." She nudged the box forward so he'd take the hint.

He scrambled for what to say to ease the tension. "Maybe you'd like to go out and do some sightseeing. As friends. You're new to Chicago, and I could show you around."

"Maybe." Her eyes shifted away. It seemed no matter what he said, he made her nervous.

"Are staying with the O'Learys again?"

"Yes."

"I'm right across the street. Stop by any time."

She nodded and he took the cake from the counter. Not quite the answer he was looking for, but at least she hadn't totally shot him down. She didn't seem *completely* un-interested.

But boyfriend?

Were they doing a long-distance thing? Tommy wondered about her relationship. This was her second trip to Chicago in under a year.

Maybe there wasn't a boyfriend and she was trying to be nice.

Shit. He hated when that happened.

He set the cake on the passenger seat and looked back through the front window of the bakery. Deirdre stood behind the counter, staring at his car. It was dark enough out that he didn't think she could still see him, but he smiled anyway.

Boyfriend or not, she was interested.

Books by Bestselling Author
Fern Michaels

___**The Jury**	0-8217-7878-1	$6.99US/$9.99CAN
___**Sweet Revenge**	0-8217-7879-X	$6.99US/$9.99CAN
___**Lethal Justice**	0-8217-7880-3	$6.99US/$9.99CAN
___**Free Fall**	0-8217-7881-1	$6.99US/$9.99CAN
___**Fool Me Once**	0-8217-8071-9	$7.99US/$10.99CAN
___**Vegas Rich**	0-8217-8112-X	$7.99US/$10.99CAN
___**Hide and Seek**	1-4201-0184-6	$6.99US/$9.99CAN
___**Hokus Pokus**	1-4201-0185-4	$6.99US/$9.99CAN
___**Fast Track**	1-4201-0186-2	$6.99US/$9.99CAN
___**Collateral Damage**	1-4201-0187-0	$6.99US/$9.99CAN
___**Final Justice**	1-4201-0188-9	$6.99US/$9.99CAN
___**Up Close and Personal**	0-8217-7956-7	$7.99US/$9.99CAN
___**Under the Radar**	1-4201-0683-X	$6.99US/$9.99CAN
___**Razor Sharp**	1-4201-0684-8	$7.99US/$10.99CAN
___**Yesterday**	1-4201-1494-8	$5.99US/$6.99CAN
___**Vanishing Act**	1-4201-0685-6	$7.99US/$10.99CAN
___**Sara's Song**	1-4201-1493-X	$5.99US/$6.99CAN
___**Deadly Deals**	1-4201-0686-4	$7.99US/$10.99CAN
___**Game Over**	1-4201-0687-2	$7.99US/$10.99CAN
___**Sins of Omission**	1-4201-1153-1	$7.99US/$10.99CAN
___**Sins of the Flesh**	1-4201-1154-X	$7.99US/$10.99CAN
___**Cross Roads**	1-4201-1192-2	$7.99US/$10.99CAN

Available Wherever Books Are Sold!
Check out our website at www.kensingtonbooks.com

More from Bestselling Author
JANET DAILEY